Travis Crim
REBEL RISING
a novel

FIRST EDITION

Designed by Virginia Mathers

ISBN 979-8-9872693-7-4

To Delaine

You've been as constant as a Northern Star
The brightest light that shines

It's been you, woman
Right down the line

– Gerald Rafferty

CHAPTER 1

Twelve Inches

Flushed and swollen was all. The boy expected bulging eyes or some other grotesque protrusion. Perhaps a dry, yawning tongue, fat from heat. Orbs burst finally from pressure, dangling down and up again, held by coiled cords of veiny flesh. Surely a stretched, misshapen mouth earned from the agony of last breaths.

There were none of these things.

At the corners, only dribbles of frothy spit. Nasty still.

The boy pulled up an old crate from the corner of the loft and positioned it directly in front of his brother. And there he sat. Staring.

It seemed like an hour, but the boy soon realized silence was bending time itself. A slight breeze set off a cascade of creaks and diminutive pops from the aged wood that ran the entirety of the barn. Here, the silence made thirty seconds feel more like the length of an afternoon.

Closest to the child, easily within reach from the stool, were his brother's grotty sneakers. They levitated with a holy, cherub-like ease, only a foot above the dusty floorboards. With this before him, Rebel was flooded with a singular thought, loud and clear as if the old funeral home director downtown stood beside him now, breathing it plainly into his ear in that sonorous baritone: *Twelve inches*, the boy thought. *Twelve inches is the only thing 'tween spit dribbles and him beatin' my ass.*

And there it was. Nagging and ever-present, like the aftertaste of sour lunch. That sticking reminder that Lee Mims would punish his little brother mercilessly. As sure as sunrise, the throttles would come, unrepentant, with varying degrees of intensity depending on mood and who was around.

"Gotta make ya tough," Lee would say.

And then, as if carrying out some ritualistic chore he was bound to for posterity, Lee would cluster his knuckles into a small mountain—his middle finger its peak—and thunder away, drilling at the same area of Rebel's puny twelve-year-old arm until the boy squealed out.

"Quit yellin' like a fuckin' girl!" Lee would bark, which always struck Rebel as peculiar, since his older brother seemed to have an uncanny ability to turn on the waterworks whenever it suited him. Just two weeks prior from this very moment in the loft, their mother had called the police to the trailer for the third time in as many months, and Lee had sobbed like a child lost. *You wasn't even gettin' hit and you cried*, Rebel mused. No matter. By the time he was a toddler, the elder Mims boy had mastered the most byzantine tactics of emotional manipulation.

"You send your own flesh and blood to jail?" Lee had moaned, wiping snot from his upper lip. He dutifully lowered his body to the living room floor, interlocking fingers behind his head. "What kinda mother does 'at shit?!" he'd hissed, standing at the slightest nudge from Officer Tiegreen.

That last punch of anger, tinged with disappointment, would usually do the trick, and Charleen would bury her face in her hands with regret. A geyser of emotional wreckage, the woman ambled toward the policeman then, begging him not to take her son away.

"John! Johnny, please don't, alright? I'm sorry. I shouldn't have called again—he's just a boy."

Tiegreen, a mountain-sized black man, gathered an absurd amount of air into his lungs and sighed it away, gently holding the woman a safe distance from her fuming son. "I come out, you know he gotta go, Charleen. Come on now," he'd said.

In the loft, Rebel marveled at his brother now, admiring Lee's work and method. He'd done it right. The rope was tied neatly around the loft's primary truss—sturdy, set up in the middle of the room so there was no way he could have reached anything to lift bodyweight and alleviate suffocation should instincts win out. Lee's dingy cut-off revealed thinly muscled arms, tattooed, and scarred from fights and a failed initiation rite when he'd tried to start a gang a couple of years before.

"What's our gang gon do?" Rebel had asked.

"You ain't in it, dumbass. Too young. And besides, I don't know. We'll probably steal stuff and just fuck shit up."

At seventeen, Lee's face and frame were not particularly attractive, but he never seemed to be without a girlfriend. Those same girlfriends would study his little brother's features and smirk. For his part, Lee never found this off-putting. He secretly loved when anyone commented regarding his kid brother's looks, assuming surrogate praise.

Rebel stood, inching closer to his brother's face. Lee's eyes were dueling slits, but the boy could tell his gaze was earnest and in the direction of the wide, windowless frame beyond. The child's arms had formed around the corpse and Rebel found himself hugging his brother. No stiffness yet. The body still warm and malleable, enough that at any moment Rebel half expected Lee to return the embrace. He did not.

The boy released slowly, grazing the edge of Lee's fingertips—tacky and flexed toward his body in a misshapen curl. The child's curiosity caused the body to turn, which offered a false sense of animation. From above, the rope complained. Stretching groans intermittent.

Twelve inches.

For Rebel, there wasn't a hint of shock. More wonderment and a foreseen sense of due course, as if this moment could well have come sooner or later and just happened to have come sooner. The way tires on their grandfather's tractor needed periodic rotation. Simply a matter of when. Not that Rebel felt his brother had nothing to live for. On the contrary, Lee Mims was hedonism personified and seemed to relish the human experience more than most. The reality was, and the child could not explain this notion even to himself; the scene appeared inevitable.

When a line of spit slipped from Lee's chin and splattered a small crater beneath his feet, Rebel thought it time to leave. As he navigated the steps to the bottom floor, it occurred to him he likely wouldn't have been the one to find his brother if it hadn't been Pony Time—those fleeting minutes when the sun bathes everything orgasmic with warm orange and amber. The boy lived for golden hour, watching as last rays kissed the horizon with womb-like hopefulness. Angels were most powerful during this window, Rebel was certain. He'd named it after Pony Boy's monologue from *The Outsiders*, the only book in his life he'd read to completion and a requirement for Mrs. Langford's sixth grade English class.

Pony Time always lured the child to his grandfather's barn, a seventy-five-year-old behemoth of splinters and pine knots.

Long for the world by any standard. Isolated from their mobile home by a hundred yards of choke-briar and high weed, this was Rebel's escape—a private castle all his own. Before their grandfather died, Lee had spent practically every waking moment there mucking stalls or bailing hay, otherwise tending to any form of callous-inducing labor. All of this in apprenticeship to an unshakable work ethic handed down by Charleen's father, Isaac Augustus Headley.

Isaac had helped his father build the barn, and in its prime it had been the envy of Chilton County—a massive structure of fresh-cut boards colored fire-engine red. Against a swath of green grass and the woods beyond, it was a spit of lava burst from the crease of a volcano. Now, sorely faded, with horses gone and manure patties deteriorated into dusty granules, it was a bygone relic.

For Rebel, Isaac's barn was a sanctuary in which he could steal away, letting loose the most fantastical daydreams his mind might conjure. He visited the loft practically every day, waiting for sun to snake orange through fissures in the pine. And with the first curvature of evening light, the long A-frame of the loft would become a thousand different places for the boy: the Portal of Enoch, or the den of an incestuous, undiscovered tribe of Sasquatch. Sometimes, the space acted as the slipknot of Heaven itself, where angels would assemble and make ready battle plans as they discussed rumors of treason within their ranks.

The boy waded through the high weed back to the trailer,

following the worn, narrow path he and his brother had beaten down over the years. At the first bend in the trail, he paused to look back. Far away, his brother was framed clearly through the bay window of the loft. A perfect silhouette. The light ebbing, Rebel imagined Lee a god on fire, alighting softly to earth where he would unleash savagery and death throughout the land upon sinners and the lazies.

On approach, the trailer looked lonelier than usual. The Mims home seemed to have more crooks and turns. But as the boy stood in the middle of the dirt, and from this distance, it was sorely plain—a bleached-out green metal box with faulty underpinning. To Rebel, never so small. Lee's original promise to maintain the yard for his mother had lasted all of one week. Soon, the cheapness of the trailer matched the shoddiness of the lawn and patches of weeds and barren earth welcomed all visitors.

Rebel shooed dogs away as he managed the pre-fab wooden steps, yanking on the flimsy screen door to no avail. The entire home seemed to rock as he kicked at the metal. He could hear steps approaching and made way. Tab flung the door open violently.

"What?" his cousin snapped.

"What, what?"

"Whatchu want, dammit?" Her eyes narrowed.

"To come inside?"

Tab grimaced.

"You askin' or fuckin' tellin'?"

"I'm...I guess I'm..." the boy balked, watching Tab become more annoyed.

"Shit, boy. It's yer house." She leaned to block his view. In the space between her arm and ribs, Rebel made out a muscular, mocha ass. It buried itself within Levi's as both jeans and owner scuttled through the window overlooking the backyard.

"He's leavin' a shoe," the boy observed.

Tab stomped away. In one fluid motion, she grabbed the shoe and fired it side-arm through the window. "Dammit, Rodrick!" she scolded.

"Was it Roddy Stockdale?" Rebel asked, stepping inside. Tab slammed the window shut and marched back through the short hallway, making sure to shove Rebel as she passed.

"I swear to God, Rebel James, you tell yer mama he was here and I'll stomp a mudhole in yer ass. You hear me?"

The boy was smiling, and she slapped him.

"Gotdammit, Rebel! You hear?"

Tab took this incessant grinning as a kind of mockery, the boy's subtle, private way of reminding everyone he was above the trailer trash they'd all been born into. In truth, Rebel smiled only because he reasoned Rodrick and his cousin were a near perfect genetic match. Both were beautiful. The girl, unavoidably so. The two brothers had discussed this perplexity many times. Tab seemed out of place ascetically, features too graceful for the starkness of their surroundings. "Too perty to come from our line," Lee would say.

Tab's face had influences both Native American and European—high cheeks with rich, sable eyes; gypsy locks were left mostly alone, at home curled around bare, athletic shoulders. Rebel felt certain someone who looked like that did not belong in a place like this, as if this kind of magnificence was wasted on those lacking the capacity for appreciation due. For those who shared this sentiment, it was agreed Tab would likely wind up in a big city like New York or Los Angeles, modeling or busying herself with whatever other silly things beautiful people find to do. But here, now, frying bologna sandwiches for her twelve-year-old cousin while her aunt worked a double? Hardly.

The Gypsy, however, couldn't have been more at home. And despite knowing full well the degree of God's grace upon her, there was no hint of elitism. This, of course, made her appeal all the more maddening for anyone she came into contact with.

Soon after Charleen hired her to keep an eye on Rebel, Lee made his intentions known by cupping her perfectly shaped ass with authority. Tab retrieved a dirty steak knife from the kitchen sink and put it to Lee's throat. This had the unforeseen effect of spiraling the older brother's heart from lust to love. In fact, as soon as she allowed the teeth of the blade to slink back from his freckle-spotted skin, Lee sprinted to the back of the trailer and into his mother's closet. He wrestled a Polaroid camera from an upper shelf in order to capture his neck up-close, blood trickling from a dozen miniature shark bites underneath his jaw. Rebel bore witness to all of this. Lee was punch-drunk, eyes glazed, studying the photo as it clunked its way out of the small machine. He snatched it from the camera, waving it impatiently in the air.

"Whatchu doin'?" Rebel asked.

"Moments like 'is, Rebellion...moments like 'is ya gotta preserve in pictures," he raved. Returning to the kitchen, he riffled through the junk drawer until he found a marker, and on the back of the picture he wrote:

> Lee, always remember I love you this much.
> Yours always, Tab '87

This would hang indefinitely, wedged in the corner of Lee's bedroom mirror. Tab's penchant for violence might have seemed strange to some, but not Rebel. He saw plainly that most girls hated her because none stood a chance comparatively. As a result, since the age of four, most of her friends had been boys. Roughhousing and fist fights became second nature for the little girl, but it was her pain fascination that marked her as unique, even among more pugnacious males. Rebel could only cull theories from mutterings he'd heard from Lee and other town gossip. Beyond fabrications of animal torture, only one incident had made the papers.

Tab was in the fourth grade when Clem Patterson asked her to stay after school one day for additional tutoring in a struggling subject. For Tabitha, this could have been any subject since she reviled education. At the time, Clem was a catch for the fledgling school, a hometown hero who'd made good at a state college, graduating with honors. Clem was also handsome, single, and eager to pour heart and soul into young minds. His was the first class that Principal Scruggs would visit with prospective families to demonstrate what children would be getting at Clanton Elementary—top-shelf instruction from the best Auburn University had to offer. Abysmal facilities and overcrowded classes be damned...Clanton had Clem.

According to the police report, at approximately 3:15 p.m., Clem stroked the child's hair while pointing at a mispronounced word. Tab looked directly at him (per the girl's report), smiled, and asked if she could sit on his lap for the duration of the lesson. Tab told the interviewing officer it was at that moment Mr. Patterson, "got sweaty on his forehead," and said he'd love for her to sit with him. Tab centered herself on his thighs, her back to his stomach. Shortly after erasing, then rewriting the word "reassurance," she reached between her own legs and grabbed the biggest handful of Clem she could manage. She then began stabbing him with a pencil he'd had her sharpen for that very lesson.

Clem's penis and scrotum were treated for eight puncture wounds and Tab got to keep the pencil. When the responding officer realized the situation, he ushered Tab into his squad car, the bloody little stick firm as concrete in the child's hand. The officer never asked for it. Clem and his punctured penis disappeared soon after. The local paper reported the "unfortunate departure of one of Clanton Elementary's finest young educators." Charleen, however, knew better, citing a private meeting she was aware of that took place between the teacher and that same responding officer. Clem took a "bad spill" down the steps of his apartment a few days later resulting in hospitalization.

As far as Rodrick Stockdale, he had the form of an Adonis dipped in a syrup of warm umber. Roddy was easily the best athlete to come out of Chilton County in the last thirty years. As a ten-year-old, Alabama and Auburn sent recruiters to several of his Pop-Warner games, and by the time he was a ninth grader, his coach was fielding inquiries from a dozen D-1 schools across the country. His senior year just ahead, Chilton County High School's stadium would soon swell to capacity every Friday night in the fall, teeming with maniacal fans and scouts.

Lee hated Roddy with a passion, but not for reasons anyone might expect. It wasn't for his incredulous athletic ability or because he was black, although Lee was a keen racist. No, Lee had sniffed out what only two or three other people in the entire town knew: Rodrick was brilliant. An elementary school teacher was the first to notice, immediately recommending a different school to his mother. Roddy's mother wrongly assumed this was a poor ruse to decamp her black son from the educator's overwhelmingly Caucasian class. But time after time, each teacher's assessment had been unanimous: the boy was gifted. Intellectually advanced and "bored" was the looping refrain. According to counselors, his mind would continue to starve unless appropriately challenged.

Growing up in West End, however, this kind of aptitude

stood at odds with his athletic ability. As a child, Roddy learned being street-smart was a foregone conclusion of necessity, while book-smarts were regarded as something else entirely—a waste of one's time at least and uppity presumption at most. And so, he became adept at hiding his mind, intentionally failing a test here, skipping due assignments there. Only a few saw through the facade, and Lee was one of them.

For Lee, it was enough to watch Roddy win the affections of Tab, who, having graduated a year before, was sticking around Clanton for only God knew why. Her presence was Lee's pain, and the infatuation with his cousin would never leave, clinging to him like an unfinished dream. But this other revelation—the smothering of genius for the prospect of cheap, shitty acceptance from shitty friends—this was too much.

His frustration culminated during a particular lunch period, now infamous, that saw him rise from his seat at an all-white table and make his way to Roddy's all-black table. The white boy eased himself into a position directly across from Rodrick and the entire company fell silent.

"Why you act like a dumb motherfucker when you ain't?"

For an instant, the two shared a look as every inch of air escaped the room. Rodrick's shock gave way to an innocent fear. He'd let the mask slip. Exposed. Lee's countenance was all earnest inquiry and sarcastic contempt: *How dare you spit in the face uh God when he done breathed his glory on ya in ever fuckin' way possible?*

This blink of mutual vulnerability evaporated as quickly as it materialized. Before the gasps had time to quiet, Rodrick had Lee's cheek glued to a lunch tray, pummeling the open side of his face with machine-gun blows until Lee lay motionless. Soon, the boy was unrecognizable, blood from his nose and mouth greasing the lunch table end to end.

In the kitchen, Tab swiped a crinkled pack of cigarettes from the bar. She jiggered one into her mouth and went to work digging a lighter from the back pocket of skin-tight jeans. Tab hopped onto the countertop.

Crossing her legs beneath her, she swung swoops of black hair from her eyes.

"Where ya been at?"

"Barn."

Tab flicked ash from her cigarette as she studied the boy, eventually extending the pack toward him. Rebel's eyes fell to the floor and he shook his head, shuffling toward the refrigerator.

"Y'know, these'll help with that," she said.

Rebel regarded the shelves inside the fridge, mostly barren save out-of-date condiments.

"Wi' what?" He retrieved an open pack of bologna.

"All them nerves and shit."

Rebel nudged himself into one of the kitchen chairs, tugging at a piece of meat from the greasy pack. The processed edges were brown and hard from exposure. Tab turned, lowering her head enough to see through the window above the sink. The dirt road leading from the trailer melted into shadow. She slid from the counter and took the meat from the boy just as he raised it to his mouth.

"Lemme fry it up for ya."

"You don't have to."

"It's fine," she murmured.

The bologna was frying in an instant and Tab gathered bread and mustard. She rummaged for a paper plate. The boy moved to the short bar dividing the kitchen from the living room and picked up where he left off on a pencil drawing of the barn and its background. It was an impressive rendering; a gift Charleen had passed down in ample amount.

He'd tried more than a dozen times to capture Tabitha's essence to no avail. She was always sliding from room to room, never alighting long enough for him to properly study her finer nuances. Rebel wondered if this constant motion was due to an overall unease, some subsurface acceptance of knowing she was never really safe. Perhaps it was boredom or that no single place held enough fascination for her to stay longer than a handful of fleeting moments.

"Where's Lee at?" she asked.

Rebel traced over the bottom edge of the barn's bay window, adding weight to the charcoal line.

"Don' know."

Tab delivered the meal and mussed the boy's hair. She folded her arms and observed him, pitching her head to one side. She sucked bologna grease from the edge of her thumb.

"You'll be cookin' for yerself soon enough."

At the sink, she shoved the hot pan underneath the faucet as flumes of steam shot toward the ceiling.

"Why ya say that?" Rebel said without looking up.

Tab sighed, peering once more through the window above the sink.

"Cuz I ain't always gon be around, and Lee ain't worth a damn, that's why. And yer mama's got more on her plate than she can handle," her voice descended into the sink.

The boy stopped blending lines on the paper and looked up at Tabitha, who moved dirty dishes around that didn't need moving.

"You gon have to step up and run shit sooner or later...so let somebody else fry ya damn bologna while they offerin'."

Tab moved to the living room and turned on the small

television, finding perch in the corner of the couch. Rebel took a bite of the sandwich, examining it carefully. He squeezed until mustard curled out from the edges of the crust.

The boy moved quietly from the stool and made his way to his room at the end of the hallway. Closing the door, he went to his bed and removed several He-Man figures from the lowest shelf that constituted his headboard. Rebel jostled the shelf board, revealing the hiding place for his most precious treasures: scores of comics, some vintage, along with a well-worn cassette player. He sat the recorder beside him along with a solitary comic, replacing the board to its tight fit.

Another bite of bologna had Rebel pressing play, and as the first honeycomb cord of Muddy Waters' *Train Fare Blues* slipped through the speakers, a measured sigh escaped the boy's chest. He lay back on his bed, feet dangling just above the carpet, and unfolded the comic above him. Successive frames made Superman appear to actually fly. Reaching overhead, he slid the window open, allowing the wet pine air to whisper over the pages.

There was Clark Kent. Rebel's eyes took in the details of this everyman. His posture, how Lois regarded him. Naive and unknowing. He flipped several pages to the action, allowing those images to flash before him for the hundredth time. Muddy sang on, a dozen stories buried within each word.

The boy finally stood, placing the remnants of his sandwich on the pressboard dresser. He leaned back against the bedroom door, peering into the small black square directly across from him. Rebel envisioned the window a gateway through which the entirety of the universe might exist. Eons of stars fixed as the canvas for bundles of planets, spread like seed across an infinity of space dust. And all their needy moons. Naive and unknowing.

That last thought danced at the fringe of his mind as the boy pushed from the door. With three rushing steps he launched himself, sailing over the bed and headlong into the abyss of the black square.

CHAPTER 2

The Tourist

He lay buoyant, sky approaching and retreating with each stretch of the canvas. The boy inhaled the vastness above him, wishing he could rise to meet it.

Lee had suggested moving the trampoline beneath his little brother's bedroom window years ago, but Rebel had forgotten about it as soon as his brother had brought it up. That was until days later, when Lee antagonized Rebel to the point of tears over something trivial, and the boy punched his older brother in the chest with as much force as his then eight-year-old body could muster. Lee feigned injury and took off like a scorched cat, screaming a staggering number of expletives in the time it took to sprint the length of the hall. He burst into Rebel's room and hurled himself through the open window. Shocked his punch had such effect, the boy ran to see what came of this mental break, only to find Lee laughing hysterically as he bounced on the trampoline, middle fingers erect.

Rebel rolled over and pulled himself to the edge of the rusted frame, then onto the ground, ripping his shirt on a wayward spring as he went. The boy reached the fence gate and climbed it, moving on then toward the woods that would eventually take him to civilization.

Smoke, liquor, and the sound of billiard balls clapping against one another filled *Larry's*, the resident pub for Clanton's blue-collar coterie. A small labyrinth of cracked leather booths wombed within clouded amber, Charleen navigated the place like its architect, delivering beers and platters of fries, gob-soaked in cheese and bacon. Larry had hired her six months prior, not at all needing the help but pleasantly surprised to find male patrons preferred her over his veteran waitresses.

At thirty-seven, Charleen was still shapely enough to warrant the occasional ass grab to which she never grumbled, milking every shift she could. Rebel studied her for much of that same six months, observing from his anchored spot in front of Galaga. Larry had ordered the behemoth for the second-rate arcade he'd fashioned within a small corner of the building. The man had played the game for twelve hours straight the day it was delivered, stopping only to squash a drunken argument. But once Rebel James Mims began showing up toward the end of his mother's shifts to ensure she made it home safely, the top six scores quickly belonged to R.J.M.

Rebel watched his mother, every detail of her process. He finally concluded that her success in this cheap-jack bar boiled down to three fundamental elements. First, she only served tables where a man was present. The boy never once saw her grace a female-only booth. Second, she never left a table until the man ordering smiled at her or until she'd touched his arm or shoulder. And third, she never spent more than 28.5 seconds at a table.

Ever. Whether his mother was cognizant of the particulars of her own system, he did not know. She never tipped her hat toward self-realization, but Rebel knew he was witnessing something masterful.

At the back of the pub, Rebel stopped long enough to help Marvin Jones pour out a tub of grease near the dumpster. "'Preciate it, lil' man," Marvin said, wiping his hands on a soiled apron. He leaned against the dumpster and lit a joint, pulling the do-rag from his head and using it to wipe his eyes. Marvin was seventeen but looked much older, long and rawboned with deep coal skin. One of Rodrick's teammates, he was perfect for the deep ball.

He extended the joint to the boy, who declined.

"Good for you, lil' bud," Marvin grinned. "Yo mama'd have my ass anyway."

"She prolly wouldn't care none."

"Sheeeit. You and me both know betta 'nat." Marvin leaned from the dumpster, reapplying his do-rag. "She in there cleanin' up tonight, boy. Y'all gon eat good dis weekin...long as dude don't mess her up."

"Who?"

"Look like a new boyfriend t'me."

Marvin tilted his head back and spiraled a flume into the night. Rebel disappeared through the back door as Marvin glimpsed a stray dog creeping along the fence for scraps.

"Git on, now," Marvin warned. The mange-ridden terrier crouched but slinked forward anyway, slowing movements as it weighed Marvin's intentions.

"Aw'ight, then, muhfuckah," Marvin searched the ground as the dog released a low growl. He snatched a chip-edged rock from the corner of the dumpster and fired it toward the animal, nailing the cur squarely in the haunches. A yelping retreat, and the dog was gone.

Rebel slid onto the padded stool that bore the indention of his small buttocks and pretended to play the game. He fidgeted with the joystick mindlessly, scanning the adjoining room for his mother. And there she was, honoring the three pillars as a loyal monk. He pushed the stopwatch button on his digital wristwatch: a table, some chat, a touch, the customer's smile, the commitment of order to memory—and she was gone. The boy pushed stop: 26.7 seconds.

As he dug deep in his pocket to find a quarter to actually play a round, Charleen whipped by a foreign table outside her normal route. Rebel started the timer. She sat down across from the customer, a man the boy guessed to be a decade older than his mother. Rebel abandoned the search for the quarter as he watched this scene play out. There were the typical flirtations. Her eyebrow cocked in conjunction with a coy grin denoting she found something amusing. Her obligatory arm graze, a touch of the shoulder. But something was off. Rebel couldn't put his finger on it until he glanced at his watch: 46.31.

The boy stared at the tiny black numbers against the scuffed gray of the screen and found himself moving toward the table. On approach, the child registered as much as he could.

Even sitting, the man stretched tall against the booth, with a Wrangler button-down that revealed a slight pudge above the belt, otherwise slender. Long hands reached across to clasp those of his mother, and gaudy, cheap rings covered the dulled tattoos marking his knuckles.

His hair was thin and wavy and black and ran into a brief mullet at the back of his neck, while a bushy goatee bent and curled with every grin. Wedged vertically above the corner of his left eye was a scar that resulted in a hairless divot, separating the eyebrow into two distinct continents. Charleen followed the man's gaze to her son. She rushed to meet the boy, wrapping him in a hug.

"Rebel!" she cooed, leading him to stand beside the customer. "Come meet my friend, Dennis. Oh, this is so great! I been wantin' y'all to meet!"

Dennis took a swig of beer and extended a rusty paw toward the child. "Hey there, young man. Nice to meetcha."

Rebel squeezed the man's hand as hard as he could, just as Lee had taught him, but the gesture was moot. The boy's offering was swallowed by Dennis' rangy grip. Rebel tried to maintain pressure but lost nerve and was the first to relax, his fingers now noodles in a bear trap. Dennis grinned and let go of the boy's hand, settling back into the booth.

"What's yer last name?" Rebel asked, stone faced.

Dennis shot Charleen a smirk. "Cleckley."

"I know some Cleckleys," Rebel observed.

Dennis let slip a laugh, the belittling kind adults proffer children when they find them cute. And it was at that very moment Rebel decided he hated this man as thoroughly as he'd ever hated another human being.

Charleen dragged the boy into the booth, situating him directly across from Dennis, who resumed nursing his beer. His mother launched into a series of flimsy details about her new friend, foaming the runway as best she could. But for the boy, her voice droned into a huddle of irksome syllables. As far as Rebel was concerned, everything he could ever hope to learn about this man was being decided in the seconds it took for his mother to babble on. "His dealership's down 'ere past *Sullivan's*, Reb. You know where I'm talkin' 'bout?" Charleen said.

"Yeah. I seen it before."

"You should come over sometime, son. I'll show you around the lot. Everything we got is used, but, if it's on my lot, it might as well be new," Dennis purred, sneaking Charleen a wink. "I hear you still got four or five years yet, but you see something you like, maybe we can set it aside... have it waitin' for you when you turn sixteen."

Charleen leaned away to take in Rebel's face. The boy forced a grin for his mother's sake, hoping this would be enough to send her away. It was. Charleen slid from the booth, her hand pressed on the boy's shoulder to ensure he understood she wanted him to stay. Rebel's eyes never left the man as he watched Dennis watch his mother go. The boy considered for a moment if it was unfair to judge so quickly. Had he grown predisposed to suspicion as a result of the litany of men that wandered in and out of his mother's life, and, consequently, his? Some had been earnest in their aspiration to care for her. Most had not. A few had even feigned interest in her sons. Most didn't bother to fake it.

But here the boy sat, examining this latest beast, trying not to be further put off by the slow-burn leer that seemed to be the man's resting expression. Subtle. A tiny simper announcing he was somehow ahead in time, as if he knew what was coming but had no plans to warn anyone.

"Your mom's pretty great," he offered, observing Charleen work the room.

The boy tried to think of a response that would convey the least amount of interest. *Damn tourist*, Rebel thought, and felt guilty for cursing the stranger in his head.

"She never mentioned me before, huh?"

"Nope," Rebel snipped. Finally, something to communicate anything his body language had failed to get across.

"That's alright," Dennis mused. "We got plenty of time to get to know each other."

At this, the boy's eyes lowered to the table like a dog beaten, and a sick pang nudged his gut. He studied the first thing his eyes found—a grimy, crust-covered saltshaker. Although the only food he'd eaten that day were the few bites of Tab's bologna sandwich, he recognized the genesis of the nausea as the man sitting across from him now.

Rebel brushed away the congealed goop blocking the shaker's holes. It was rare that a particular individual stirred such repulsiveness within him. Something else. A lingering void perhaps, inevitably occupied by a parade of men feigning good will. The cycle was easy enough to spot. At some point, the man would try to instruct Rebel in whatever grease-monkey wisdom he'd picked up throughout his own rugged life. That was the obligatory effort made. Check. But soon—and the boy often considered timing this in the same way he did the pillars of his mother's work—any hint of goodwill would vanish and their essential nature would lay bare, raw and unfiltered to the world. This recognition would come first to the sons. Always the sons. Perhaps because they could smell instinctively what was native to their own souls—a kindred, primal connection to that same ugliness.

"My mama says y'all's friends," Rebel ventured.

Dennis leaned into the table, edging his beer aside. "Well, I hope we end up bein' more than that, son."

"I ain't yer son."

Rebel froze. The statement slipped before he realized he'd formed the words. He shrunk against the seat, his spine flinching from shards of the booth's cracked leather. His eyes fell again to the table. Dennis only grinned, glancing around the room to ascertain Charleen's whereabouts. The man lowered his head to meet the child's cower.

"You know what…you're right about that. You sure are. My apologies."

The Tourist reached for his beer and Rebel watched the leer vanish just before he touched lips to glass. This new look was something else, something primitive and lifeless, an expression the boy knew he would see again. Dennis wiped his mouth with the back of his wrist.

"But you know what I think?" Dennis scanned the room once more. "I think you're a smart kid. And I think you and me both know I'm probably gon be stickin' around."

The boy shifted against the cheap padding, trying to digest the implications of this remark. And now it was Rebel's turn to look for his mother, but Charleen had flitted to the far side of the bar. He pulled up straight as he could.

"We're fine like we are," Rebel said.

"'Course you are!" Dennis shot back. This sudden burst rattled the boy. "I know you and Lee got everything squared away."

Rebel's ears perked.

"Yeah. Your mom told me all about your brother. The infamous Lee Mims…said you two are thick as thieves."

"That's what I mean. Lee looks out for us. We don't need no help." And, for the first time, the boy felt real sadness. An intangible, cavernous loss, heavy around his neck and shoulders. It was as if Lee's name leaving his own tongue shook loose the mortar, and his upper lip gave way to the smallest quiver. "I gotta go, I guess," Rebel said.

Dennis tilted his beer as the boy stood. Before he reached the arcade, Charleen had accosted him, euphoric, searching her son's face. "Well? How'd ya like him?"

Over her shoulder, Rebel watched the Galaga spaceship launch missiles at alien enemies. "He's aw'ight," Rebel grunted.

The woman knew not to press. "You stayin' 'til close?"

"I think I'm gon just head back," the boy said, glancing at The Tourist. "You got somebody lookin' after ya."

"Rebel, are you kiddin' me? He's just a friend. But I'm glad y'all got to finally meet. He's real nice. Trust me."

"Okay." Rebel pulled himself toward the hallway. "Hey, is it aw'ight if I sleep in the barn tonight?"

Charleen sighed. "You know I hate when yer out there at night, baby."

"Come on, Mama. Please?"

The woman retied her apron before propping her hands on her hips. Charleen recognized the child's countenance, by far the harshest critic of her choice in men. "Alright." She hugged him and the boy kissed his mother's cheek. "But sump'm crawls up 'ere and bites yer ass, don't come cryin'."

"Yes, ma'am."

Rebel flung the back door wide and slapped hands with Marvin who was enjoying the last of his blunt. The black boy flicked ash in the child's direction. Rebel reached out for the tiny rolled paper, causing Marvin's eyebrow to pique. A smile spread across his wide mouth. Marvin extended the smoke and Rebel took it. The boy analyzed the joint as he trekked the dirt drive behind the bar. Reaching a trailhead, he watched the tip of the smoke dwarf to a tiny glow as he ambled into the dense woods.

The boy coughed and choked at the joint as he followed trail after trail. From a distance, he finally made out a trio of pocket-sized squares glowing orange—the rear windows of the Mims trailer. He would need his sleeping bag and pillow before rejoining his brother in the loft, but first required Tab's whereabouts.

Frustrated attempts to capture her to paper had left him searching for occasions to find her unaware. Traversing the last bit of brush and briar, he reached the best climbing oak nearest the trailer and made his ascent. Four branches from the ground, he found the spot where he'd nestled a dozen times before. This was the seat he'd spied from when Lee had been drunk and violent with blind, lurching swings that had barely missed Charleen's nose. This was the spot from which he'd watched Tab and Roddy have sex once.

He could make out the top of Tab's head in the living room, the glow from the television casting turns of color from her brunette palette. Farther out, he would have a better view, and before scooting forward, he dug a wrinkled piece of ruled paper from his back pocket and a dull-stubbed pencil from his sock. Rebel clenched the pencil with his teeth, inching farther out until the branch lowered from weight. The window framed the scene now and he saw most of his cousin coiled perfectly on the couch.

Without looking down, he unfolded the paper, flattening it on his thigh. Moon glow would suffice for light. The boy strained to catch her eyes. In truth, that would be the lion's share of what was needed, since within those eyes lived all that she was. Two minutes of stillness...and those eyes. He was certain he could piddle out the rest.

He watched as her eyelids bobbed and rose drunkenly, head tilting as she trained her stare forward. The boy found himself beginning to stand and followed the subtle movement of her shoulder all the way down to her waist and on to a hand that was plunged deep into the open v of her jeans, slipping down and back, down and back again.

Rebel remained paralyzed in a crouched stupor, unable to look away. He followed her gaze long enough to make out the figure on the screen across from her: the familiar caramel- furred creature with the ant-eater snout. ALF shook devilishly, laughing at his own corny joke. With that realization, weight suddenly left the child's legs and the tree limb beneath his feet gave way. A piercing crack and the boy dropped, groping wildly in search of a branch that was never there. An offshoot sliced through the pant leg of his jeans and into his thigh as he fell. Rebel met the ground with an unforgiving thud as every bit of air escaped his small chest. Rolling onto his back, he stared open-mouthed at the celestial, clamoring for oxygen that refused him.

The sound of the back door opening jerked his attention sideways, long enough to see Tab descend the short steps of the back porch. Under one arm, she bore Rebel's sleeping bag and pillow, the other busy with a fresh cigarette. She took her time, and Rebel knew this was to elongate suffering.

Tab stood over the boy, finally, cocking her hip into a relaxed position as she took a deep, methodical drag. She hadn't bothered buttoning her pants and they were just beginning to slide off her hips on one side. *What a bitch*, Rebel thought through choking moans as he pointed to his throat.

"Yer mama called and said you's gon sleep in the barn," Tab said coolly. "First of all, you should'a told me you left." She switched to rest on the other hip. "Second," Tab balled up the loose sleeping bag and pillow, "here's yer shit." She dropped the fluffy mass on top of the child and walked back to the trailer.

The trek to the barn was always more precarious after dark. On more than one occasion, he'd met with coyotes and a few surly raccoons. The path was a curving line of meandering twist-weed. He managed by the faded glow of Isaac's old work flashlight. Barely up to task, Rebel throttled the yellow stick in his hand, shaking it periodically so that it showered punches of light on the more nefarious turns.

All seemed quiet and godforsaken, as if regular nocturnal traffic saw fit to show reverence in honor of Lee's passing. Rebel lugged his gear over one shoulder and from the ground cast light up onto his brother. Lee remained suspended as before, a frozen marionette, without the slightest turn of direction since Rebel last saw him.

Upstairs, the boy observed his brother as the blackest silhouette. Moon poured through the bay window and traced Lee's body in a leaden glow. This was bright enough for Rebel to shut off the flashlight. He walked to the other side of his brother, looking for changes. More spit splatters beneath, but beyond that, the only difference was color. Blood-rushed cheeks and cherry-splotched skin had given way to a serene viridescence, made all the more phantasmal by moon shade. Lee's blue eyes served as the barn's beacon now and reflected a luminescent moon.

Seeing the trailer in the distance reminded Rebel of his encounter with Tab. All of it might have scarred him for life if he thought for a second that she gave a damn. But the boy knew better. He knew that if he'd walked in on her directly and stood there in front of the TV, mouth agape, innocence lost, she would have regarded him only with annoying disdain. And not for pubescent voyeurism, but for interrupting. Lack of manners.

Rebel unfurled the slipshod bag onto the floorboards, situating himself between Lee and the bay window. He dropped his pillow on the side that felt most natural and lowered himself onto his bed. The boy stretched long, flexing muscles to relax and wincing at the wound in his thigh. It turned out to be shallower than he'd imagined, only requiring Band-Aids scoured from his mother's bathroom. Rebel knew his mother would rant about the rip in his jeans, about lack of money for new clothes.

He lay there, bathed in moon, concluding that Lee looked taller. The day's hang had elongated space between vertebrae, and his feet were closer to the floor than they had been. The boy rolled his head to the other side, casting his stare through the massive opening of the bay. It was then the questions finally came.

Not, *Why would Lee do this?* Rebel could work that out later if he cared enough to investigate. Lee's mind and ways, as far as the boy could tell, had always been a haphazard concoction of misfiring neurons and animalistic trigger-responses with no pattern or through-line. *But why leave ME?,* Rebel wondered.

He regarded the expanse on the other side of the frame, trying to decipher if the length from star to star was equidistant. For all of Lee's hell-raising vice, for all his hate and vengefulness, in spite of the tireless beatings and emotional havoc that trailed after the older boy...Rebel knew his brother loved him. The child raised a finger and traced a methodical figure-eight along the whitest dots beyond his hand.

"Hey, lil' brother."

The boy's hand stopped. The looping motion of his finger frozen in time as he attempted to register what he just heard. The question of its realness was barely beyond his own breath, daring him to look. Lowering his arm, Rebel steeled himself. He snapped his head toward the dead body.

The corpse was smiling down at him. With some effort, Lee curled his hand further up from his hip, pointing at his own broken neck.

"Ain't this some shit?"

CHAPTER 3

Supplanting Chandalare

Rebel remained slack-jawed, immobile against the base of the bay window, having scrambled against it at the sight of his brother's talking corpse. Lee's expression changed as he made efforts to look down, examining his own condition.

"You gon help me down or sit there like a damn fool?"

Rebel's mouth grew wider still, making way for words that would not come. The boy clambered to his knees and pushed back against the rough pine. Forcing himself sideways, he scraped against the perimeter of the loft, never taking his eyes off his brother. Lee tried swinging his weight, struggling to turn his torso in Rebel's direction.

"Where ya goin'?" the dead boy said.

Rebel sprawled from the bottom of the barn, careening headlong into a wall of chest-high weeds. Righting himself, the boy used his arms like machetes, whacking at the dark brush until his feet finally touched the smoothness of the path. He sprinted.

When he felt he'd put enough distance between himself and the barn, he glanced back, half expecting to see his brother galloping after him like a necromantic Ghost Rider, his face aflame, on a horse with burning, cavernous holes where eyes should have been. Rebel saw only the black square of the bay. The boy skirted around the trailer and mounted his bike, speeding down the dirt road and away from home.

The whip of the Huffy's chain against the cheap plastic guard was the first thing to usher the boy back to reality. The bike was a hand-me-down from Lee, who'd treated it mercilessly. Its bright red paint long vanquished by rust and hard sun. Rebel had tried in vain to dress it up, make it his own as much as possible. But Lee's abuse had won out in the end. Her frame was sorely bent, the handlebar often slipped unexpectedly, and the tires were so re-patched they retained little original factory rubber.

Rebel finally skidded to a stop in front of *Grayson's*, an antiquated two-pump gas station helmed by none other than Grayson himself, a seventy-six-year-old Clanton relic. The old man had driven away most of his customer base over the years, and certainly not because his fuel was pricey. In fact, his was the cheapest in town by a good thirty cents. Gaudily underpriced. The steady depletion of business was due in large part because the old man simply loved to talk, and this he owed to a genuine fascination with people.

He was enamored with the mundane goings on of each life that passed through the washed-out glass double-doors of his store. This, of course, would endear him early on to anyone venturing west of the interstate in search of bargain gasoline, but soon felt like a chore the first time a person found themselves in a hurry. For many, the guilt of rushing off was too much. Cutting an anecdote short left most feeling disgusted with themselves afterwards, as if they'd shunned a venerable bear waving over passersby at the zoo.

The clang of cowbell against the old glass signaled the boy's entrance, causing Grayson to shuffle nearer the cash register for a better view. The old man pushed outmoded spectacles further down a long, shovel-shaped nose and grinned with recognition.

"What say, Johnny Reb? Comin' in late today," Grayson said warmly. Rebel made straight for the cooler in the back of the store without looking up. He glanced through the windows to the parking lot outside. The old man watched Rebel pace, following his eye-line in search of what was troubling the child. Outside, only the neglected fuel pumps and the narrow stretch of blacktop camouflaged within the dark.

Grayson cocked a white bushy eyebrow. "Who ya expectin'?"

The boy collected his bottle of chocolate as the cold of the open cooler chilled the sweat on his arms and face. He held the door, staring at the neat rows of sugary drinks.

"Nobody," Rebel said. He let go of the metal handle, waiting for the familiar sound of rubber suctioning hard against more rubber. He lifted his eyes to see Lee standing behind him, neck rung red from the bristly rope hanging loose around a pronounced collar bone. Lee waved at his little brother and Rebel gasped, hurling his Yoo-hoo hard against the dead boy's smiling reflection. Shards of the bottle and chocolate exploded in a thousand directions.

Grayson shoved from his elbows, moving as quickly as possible around the counter. "Damn, son!" He hurried down the aisle. "What the hell happened?"

Rebel swung around in search of the ghost only to find the old man ambling toward him. The boy turned back to the cooler and wiped his hand through the syrupy chocolate coating the glass. All he could see was his own terror-stricken face. Rebel stumbled backwards and into an overstuffed rack, sending bags of chips and candy spilling to the ground. Grayson reached out to steady the child.

"Whoa! Calm down."

The boy swatted the old man's hand away and scrambled to his feet. "I'm sorry, Mr. Grayson." The child's voice quivered as he backed toward the double doors. The old man shook his head, taking in the extent of the disaster. Outside, Rebel slipped in the loose gravel in route to his bike, raking skin from his palms.

Twenty minutes later, the boy was alternating lifting his hands from the handlebar, allowing wind to ease those burning palms. An urgent breeze pushed hair from his eyes as he questioned the validity of what had just happened. *No...no way.*

He rested his forearms onto the handlebar, opening his palms to the wind as he rode, in worship of something invisible that beckoned him farther along the dark road. By the time the pain in his hands abated, he figured he was miles from home, already past the high school and long past Larry's bar.

He realized how far he'd ridden when the scenery began to morph. Busted curbs gave way to pristine concrete edges, and derelict structures were replaced by freshly minted two-story homes. Lush, extravagant landscaping. All of this carved into the choicest tracts of land on the fringe of the East Side.

This was Riverchase, the newest development beyond Chandalare. He remembered Lee once ran with a boy from Chandalare. When the boy's mother laid eyes on Lee—those freckled, sun-scorched shoulders protruding like knobs beneath a grungy wife-beater—things changed. She was all smiles and Southern hospitality at first, presenting her son and his new friend with a snack plate full of carrots, apple slices, and caramel while the two played Atari.

Almost immediately the boy's mother caught Lee ogling the finer parts of her ass, one she had tucked firmly into white skintight jeans. This she would have let slide, but Lee could never win out against his baser compulsions. He promptly found the largest carrot on the plate, made sure to lock eyes with the woman, and proceeded to slide the orange stick back and forth in the hole he'd formed with paper-thin lips.

But this was Riverchase, a newer development by more than a decade and one that would shame Chandalare into obsolescence. Rebel sped up enough to coast, soaking in the opulence of a lifestyle he knew was not his. The homes and the yards where fresh sod had recently taken hold. Driveways anchored by Mercedes and BMWs. Others were still skeletal in growth, framing studs desperately trying to keep pace with the changing whims of excited homeowners. Drywall awaiting its mud.

The boy made the bottom of a small hill and coasted onto a new street. He steered himself to the sidewalk, tires whirring against the virgin concrete. The houses here were mostly finished, and ahead, on the other side of the street, Rebel noticed a kid shooting basketball in a driveway. Sailing nearer, he realized it was a girl with hair pulled into a tight pony. He guessed her to be close to his own age and he slowed. From the edge of dense brush, she drained a basket. The ball bounced off the goal post and rolled to a stop against the bumper of a large U-Haul. Two movers trekked down a ramp leading from the truck to the ground, leveraging a massive rosewood chest as they went.

The girl jogged to retrieve the ball and Rebel pushed hair from his eyes, desperately hoping she was as pretty as he expected a rich new girl to be. She plucked the ball from the ground, examining this curious boy as he rode by. She offered a small wave which made Rebel sit up straight. He glanced shyly to the sidewalk below. A rustling from above called his attention. He looked up to see Lee hanging upside down from a tree branch that extended across the walk.

"Hey, Reb!" Lee gushed, reaching out for a hug.

Rebel inhaled sharply and yanked the handlebar to miss his brother, launching himself headlong past the bike. Everything slowed in the air, a cruel postponement of the pain to come.

His body hammered against the grey slab—more skin lost—and rolled into half a dozen newly planted shrubs. The collision yanked the bushes clean, chasing after the boy like verdant tumbleweeds.

The crash finished with the child on his back, breathless—the second time since nightfall hard earth stole his oxygen. Rebel beat a fist into the grass as he lay there, bare to the world, and wondered why today, of all days, had turned into such a strange and uncontrollable shitstorm.

CHAPTER 4

Of Manookie

His small lungs started to finally inflate, and a sweet, winsome face came into view, blocking out the glow of stars. As Rebel's eyes adjusted to the silhouette, he realized it was the new kid, and in spite of the pain, he was euphoric. She was even prettier than he'd hoped. Two dark locks had escaped her ponytail and they curved around rich, mahogany eyes that matched her hair. Her jawline sloped in crescent to a chin that was home to the faintest dimple. Before regaining his first full breath, the boy decided he would love this person for the rest of his life.

"Are you okay?" she asked, her brow furrowed with worry.

Still fighting for oxygen, Rebel rolled to his knees and held up his hand. "I'm alright," he choked, glancing at the branch. He knew he would see nothing there. The boy pulled himself upright, using the last bit of strength he had to pretend he was not as hurt as he was. He teetered over to his bike to assess the damage. Every angle of the thing was wrong and misshapen. This assault was surely the last, he feared. It struck Rebel as fitting that this final act of violence upon her would ultimately come from Lee's hand.

"You're bleeding," the girl said.

Rebel pulled up his pant leg and watched as micro-rivers of crimson divided and branched down his shin. "Oh." He looked up at the girl and felt like standing there for as long as she would allow. "It, uh…it'll dry."

She grinned and the boy did too.

"Come over to my house and at least put some Band-Aids on it," she said, moving that direction and waving him along.

Rebel looked back at his bike.

"Just leave it for now. Come on," the girl said. Rebel walked after her and crossed the street, finally registering the enormity of the house. It was a white Colonial with long black shudders which made it seem older than the other homes, although crisp as the rest.

"My name's Kip," she said, glancing to make sure he was still following. Rebel couldn't help imagining the thousands of hiding places in what was, in his estimation, a true mansion. Lee had always been amazed at the crannies his little brother had managed within the trailer. With no architectural nuance to speak of, mobile home hiding was relegated to cupboards and furniture or piles of laundry, and Rebel stretched creativity in these spots to a snapping point.

"What's yours?" the girl asked.

"My what?" The boy noticed she had stopped walking, allowing him time to gawk. "Oh…Rebel."

Kip's face eased into a mischievous grin. "For real?" she asked.

Rebel looked down at his Pumas and realized the ratty sneakers were sunken deep into the thickest, greenest cut of grass he'd ever seen.

"You're saying, like, that's the name on your birth certificate?"

"Yeah," the boy replied. He could sense her fascination, rolling this information around in her mind.

"So, you're destined to be an outlaw, huh?" she smiled.

For the first time, the boy felt painfully self-aware, his clothes cheap and spent compared to hers. He was as out of place in this neighborhood as much as she would have been in his. "I guess," Rebel offered shyly.

Kip bounced up a series of steps to a landing on the side of the house and turned to him. "Well, come on in, Jesse James."

"That's actually my middle name."

"What?!" she laughed, "Jesse James is your middle name?"

"Naw, just James...I mean James is my only middle name. So it's Rebel James," the boy said blushing. He remained at the bottom of the steps as if some imaginary wall made approach impossible. Rebel knocked some dirt from his Levi's. The girl descended the steps, taking him by the hand to tow him along. Her hand around his felt oddly familiar, as if this was supposed to have happened a long time ago, but this kind of bliss would have overwhelmed the boy had it come sooner. Her palm was warm against the top of his hand and her fingers rested on the scrapes of his palms, setting them ablaze. He did not care.

The side door led them into a spacious kitchen. White was everywhere. The walls. The floor. The ceiling. Omnipresent. It would have felt antiseptic if not for a handful of precisely placed plants and other immoderate garniture.

Kip moved to a white wooden stool and patted the seat of it. "Here. Hop up here for a minute," she ordered.

Rebel looked down at himself. "I don't wanna git nothin' dirty."

She flexed her brow in annoyance. "You're fine! Come on." She patted the seat again. The boy complied, watching Kip rifle through some moving boxes on a massive island. He envisioned this same island in the kitchen at his house and reckoned there would be two, maybe three inches of space left between it and the walls of the trailer. Here, it made sense—a center anchor for a room large enough to dock a cruise ship. Kip fished a small box of Band-Aids from a much bigger box. She went to the sink and wet a washcloth.

"Yer accent is different," Rebel ventured. "Where y'all from?"

"Houston," the girl said, wrenching the cloth of excess water.

"Houston, Texas?" the boy's eyes grew. Kip grinned. "If you from Texas, I thought you'd talk like us," he said.

"Well, Texas is huge. And we lived in the city so there were all kinds of people there."

"Who's this?" said a voice. It was terse and precise and belonged to Kip's mother. Rebel felt his body go rigid against the stool. He looked to the door through which they'd entered, making ready his escape, and immediately felt foolish for doing so. The woman was tall and elegant and matched the house. Her hair was long and blonde, curled to perfection atop a fancy sweater the boy thought ridiculous for summer in Alabama. Rebel recognized right away features the lady had passed on to the girl he now loved. They were unmistakable, the dimpled chin and the graceful lines that created the shape of her face.

Kip said, "This is Rebel, Mom." And Rebel watched as her mother gave him the once over, discriminations in nanoseconds as he sat helplessly. A bird on display. He knew this look, having seen it before, many times, especially when he'd gone places with Lee.

Sometimes it was the mall, but mostly it was when Charleen

took the boys to visit their aunt in Mountain Brook.

Technically, Charleen's Aunt Lou lived in Homewood, but she always claimed Mountain Brook. "We're on the line," she'd harp. Aunt Lou had married a wealthy man long dead and now lived pleasantly alone. On visits, she demanded they all eat out every meal at the swankest establishments Birmingham had to offer. Lee found it annoying, but Rebel relished the experience with supreme zeal. The glances, however, were always the same. A subtle mix of condescension and contempt; two-thirds unspoken class distinction, one-third how-dare-you-make-us-feel-uncomfortable insinuation.

Here it was again.

"Well, hello there," the woman said. "I'm Laura, Kip's mother." She stared at the child's face, mentally affirming her assessment. "It's awfully late for company, don't you think, sweetheart?" She said this while glaring at Kip, but it was wholly directed at the boy and the boy knew it. Rebel began to inch from the stool until Kip shot him a commanding glance.

"Looks like somebody's had an accident," Laura noted, determining Kip's intentions with the washcloth. Just as Kip reached to wipe blood from Rebel's leg, Laura snatched the cloth from her hand. "Let's use paper towels, sweetie, so we don't ruin the linen."

"Oh..." Kip said. "Whatever." And the girl began rummaging through more boxes. Laura folded her arms. Rebel recognized the stance too. He'd seen it just hours earlier as Tab had towered over him after his fall from the tree. It was dominant. A suffocating posture that removed all question with regard to who was in control. The boy watched a smile form on the woman's mouth.

"So, Rebel, do you live in the neighborhood?" she asked. And now it was Rebel's turn to grin, aware of the game. She wanted him to say it, to say he lived exactly where she already knew he lived, as if releasing the words into the ether solidified the chasm between worlds. He would play.

"No, ma'am," Rebel said softly. "I's just ridin' through."

Kip was busy dabbing blood from his shins, and the coldness of the wet paper prompted him to sit up straighter. He observed the top of Kip's little brown head—a perfect sphere teeming with life the breadth of an ocean, he was sure. The boy was eager to discover it all.

"I live over in Manookie," he said.

Kip's face popped up, and she looked at Rebel curiously, then her mother. "That's a weird name," the girl observed.

Laura seemed to uncoil as she leaned against the island. "What's your last name?" the woman asked.

"Mims."

Kip's mother lowered her head and Rebel could tell her face was changing beneath. Whether this information was pleasant or alarming, he did not know. "And your mother...what's her name?" she asked, holding her stare of the white tiles underfoot.

"Charleen Mims."

A muffled laugh from the woman, indistinguishable, as a man walked into the kitchen. Thick-chested, his hair was short and newly clipped, too dark for his age. Rebel guessed the man much older than the woman. His attire was immaculate, and the boy couldn't get past how pristinely pressed the man's slacks were. Jet-black suspenders held them up and lay against a snappy pin-stripe shirt. He pulled at a loose tie as he smooched Laura's cheek like a woodpecker.

"What's going on in here?" declared the fancy man. Rebel had never witnessed someone who so blatantly reeked of confidence. It was palpable, and the child watched as this person's presence vacuumed up whatever space was left in the giant kitchen. In two strides, he was beside Rebel, grinning as he slapped the boy on the shoulder. "Damn, Kipper, we're here all of two days and you're already beating the hell out of boys?" the man smiled.

"Steven," Laura reprimanded.

"I'm kidding! The kid knows I'm joking," he chortled.

A phone rang in another room, and the confident man was already moving that direction. "Is Balboa staying for dinner?" he quipped before disappearing. Kip stood, having done the best clean-up job she could, and looked hopefully at her mother.

"I don't think so," Laura said.

"Mom! Come on."

"Honey, it's late and I'm sure his mother is worried about him," Laura said with finality.

Kip eased, then said, "Well, we at least need to drive him home."

Rebel had been studying Laura's face intently and felt cued to exit before the woman was forced to conjure an excuse. "I don't need a ride. I got my bike. Thanks, though."

Kip's eyes narrowed at her mother.

"Nice to meetcha, ma'am," the boy offered, and left. He could hear an emotional exchange happening inside as he trotted on toward the lawn. The side door slammed, and Rebel turned to see Kip running after him. He turned back to hide an irrepressible smile.

"Rebel James Mims!" the girl yelled. They crossed the street together, well-lit by dozens of ornate fixtures lining the curb. "Sorry about that," Kip said.

"'Bout what?"

"My parents. My mom especially...she can be a jerk sometimes."

"She's alright," the boy lied. Kip looked at him. Rebel grinned.

"She's not like that all the time!"

"I didn't say anything," Rebel laughed. The girl surveyed the mangled bike.

"Now, my dad…my dad is definitely always like that."

"What's he do for a livin'?"

Kip studied the crushed metal; a surgeon observing the bones of a failed skydiver. "He's in oil," she said. "In Houston…that's what he does. He makes deals with big companies who want oil or something like that. He's only here for a couple days and has to fly back for work. My mom says he'll probably be flying back and forth for a while."

She tried spinning the rear wheel with her foot. It failed to make a full rotation, screeching to a halt against the warped frame. They giggled. "You realize this thing is totaled, right?" she asked.

"Yeah," Rebel lamented. "She was good to me while she lasted."

"Looks like it," Kip looked to the house. She gnawed at her bottom lip, debating an idea. The girl smiled slyly at her new friend. "Come on," she said, darting toward the house.

"Wh…where you goin'? I gotta go."

"Just come on!" she said in a hushed tone.

Kip circumvented the house, rushing past a lush hedgerow bordering the four-car garage. She stopped short before the greenery ended, peering around its edge like a proper spy. Rebel caught up, falling naturally into stealth mode along with the girl. Whatever she had in mind didn't matter. They were together. She was crouched and urgent, and Rebel loved everything about everything that was happening. She leaned forward to check the perimeter, then suddenly grabbed her new friend by the hand and sprinted into the dark.

Rebel marveled at how much ground she covered, the tips of her pony teasing his face. They ran across the backyard, hand-in-hand, until they reached an elephantine pecan tree where they hid. The boy poked his head out slowly and spied Kip's mother through the kitchen windows.

"Look up," Kip breathed heavily.

Rebel raised his head to see an elaborate, expansive tree house some fifteen feet above them. His mouth fell wide as he leaned back to take in the whole of it. This airborne domicile was painted white as well, in genre with the mansion and meticulously detailed. "Wow," Rebel gaped.

"Get ready," Kip said. A soft, ethereal glisten had formed around her face and her cheeks were thoroughly flushed. Here, behind the tree, she looked like a true Indian princess, all her dark features heightened by this rush of adventure. The boy resolved then that if she was leading them off the edge of some bottomless, eternal gorge, he would go there with her.

"Over there," The Princess said, pointing to what she would call a shed, but Rebel thought it looked more like a diminutive version of the main house. They ran again, darting through the open double doors of this building and ducked from sight. Scanning the space, Rebel saw boxes that would eventually be unpacked, along with brand new lawn equipment and outdoor lounge furniture. Kip skirted around a box large enough to make her disappear.

"Where'd you go?" Rebel whispered. The lights from the backyard barely reached this building and he navigated in her direction as best he could. He turned sideways, sliding between stacked boxes that were taller than him. On the other side, Kip stood proudly between two bicycles. One was a dirt bike, white with a dozen hot pink decals and virgin tires and not a scratch on it. The other was a yellow beach comber, kid-sized, but rangy still with a thick, plush banana seat.

"Take your pick," she beamed.

Rebel stood mute, piecing together the girl's intentions.

Kip nudged the dirt bike with her sneaker. "This one's newer," she revealed, "but this one rides way smoother." She patted the banana seat.

"I can't..." Rebel shuffled his feet, "I can't take yer bike."

"Sure you can," she said, as if he'd uttered the oddest thing she'd ever heard. "And you're not taking it forever, just borrowing it. I have two and don't even ride them that much. I like my skateboard way better."

Rebel considered her face carefully, trying to ascertain if she was serious. He'd grown accustomed to elaborate pranks and subsequent monumental let-downs, thanks to Lee's impishness. The older Mims brother was notorious for carrying larks to the brink, especially at the expense of his little brother.

Kip's brow flexed as she glanced toward the house. "Come on, hurry!" she coaxed. "They're gonna come out looking for me soon."

"Are you for real?" Rebel hesitated.

"You know what," she flicked the kickstand up on the dirt bike and rolled it to him. "I'm picking for you. This looks closest to your old one so just take this one." In an instant, his raw palms were touching the rubbery waffle grips of the handlebar.

"Thanks," he mumbled, and an unforeseen surge of embarrassment crept over his entire body. He couldn't bring himself to look her in the eye as together they navigated the bike around boxes.

"I'm gonna go inside, so wait here for a little bit and then go, okay?"

"Alright," he said.

Kip craned her neck, surveying the backyard. The lights were still on in the kitchen, but Laura's blonde head was nowhere to be seen. The Princess glanced back at the boy and smiled, crouching for launch.

"Hey!" Rebel whispered, grabbing her arm. She looked at him expectantly, as if she knew he was going to stop her all along. "I'm gon take good care of it. I promise."

"I know," she said grinning, and sprinted away.

Rebel watched her run all the way to the house, up the back steps and into the kitchen. He'd practically held his breath as she ran, finally allowing himself to collapse against the wall inside of the storage building. He gathered himself, replaying every significant moment of the last six hours, scenes flashing before him and, between each, the pulsing drum of his own heartbeat.

The few moments the boy agreed to wait turned into twenty. Rebel remained until every light in the giant house went away. He allowed night to settle until the volume of crickets gave him confidence and then straddled the new bike for the first time. Its frame was strong beneath him, and this brought about an odd hopefulness.

Sprinklers had by now bathed the backyard in a sheen of gossamer mist and Rebel watched beneath as the new treads lay ruts in the sod. On reaching the street pavement, water flew up at him from the tires, generating a chill that rippled to the top of his neck. He marveled at how much more secure Kip's bike felt, as if its strength had earned a kind of mutual connection to the earth below. Lee's hand-me-down lost rights of security years ago, a wayward child unjustly responsible for the vices of its father.

The bike coasted along, and Rebel realized he was making no effort to propel it forward anymore. He extended his legs, allowing the bicycle to finally creep to a halt in the middle of the road. The neighborhood slumbered, calm and satisfied with itself.

The child reached the same lavish dual-stone entrance he passed on the way in and paused to consider the trek back home. The boy could not find motivation to move his feet onto the pedals, and instead rested his chin on the meaty pad velcroed to the handlebar. It was as comfortable as a pillow, and he imagined he could have continued to enjoy himself like that for the next hundred years, balancing the bike and its pillow, as the neighborhood remained idle.

He lifted his feet enough to let gravity carry him and crept slowly in the direction he'd just come. Rebel pedaled leisurely past the stone towers again, back into the labyrinth of newly colonized properties, back to the house of his new friend.

Hiding the new bike behind the storage building, he meandered to the base of the huge pecan tree. Looking up, the bottom of the treehouse looked like the undercarriage of a monstrous spacecraft with white-washed boards spindling out in every direction. On the backside of the tree, he found the ladder nailed to the trunk.

On cresting the loft floor, Rebel was amazed by its spaciousness. Its height felt appropriate for most any child, with several hand-crank windows and waist-high walls. The boy sat down in one of two miniature rocking chairs situated in front of a wide windowless opening. This view overlooked the backyard, perfectly framing the master house beyond.

Rebel eased back into the little seat, allowing the top slat of the chair to prop his skull just so. For the first time all day, he felt the weight of his eyelids and looked down at his watch: 10:48 p.m. A clatter against the floorboards, and he noticed a small mound of pecan shells gathering beside his feet.

The boy turned his head sleepily to observe Lee in the rocker next to him. The dead boy cracked pecans with practiced methodology. The night offered indigo and seemed to mute the red violence Rebel had encountered earlier. Lee appeared more normal. The Lee that Rebel knew. He watched as his older brother used his tongue as a toothpick, trying unsuccessfully to dislodge a piece of rogue pecan from a molar.

"Damn pecan," Lee observed, "stubborn as hell."

Rebel turned his gaze back to the mansion, imagining it now as the retreat of some notorious mob boss, one who conducted many of his felonious activities in broad daylight but whom no cop dared confront. The treehouse was the compound's lookout tower. But the boy knew Lee would make a terrible sentry. At the first hint of responsibility, Lee had always faltered, losing focus as soon as the task at hand bored him. Rebel tired of watching his brother's struggle.

"Pluck a piece of yer rope and fish it out," the boy suggested.

Lee regarded this advice for a moment as he continued wriggling his tongue. The dead boy maneuvered his noose around to his chest for examination. He'd somehow cut himself down, and the noose now hung mangled around his neck as a mismanaged tie. Lee pulled at the frayed tip, yanking out a strand he judged worthy, and began flossing the nut free.

Rebel sighed in resignation. In various situations—hundreds, the boy ventured—Lee would struggle in vain against some indiscriminate force. Always conquerable, Rebel surmised, if not for his brother's pride. A slight popping sound, and the pecan piece sat in Lee's hand. "Tough-ass bastard," the dead boy remarked.

"This real?" Rebel starred at the Colonial.

"Well hell, Reb," Lee said, pushing the pecan particle around his palm, "I tried to tell ya as much three or four times but ya freaked the hell out."

Rebel took in the dead boy, relaxed as ever. Nothing ever seemed to rattle his brother. It was as if Lee knew that any given circumstance on any given day would inevitably devolve into its worst outcome. Therefore, a person might as well settle in. A nihilistic, morose view of Murphy's Law was his at all times, but somehow never overcame his gusto. Lee's philosophies seemed at odds with one another, yet stitched together his psyche like a malfeasant romance. Not much surprised Lee. This afforded his countenance an ironic cynicism masquerading as wisdom. In turn, most people wanted Lee Mims to like them, and the boy reckoned this was his brother's superpower.

The dead boy surveyed the treehouse as he cracked wide another pecan. "Damn," he said, "These people rich as hell."

"You been wi'me all day?" Rebel asked.

"On and off." Lee spat an errant piece of shell through the giant opening. "You just 'bout give Ol' Man Grayson a damn heart attack," the older brother said.

Rebel grinned. Lee smirked.

"And don't thank I don't know why we out here in the damn Ritz Carlton," the dead boy continued.

"Shut up," Rebel dodged, stuffing his smile.

"Shut up, hell," Lee nudged the boy playfully. "She's perty. I give ya that." The dead boy watched a blissful calm come over the child. "I'm just pissed ya didn't introduce me to her mama."

"You gon git yerself shot, you mess with her!" Rebel laughed, throwing a pecan shell at his brother.

"Shit...whatever." Lee rocked back and forth, playing with the rope around his neck. "I done been to the other side little brother, and lemme tell ya...it puts all this bullshit in perspective."

"Whatcha mean?" the boy asked.

"I mean time ain't whatcha think it is. And shit on this side carries over. So if sump'm needs doin', you don't fuckin' wait." Lee watched the humidity swallow his little brother's affable demeanor. "You like that little girl, you tell her. And if you gon love her, then love the hell out of her. But ya better git to it."

The dead boy stopped rocking and looked intently at the child. "And I tell ya sump'm else…" Lee leaned in, "…that slimy sumbitch mama's takin' up with?"

Rebel met his brother's gaze.

"We gon kill that motherfucker."

CHAPTER 5

Le Cirque

Biking home the next morning, Rebel couldn't turn his gaze from the vapors escaping the blacktop. Gases danced off the surface, seducing the boy as he tried again and again to disrupt his stare. The heat was merciless, forcing him off pavement and onto wooded trails Lee had shown him over the years.

By the time he reached the long dirt drive that would take him to the trailer, the boy expected bustle and traffic the likes of which this desolate stretch of road had never seen. The home came into view, and all he envisioned came to pass: two police cars sat empty at the end of the drive, while beyond, a firetruck—new for the county—edged below the bay window of the barn, as if Lee's corpse might decide to jump after all.

Rebel had heard about the new firetruck. He remembered when it still sat cradled in the Fire Department's garage, not yet called upon for duty. Lee had suggested they sneak into the garage and christen the vehicle by pissing cross-stream on each tire. This would turn out to be one of the few plans Lee failed to execute since, on the whole, Lee's ideas were more like inevitabilities luring bystanders off a cliff edge. But now here it was, in action, crisp red paint like fresh flame against the weathered burgundy of the barn.

Rebel didn't bother stopping at the trailer, making straight for the barn. Through the buzz of activity, past the officers and firemen and several important-looking people in suits, the first familiar face he made out was Tab's. She sat hunched atop a dry-rotted tire, itself attached to an antique John Deere that was once Isaac's most prized possession.

The Gypsy watched this hustle—the serious, purposeful walking and the hushed, serious conversations. She observed with casual disaffection as she burned through a Camel, firing warning glares to men who might approach, drawn irresistibly in spite of their work. She watched them grapple, often right up until the moment of decision, with the mental gymnastics required to justify finding themselves in her orbit. She was kin to the deceased. *Thank God*, she could see them thinking. That alone had to be reason enough to engage the girl, even to speak. Nerves most often won the day.

The boy found his mother, a heaving form of streaked mascara. She talked with her hands to an officer, animating toward the barn. Then Rebel noticed behind his mother...The Tourist. Dennis stood, arms folded, casting shade for the left side of Charleen's body; the paragon of quiet comfort. Rebel felt the same nauseating helplessness he felt when he'd sat across from the man in the booth.

Tab nodded as the boy coasted by on the new bike. He rolled to a stop a few feet from the hysterical woman. Charleen caught sight of her son and let go a godawful yelp—a sprinting cat stopped short from barbed wire.

The sound grabbed the attention of the entire company. She rushed from the officer toward the boy, her expression transitioning to rage. Charleen slapped the child across the cheek, quick and certain, only to return immediately to the crying heap she was before.

"Where the hell you been?" she said, shaking him by the shoulders. She yanked the boy's head to her chest and sobbed, pressing her son hard against her body until Rebel felt the trinkets of her bracelet plow into his ear. Her cleavage smelled like country-fried steak and the boy tried pulling away. This was the go-to dish at *Larry's*, by far the best item on the menu. Charleen served it incessantly, and as a result, wore the scent at all times. She released her son, her blue eyes bloodshot and set deep in their sockets. Her face grew soft and sad and she caressed the cheek she just smacked.

"You know what happened?" she asked.

"Nuh-uh," Rebel remarked.

He watched her face change again, tears building then teeming. Dennis stepped closer and placed his hand on the woman's shoulder. Rebel leaned away from this gesture, stumbling over the borrowed bike and falling to the ground. He was up in an instant, furious he'd put the bike's condition in jeopardy. Rebel surveyed its frame for scratches, convinced Dennis would be to blame for the slightest scuff.

"Rebel, yer brother..." Charleen said weakly, "Lee had a accident."

"Okay," Rebel said, examining the bike.

"He...uh, h..." she stammered.

Dennis started to speak but the boy held up his hand. The

child held a cold glare, repulsed by this forwardness. By his brash presence in this place. No, The Tourist would not be the one to say it, Rebel decided, and if he tried to, the boy would scream as loud as he could until whatever the man said was drowned out. "What, Mama? What happened?"

The woman snorted back enough snot to speak clearly. "He died, baby. Yer brother's dead."

Rebel could tell she was waiting, anticipating a reaction. Ready to hug him too hard for a second time, consoling his crushed heart. But the boy could only think to look down and so he did. He studied the matted grass, intrigued by how quickly it had been trampled into a flat shag by the strangers. "What happened?" Rebel asked.

Charleen cupped her son's hands. "It was...it was just a freak accident and he hurt hisself," she said, glancing at Dennis. "That's all ya need to know, alright?" she reassured.

"Sorry, kid," Dennis said in a low murmur.

Charleen hugged the boy again, crying onto his back. As her body bounced against his, Rebel looked up to see Lee sitting on the ledge of the bay window, legs dangling. The dead boy drummed his heels in rhythm against the pine boards. He smiled at his little brother below, waving as he took a drag from a cigarette. Rebel squinted against the sun, smiling in kind.

"I'm so glad you didn't stay in the barn last night, baby," Charleen said, combing his hair with her fingers.

"I told her how ya wound up sleepin' in the house after all," Tab piped in as she approached. She tossed bangs from an eye and lit a fresh cigarette. The cousins shared a look. Rebel's face flushed hearing the lie.

"What made ya change ya mind, sweetheart?" Charleen asked.

"I don' know," the boy replied sheepishly.

Rebel watched Tab look up toward the bay window as well and his eyes grew wide—*She sees him too!*, he thought, and looked along with her. For his part, Lee energized at the sight of Tab staring his direction and sat up straight. He waved to his cousin. Rebel studied The Gypsy, only to watch her eyes return to ground level.

Lee scrambled to his feet. "Hey! Tab!" the dead boy snapped. Rebel searched his cousin's face, desperate for her to hear the same yelling he did. She did not. "Tabitha Jane!" Lee screamed, waving his hands above his head. "I'm right here, you beautiful bitch!"

A new officer engaged Charleen, and Rebel caught the words "hospital" and "coroner" as the man ushered his mother toward an ambulance.

"Sorry," Dennis said to Tab. "I know he was your cousin."

Tab remained silent, staring stoically ahead. Rebel felt comforted seeing this, surmising Tab found Dennis equally as loathsome. This was no small victory; it was a key battle Dennis had already unknowingly lost. Winning Tab's fondness was strategic for any of Charleen's suitors, the boy knew. She was blood, and this unseen arbitrary bond carried a silly amount of weight with the Mims clan. This was due in large part to Isaac.

Rebel's grandfather had been a master of oral family history, most often recounting the Mims lineage of crime and other nefarious deeds against humanity. But in the end, "If'n they blood, they's blood—fer better n'worse," Isaac apprised. This sense of blood loyalty would ferment into posterity.

Dennis regarded Tab with distant affection, posturing himself as indifferent to the girl's allure. Rebel was dumbfounded. If ever there was a swinging dick guaranteed to ogle Tab into oblivion, it was this asshole, the boy surmised. Rather, Dennis found anywhere to look but the girl, as if he would refuse her the satisfaction. Rebel had never witnessed such self-control, making the man annoyingly more interesting.

The Tourist walked away, searching for Charleen's whereabouts. Tab seemed equally as baffled by the encounter as she watched the man go, a zookeeper perplexed by the behavior of a new primate. "That's Charleen's latest, huh?"

"I reckon," Rebel said, crawling onto the bike.

Tab motioned with her cigarette to the bay window. "You alright?" she asked. The boy looked up to see his brother. Lee was glaring at his cousin, and upon seeing her gesture his direction, took a quick drag of his own cigarette. He blew smoke into his hand as if to trap it, then lowered the cigarette to his crotch so it stuck out like a tiny paper penis. He used the hand full of smoke to throttle back and forth over the cigarette-penis, ejaculating cancer into the air like a galled dragon.

"Yeah," Rebel answered, turning to hide a smile. He observed Charleen walk away from the cop, leaving Dennis to finish the conversation. The boy knew this was the walk his mother enlisted when she had a plan in place and something to get done. This was Business Charleen, the most uninteresting version Rebel had come to know. She rubbed her son's shoulder reassuringly while looking at her niece.

"Listen, the officer says I have to go with 'em to the hospital for the coroner and all. And I gotta fill out some paperwork. Said he wants you to come too, Tab, so they can gitcha full statement."

"I done told 'em what happen three damn times," Tab said.

"I know, sweetheart, but ya gotta tell 'em again," Charleen turned her attention to the boy. "Now listen, Rebel. I asked Dennis if he'd stay with ya while we gone and he said he'd be glad to."

"No! Mama, please!" Rebel winced, shrugging her hand from his shoulder.

"I don't want ya at the house alone after this."

"Then lemme come wit y'all then!"

"Absolutely not. I don't want ya around this no more than ya have to be, baby."

Tab released a sigh whose message was clear: resistance was useless. Business Charleen was impregnable, only able to hear or see what was sensible and efficient for the occasion. Rebel flipped the bike around dramatically and made for the trailer before his mother could say anything else.

At home, the boy charged down the hallway and flung his door wide, the knob sinking neatly into the hole notched out in the wall from slammings past. Rebel threw himself onto the bed, tears making his face hotter than it already was. He could feel heat escape his body and float to the ceiling. He looked to see if it would pool there—a temper cloud of fire and static intermittent. Only the gimcrack pattern above. Rebel could hear someone enter through the front door of the trailer, and his eyes glossed anew.

That motherfucker didn't even knock, the boy thought. Rebel inched light-foot down the hallway, edging his way to the corner of the kitchen. Dennis stood in the center of the tiny living room and surveyed the place. The boy regarded him carefully, convinced the look he saw on the man's face now was one he'd worn dozens of times before, in other homes that belonged to other boys.

Dennis examined the sofa and the television, then cranked the air on the window unit that cooled the hull of the trailer. Rebel could tell he was sizing up what he had to work with—what he would have to get used to, what he would eventually decide to change. The boy allowed his shoulder to slide from the corner, announcing himself.

"Hey there," Dennis said without fully devoting attention. "Your mom and cousin went to the hospital."

"I know."

Dennis glanced at the largest bedroom behind him—Charleen's—before joining the boy in the kitchen. Rebel shrunk into the chair closest to him. Dennis opened the fridge, tawny and narrow, and took his time, perusing with an ease and familiarity that disgusted the child. Rebel glared at the stranger, in awe of the arrogance required, the level of brazenness needed for someone to instantly make themselves at home like this.

"Your mom ain't much for keepin' a full fridge," Dennis mused, taking a beer and allowing the weight of the door to close itself. Rebel watched the man wrench the cap clean from the bottle and toss it onto the counter. He joined the child at the table. The boy hated that he admired the way The Tourist was with furniture. Dennis sat now the same way he had at *Larry's*, sidling up to the chair like an old mare. His hand grazed its frame with something near grace before he sat. Then came a supreme, enviable comfortability. Dennis sighed before taking a long swig.

"Where's your old man?"

"I don't know."

"Your mama says he ran out on y'all."

"She don't know that. Nobody knows what happened to him."

Dennis looked intently now, measuring. "You miss him?"

Rebel tried to match the man's stare but couldn't, his eyes darting to the window and the natural world beyond. "I guess," he said.

"Naw...I don't reckon you do much guessin'. You strike me as a man who knows his mind. One who likes bringin' his own ideas to a thing then see if they line up," The Tourist said calmly. He took another gulp. "You know…" Dennis trailed. Rebel could tell the man was mulling a choice, turning it over in his mind. Dennis leaned a sinewy shoulder toward the table.

"You're gonna have a lot of dumbass people say a lot of dumbass shit about what happened with your brother. They 'can't believe he would do something like that,' 'He was a coward for doin' it…' Shit like that. People feel like they're supposed to say something. But what's underneath all that bullshit is buncha assholes scared shitless 'cause they don't know what comes next. Nobody does."

Dennis paused to light a cigarette, enjoying it for a moment. "But I'm gonna tell you something they won't," he grinned, "'cause I can see you got more goin' on up there than you let on." He took a deep drag, allowing smoke to slide in and out of the thatch-work of his goatee. "It don't matter."

The boy was still.

"It don't make shit difference why he did it. He was too sad… too happy, mad at his old man, pissed at some girl, bored, jealous, screamin' for attention…" Dennis shook his head. "Don't matter."

The man took in the boy's face. A canvas of embittered confusion. The Tourist tilted his head then, examining the child like a puppy he hadn't decided yet if he would keep. "This is all just one big fuckin' circus, kid. You carve out your space in some shithole…do whatever the hell it is you're gonna do…then get out of the way so another clown can come in and take over your shithole. Your brother…he was just stepping out of the way. And I gotta tell ya, I respect the hell outta that. I don't judge it. Nobody else should either."

Dennis caressed his goatee into a point, the corner of his mouth forming a grin. "But at the end of the day, we're all in the same shitter, right?" The Tourist rose and made his way to the refrigerator once more, his arm leaning on the open door.

"Yer outta beer," the man observed. "Let's run to the store and get a six-pack for your mom."

"I can just go git it," Rebel said quickly.

Dennis turned, cocking an eyebrow. "You pass for twenty-one?"

"I know a guy that works at this place...he always gives me and Lee whatever we want," the boy said.

Dennis laughed. "You know a guy that works at a place, huh? Well damn, son. You're already runnin' the circus." The man dug a wallet from his back pocket and riffled through the dingy leather, handing the boy a twenty. "Alright, P.T., anything left from that is yours," Dennis added, the cigarette bobbing with each word.

"Whatcha mean, 'P.T.'?" Rebel asked.

"P.T. Barnum. Circus showman. That's you. The ringleader." Dennis turned up his beer and moved to the couch. "Go see your guy you know at that place," the man grinned. "Let's see what you come up with."

The boy turned the handle of the front door and sun consumed him. He closed it, standing alone there on the small wooden porch. For a moment, he studied his feet. Matching slabs of worn rubber atop the drywood. Then he left.

CHAPTER 6

The Princess

The trip back to Riverchase seemed to pass in seconds. Barely midday, this made the second time he biked it. In truth, he was ecstatic when Dennis had mentioned the lack of beer, immediately recognizing a window for escape. Never in the boy's life had he been happier the refrigerator was bare. Rebel knew the real reason Charleen could never keep stock of alcohol was Lee. No matter how much or little she purchased, it would never last beyond a couple of days. Lee would bide his time, waiting for sleep or work or an errand to take his mother away in order to empty the kitchen of any deposits. The barn loft thus became a depository for empty cans and bottles, constituting target practice for the boys by rock and sling-shot.

Coasting a soft descent in the trail, Rebel smiled as he recalled his brother. It occurred to him that maybe Lee was never intended to be long for this world. *What if God sends certain people to earth to be short-fuse shots of lightnin'?* he thought, as he whipped passed the brush. Certainly God plans for most humans to live long, full lives. But he wondered, what about those bottle-rocket souls? The Lord's special accounts, designed to dislodge all that is regular when life gets too boring. Birthed to remind us that God is color and blood and fire.

These were the thoughts the boy had as he leaned this way and that, avoiding limbs and wayward branches that whizzed by him in blurs. He knew exactly why time seemed so fleet: a thirteen-year-old Texas Indian princess had stood over him in bronze silhouette last night. She would be the salvation of any twelve-year-old boy, Rebel figured.

Aside from his interaction with Dennis at the trailer, he'd thought of nothing else besides her—not even Lee—replaying every nuance of their encounter beat by beat. She seemed beautifully alien, and choosing the trails that led to her neighborhood felt as instinctual as breathing. He would go to her first, before fulfilling any agreement he'd made with The Tourist.

The dual-stone entrance appeared twice as large in the day, and Rebel could see the name "Riverchase" engraved regally into the nucleus of the rock on either side. Night had cast shadows about, acting as a buffering cloak. Coasting into the development now, however, the boy felt woefully out of place. He watched several cars pass, parents and children alike offering opinions with cut-glances. The sight of construction soothed him somewhat, as clunky dozers nudged and clawed at the rich red dirt of developing plots.

Kip's house came into view and Rebel took a deep breath.

Finishing the same low hill he'd discovered the night before, he scrambled to think of how he might approach the house in the day. Last night had been haphazard and rightly excusable— he was on the run from a ghost. Lee was a resilient bastard and had practically driven him into this neck of the woods. This was different. Now, he was willingly seeking out the attention of a kid in this neighborhood—a girl no less—and with that thought came paranoia.

It was hard to miss the white Colonial. Rebel rolled to a stop in the same spot where he crashed. He glanced up at the branch from which Lee had swung nimble as a chimp. Kip was nowhere in sight. The house looked closed up; distant and repellent to strangers. The boy leaned the new bike against the tree and ran across the street, taking cover behind the same hedgerow.

He walked the length of it, allowing his hand to graze the foliage, full and rich with hydration. At the end of the row Rebel crouched, peering around the last bush. The backyard was bigger than he realized, and in the sunlight he could see the sod had not yet fully grown together. Long rectangular patches lay puzzle-like across the expansive yard. Boxes—some empty, some untouched—sprawled along the massive deck that protruded from the back of the house.

He remembered the vantage point of the treehouse and scurried along, trying his best to stay near the privacy fence. The wood of the fence smelled new, and as he ran, Rebel could see where painters had begun staining the spruce. He scaled the tree's ladder and army-crawled to the edge of the large opening.

From up high, the child was taken aback by how green the lawn was. Elevation afforded the sun its fullness, galvanizing the spacious lot to look more like a rolling emerald carpet. Rebel felt invulnerable for a moment, taken by what he guessed to be the most beautiful place he'd ever seen—and this was only someone's lawn. Movement through the kitchen window caught his attention and the boy crouched out of sight. He peeked over the edge of the half-wall to see Kip's head bob in and out of view.

Rebel thought through how he might gain The Princess' attention without alerting her parents. He knew walking right up to the front door and rapping confidently on the metal snout of the lion's head would be madness. He'd picked up an unspoken canon from his brother informing this mindset: avoid parents of any kind at all costs. In his short seventeen years, Lee had damaged, marred, or otherwise terrorized most of the adults he'd come into contact with. In at least half of these encounters, Rebel had been present and bore witness. As a result, the younger Mims often found himself aggrieved by association. No, he would not knock on the front door.

He waited until Kip walked out onto the deck and watched her peruse a maze of moving boxes. "What's it say on it again?" Kip yelled to the kitchen. Rebel could hear her mother call out something muffled in return. The boy scanned the floorboards, searching. In the corner, he saw a beach bucket filled with pinecones and mulled through the collection, selecting one he thought most aerodynamic. He hurled the cone side-arm through the opening. Nothing.

The girl tilted one of the boxes to read its label. Rebel retrieved another cone and waited patiently until she turned his direction. He fired the new cone as hard as he could. It sailed farther than he thought it would, coming to rest just feet from the deck. Kip caught the last of the cone's roll and descended the steps to pick it up, this tiny meteor fallen from space.

She surveyed the yard and spotted a waving hand from the treehouse. The Princess smiled, then ran back into the house. Rebel's own smile faded, unsure what this meant. Suddenly, Kip reappeared, bounding from the deck and sprinting across the puzzle pieces. She was already finishing the last rung of the ladder when Rebel met her at the floor's opening.

"Stay down!" the boy said crouching.

Kip frowned. "Why?"

"Yer mama's gon see us up here," he pleaded.

"So? I told her I was going to the treehouse and that's what I'm doing. How long have you been up here? You spying on me?" she grinned. He was convinced she was even prettier than the day before. The girl sat cross-legged in front of him now, pushing brown wisps from her face. She'd wrangled the rest into dueling ponytails.

"You look like a Indian princess," Rebel confessed and immediately reddened. He'd meant to think this and not say it, but there it was. And now, he was trapped with no way of escape in the white spacecraft. He looked away but could tell the girl was smiling at him.

"What do you mean?" Kip asked coyly. Rebel made a poor play at misdirection, ordering the pinecones into formation. "I always get really dark in the summer," the girl said, pulling her ponies tight and wiping a small bit of sweat from her temple.

"I get suntan too, but my brother don't. He just burns up and gits red. He just gits more freckles," the boy said.

She laughed and the boy wondered why.

"You wanna come inside?"

"Naw," Rebel said, sitting up. "I was gon see if you wanted to come with me. I gotta go git sump'm fer my mama from the store."

He expected her to think, to mull and scheme as Lee would, strategizing best options for escape and concealment. He would give her the time she needed to formulate the most believable lie for her mother.

"For sure. Let's go," she said, descending the first step of the ladder.

"Whoa—hold on!" Rebel whispered, grabbing her arm.

"What?"

"What about yer parents?"

"I'm gonna tell my mom I'm running an errand with you. Which is exactly what I'm doing. Come on."

Rebel was still processing the apparent limitless amount of trust Kip enjoyed when he realized she was gone. The girl was in and out of her house in seconds, heading then for the storage building. She reappeared with the beach comber. Rebel met her mid-yard, gun-shy.

"Where's your bike?" she asked as she slid onto hers.

The boy watched Laura step through the kitchen door and onto the deck. She held a dish towel, folding it with the precision of a cadet at rifle drills. Their eyes met. Rebel waited, expecting at any moment the woman would descend upon him like a begrudging vulture, swatting at him violently. She only stared, waiting until Kip turned to wave goodbye.

The Princess pushed off the thick grass, waving at her mother as she rolled along. Laura and the towel disappeared into the kitchen. Kip slowed halfway down the drive, balancing onto one foot as she looked back at her friend.

She smiled. "Ready?"

CHAPTER 7

'Spect Some Wolfs

Heat followed the pair. Deep into summer, most folks huddled indoors, seeking shelter from the suffocating humidity. But the two pedaled on, resilient and without complaint. Rebel took the trails he was most proud of, ones that hugged the edges of creeks and dilapidated shacks overgrown with nature.

The boy often glanced over his shoulder to check on his new friend, hoping she was impressed with the sights and his navigation of the wooded labyrinth. Many of the paths he'd carved himself with Lee. The brothers Mims would explore until Lee spied something of interest—an old well or an abandoned school bus. A hobo's camp. Rebel would be the one to suggest its use. The well became home base for an elaborate game of war with neighborhood rivals, the old bus their newest fortress, and the hobo's encampment a demilitarized zone where no one was allowed to be tagged.

For all the spots the boy was eager to show off, there was an endgame. Mazell "Brown Bear" Armstead was the obese owner of an all-purpose gas station at the edge of Highway 22. Beyond this highway lay West End, home to the majority of Clanton's black folk. Over the years, Lee had earned a level of respect with Brown Bear, who eventually acquiesced to selling the boy beer when he was in the mood.

There was a distinct, halting line of demarcation between the edge of town and Mazell's place: a lone stretch of worn blacktop fixed like a sickle in the earth, traversed mostly by lumber rigs. This road was called Enterprise, famous for serving as the mud-slogged path of escape for General Chilton. A Confederate commander, Chilton had been temporarily outflanked by a brigade of Union soldiers. The general's retreat turned counter-flank, thanks to this path, unknown to the Union.

Years later, the road would court infamy as stage for a raucous Klan rally, and just a few years after, an even livelier Civil Rights march. It remained mostly undisturbed now, save the large trucks adding to the potholes in the busted pavement. Mazell liked Rebel but suffered Lee, refusing to discuss trade until the older brother gave him at least one reason why the Black Man should be in charge of things.

The store owner had smelled Lee's racism a mile away, and the first time the older boy had approached the store was out of sheer desperation. His regular liquor stop had closed when the county voted to go dry, but everyone knew the fat man sold. The brothers had crossed the road with Rebel protesting vehemently. But Lee had called him a pussy so that was the end of it. The freckled white boy had walked into the man's place of business a stouthearted peacock, eager to negotiate.

Rebel was clammy, his eyes darting continually to the way of egress. Mazell's bulbous eyelids did not rouse at the sight of the two. Several black teens already in the store snickered and slid into position, ready to be entertained. By the time Lee postured himself across from Mazell, any sales pitch he'd prepared left him abandoned. Threadbare overalls covered as much of Mazell's mass as was manageable. The rest of him bulged and spilled free at every opening. Arms large as hams were covered by a short-sleeved shirt, unbuttoned and waving from the metal fan on the counter.

Mazell gummed the quarter inch of cigar left at the corner of his mouth. He nudged his soiled fedora higher up on his huge head, studying Lee. "Damn, son. You act like you ain't neva' seen a nigga be-fo'," Mazell said. The black teens cackled. Lee straightened as Rebel fidgeted with the pockets of his jeans.

"I's wantin' to git a six-pack," Lee said.

Mazell looked the boys over casually, then nodded to the door. "Boy, git yo' ass up outta here," the man snorted. He retrieved a crumpled newspaper and buried his large head within it. Lee shot a defiant glance at the other boys. The chuckling stopped in an instant and the teens stood. One boy, sporting a tall fade and muscle-tee, stepped to Lee, nose to nose.

"The fuck you lookin' at, white boy?"

Lee clenched his teeth, his thin lips growing thinner. "I'm lookin' at yo' black ass..."

"Hey!" Mazell shouted. "Step the fuck back, Duron, fo' I beat the hell outta both y'all."

Duron scowled, inching back dutifully.

"Look here, boy," Mazell coughed, "Answer me 'dis an' I sell ya sump'm."

Rebel closed his eyes in defeat. The decision to cross Enterprise had been a mistake, no doubt. But now, their fate would be left to Lee's sense of diplomacy. "Alright," Lee said.

Mazell shifted one of his boulder-sized butt cheeks. "Why

should the Black Man rule the world?"

Laughter again from the teens, and the room was quiet, save the clink and buzz of the old metal fan. To Rebel, the blades may as well have been steel turbines grating in that silence, as an anxious sweat streamed down the small of his back. The boy could tell Lee was stumped. Any other time, in any other situation, his older brother would have fired back in nanoseconds some snappy retort girded with enough derision to blush sailors.

Rebel was keenly familiar with Lee's view of the Black Man. His was a mixed bag of repulsive contempt and deep-seated respect. For as long as the boy could remember, Lee had schooled the child on reasons to dislike black people. Some of his brother's ideas had seemed logical, but most did not line up with Rebel's own personal experience.

For the boy, the negative conjectures of his brother never took. In as many ways Lee saw disparity, Rebel saw kinship. In the child's estimation, the black friends he had were as poor as he was, and, like him, not particularly welcome in an upper-crust milieu.

"Well? Why should a nigga run shit instead a whitey?" Mazell asked again. The boys stood paralyzed with Lee mute as stone. Rebel could hear the teens muttering behind them as Mazell snapped his newspaper straight.

"Y'all got big dicks," Rebel blurted out.

The room was noiseless for a moment, until Mazell and the teens howled in laughter. The entire length of the counter moved back and forth, keeping time with Mazell's heaving belly as coffee-colored rolls nudged the bar.

That was three years ago. Rebel crossed Enterprise now for the first time without his brother, accompanied only by a Texas Indian Princess. Kip was the picture of calm. Along the journey, she'd taken in every sight, enclave, and detour as if each was a remarkable discovery unto itself. These were the findings of a faraway world she was meant to see since before she was born. Her genuine interest fed the boy, and Rebel supposed that even if he had not wished she was his girlfriend right away, they would have inevitably become best friends at least.

The snap of loose rock under rubber turned Rebel's attention to the task at hand. He swerved to miss a large divot in the parking lot, looking back to make sure his new friend avoided it as well. The boy rolled up to the store's edge and leaned his bike against a corroded septic tank, overgrown with weed stalks. Kip slid in next to him and propped hers on its kickstand, which reminded Rebel to use his as well. He flipped the kickstand out, allowing the bike to rest independently. A strange sight, he had to admit.

"Don't be scared or nothin'," Rebel reassured the girl. "It's just Brown Bear."

"I'm not," Kip said, and Rebel could tell she had the utmost trust in his guidance. This lent the boy an unreasonable confidence, and he walked more casually than he otherwise would have.

A patched out-of-square screen door was all that separated patrons from the inner sanctum of Mazell's establishment. An archaic ice cream chest with cedar trimmings hummed pleasantly at the head of three aisles full of chips and candy. Periodically in sync with the clip-clank of the metal fan, the buzz of the chest made the place feel as if it were in constant song—a symbiotic stream of integrated noise reflecting the sins of Enterprise.

The store was empty except for Brown Bear, and the boy caught himself thanking God aloud. Rebel offered Kip a smile and headed straight for the fat man. Brown Bear slouched within the same overalls and fedora he always wore, poured onto the same rickety chair. Rebel could swear he sat now in the same position he did three years prior with only the length of his cigar altered. A fresh, robust Cuban filled every crevice of the building with Havana. The fat man ruffled his paper in acknowledgment and cast a bored glance to the young white girl perusing his store.

"What's a'word on the street, lil' man?"

"Nothin' to it. I come to git a six-pack," Rebel said. Mazell peered over the boy's shoulder to locate the girl. "Where Lee at?"

"Who knows. He's all over the place."

"Who ya friend is?"

"She just moved to town. Her family moved from Texas to that fancy neighborhood they buildin' out on the East Side."

"M'kay, m'kay," Mazell stalled.

Rebel dug into his jeans pocket and produced the crumpled twenty. "I got money."

"Boy, put yo' damn money up," Mazell grumbled. He fished a lighter from somewhere within a fat roll, adding fresh fire to his tobacco. The small log flamed to life as smoke billowed toward the ceiling. "How you likin' Muddy?"

"Best so far," said the boy, "better'n Howlin' Wolf."

"Is 'at right?" Mazell grinned.

Kip came to stand beside her friend. She smiled warmly at the mass behind the counter and said hello.

"Hey der, lil' girl. What's yo' name?" Mazell asked.

"Kip," she said.

"This is Brown Bear," Rebel said.

"What you runnin' around wi'da Mims boy fo'?"

Kip laughed. "He was riding his bike in my neighborhood late at night, being all creepy...but I decided to trust him anyway," the girl said.

Mazell grinned, wider than Rebel had ever seen before. He shifted on the chair buried beneath him and reached beneath the bar, eventually tossing a scratched cassette onto the counter. "This

Son House." Mazell said, catching his breath. "Lemme know what ya thank."

"Yes, sir. Thank ya," said Rebel, stuffing the tape into his pocket. There was the sound of cars in the parking lot. "Can I git a six-pack and these?" Rebel asked eagerly. He took the chips Kip was holding and placed them on the counter. "You want sump'm to drank?" the boy asked his friend.

"No, I'm fine," Kip said. "I have money. You don't have to get mine."

"Naw, I got it."

Mazell leaned to take a warped cane, using it to reach the tattered curtains that blocked the outside heat. He pushed them aside, bending low to see Roddy Stockdale exit his '84 Buick Electra.

"Why you like Muddy mo' than Howlin' Woof?" the fat man asked.

Rebel knew whoever pulled up would soon be inside and any tenuous sense of control he felt he had over this transaction would be lost.

"Whatcha mean?"

"Prove to me you been listenin'," Mazell gnawed at the cigar. The screen door creaked wide, announcing the arrival of a young black man with a steep side-slope fade. A white muscle shirt and bright red gym shorts hung loose around his stocky frame. Rebel did not recognize this person from his liquor runs with Lee. Mazell nodded to the customer. "Gimme a reason and I git ya drank fo' ya," Mazell persisted.

Rebel watched the young man double take when he saw them. The customer made his way slowly up the aisle in their direction. Sweat gathered on the child's upper lip in an instant, frustrated Mazell was dragging this out. But Rebel had come to know that anything Brown Bear did he did without haste. The boy sighed, his brow furrowing as he thought for an answer that would appease the man.

"Howlin' Wolf is raw…like sandpaper goin' at a two-b'four. He got edges in his voice. Hot like he's lookin' to fight. Muddy's diff'rnt. He sounds like he's done on the other side of ever'thang, like a rock smoothed out from water over a long time. And he just wants to rest."

The fat man slowly took the cigar from his mouth, another thing the boy had never witnessed. Rebel watched as the place where the cigar had been pull into a wide grin. Brown Bear surveyed the boy as if for the first time, investigating the blue hues of the child's eyes. He disappeared into a side closet.

The young man now stood directly behind Kip, so close that the Gatorade bottle he turned over in his hand nearly touched her. Rebel could feel Kip inch forward to create space between her and the customer, and the boy forced a glance at the young man. On his forearms were a series of raised, bulbous scars, long and side by side as if he'd tangled with a bobcat and lost. The young man eyed the back of Kip's head, cutting eyes to the boy in defiance. Rebel slid his arm around Kip's shoulder, unsure himself as to what this action would actually achieve. Kip did not flinch, emboldening Rebel to pull her firmly to his side.

The young man's lip curled and he sniggered. "Ain't nobody tryin' to git up on yo' skinny ass bitch, boy. Calm down wit' yo' punk ass," the customer said.

Rebel stared straight ahead, noticing for the first time the plethora of cigarettes that lined the wall behind the counter. These were normally blocked out by Mazell's mass, but now the boy could see Marlboros stretching the length of the wall itself.

Stiff as he was, Rebel could feel his heartbeat in his throat, the space inside his ears compressing with anarchic energy. An idea was forming in his head: he would not say or do anything unless the young man touched them, at which point he would swing wildly and not stop. With luck, Mazell would return before the customer overpowered him.

"What, you can't speak? You was talkin' to big man a second ago, but you can't speak to me?"

The boy felt the young man's breath lift from the back of his neck as the customer turned his attention to the girl.

"How 'bout you? You can't speak neither, bitch?"

"Hey!" Brown Bear barked, having magically reappeared behind the counter. "You gon buy sump'm or keep runnin' yo' damn mouth?" he asked the customer. The Cuban had returned to its rightful place. He tapped the counter casually with the barrels of a sawed-off shotgun. A short gasp from the girl, and Rebel gently pulled her to the side, making way for whatever was about to happen. The boy noticed a six-pack of Coors and two bottles of Coca-Cola on the countertop next to the gun.

"Oh, so now *you* can't speak?" Mazell snapped. "Nigga, git yo' ass up out my sto'," Brown Bear said, using the shotgun as a pointer. The customer sneered at the fat man and crammed the Gatorade into the nearest aisle full of chips.

"Man, fuck this," the young man said, staring at the boy as he went.

The children sighed in relief. Brown Bear turned his cigar over in his mouth, grinning as he watched the two finally breathe.

"Son, you come this side of the woods, you betta 'spect some wolfs." Mazell chuckled. He nodded toward the booty on the counter. "Take this and y'all git on. Gon git dark fo' too long, and y'all betta have yo' ass on the other side of town.

Rebel used both hands to gather the six-pack and drinks.

"Thank you, sir," the girl said, smiling at Mazell.

"Brown Bear," Mazell replied. "My friends call me Brown Bear."

"Well, thank you very much, Mr. Brown Bear," Kip said, waving goodbye, and followed the boy out of the store. In the parking lot, Rebel was relieved to see the customer leaning into the passenger window of a car close to Roddy's, immersed in conversation. The pair tried wrangling themselves onto their bikes, balancing loot awkwardly in one hand while managing handlebars with the other. The boy made sure Roddy noticed them with a wave. Rodrick's face brightened and he jogged across the lot.

"What in the hell are you doin' here?" Roddy asked, clasping the boy's hand as he hugged him. Rebel was reminded again how handsome and well-formed Rodrick was, and immediately regretted gesturing for his attention. If Kip were smitten, it would be no fault of her own.

"I come to git Mama some beer," the boy replied.

"I hear ya. Brown Bear hook you up?"

"Yeah."

"Good. I didn't know you had a girlfriend," Roddy smiled.

"We're just friends," Rebel blushed.

"I'm Kip," the girl said, shaking the older boy's hand.

"Liquor run's a shitty first date, don't ya think, Kip?"

"Shut up, Roddy!" Rebel shoved him playfully and Rodrick laughed as he walked backwards toward his car.

"Gotta step up your game, Reb!" he grinned. Rodrick lifted his hands as if conducting an orchestra, and then, in the most hoity-toity accent he could muster, "Love him and let him love you. Do you think anything else under heaven really matters?'"

"Come on," Rebel said to the girl as he realigned himself on the bike, "he's bein' a idiot."

Kip watched Rodrick go, held fast by this last sentiment. "That was really pretty," she called out.

The older boy spun around. "James Baldwin," Rodrick yelled back, and disappeared into a cluster of friends.

In spite of the legendary lunchroom altercation with Lee, Rodrick never assumed Rebel guilty by association, and the boy had always been deeply appreciative of such objectivity. It was Lee who turned Rebel's attention to Roddy's intellect, coaching his younger brother on what to look for, how to identify various ways in which the gifted boy would reveal his hand.

"A thang's gotta be what it is, Reb," Lee told him. "If it ain't, then the truth of it comes out sideways and steals from ever'body else. And that ain't right."

When Lee had said this, the boy was sure he had no idea what his brother was talking about. Lee often garbled nonsensical philosophy he thought worthy of print. But soon enough the child began to catch on, noting Rodrick spoke one way around his teachers and Tab, yet seemed reticent around his friends. In truth, the events leading up to the lunchroom beating were never revealed to anyone besides Rebel, who still struggled to fully believe them.

Once it became clear that Tab and Rodrick fancied one another, Lee set out to see exactly what he was up against. In the beginning, he tracked the pair's every move. Their first real conversation Lee had eavesdropped. The first time they'd had sex, Lee was there, hidden, yet present all the same. Increasingly, Rebel was coming to realize his own fascination with human behavior—examined from afar as not to encumber its natural course—he'd learned quite by example.

The boy had watched when Lee dressed himself in black from head to toe, painting his face as well, so only the whites of his eyes had shown. Then, from Rebel's own bedroom window, Lee disappeared into the darkness of the dirt road and into the woods beyond. Of course, for everything that happened from that point on the child would have to take his brother's word. Lee apparently made his way across town to West End. Once there, he trekked deep into the neighborhood until he came to Rodrick's house. Under the cover of night, he broke into and combed through the entirety of Roddy's Buick.

Just before dawn, the boy heard the stretch of trampoline springs and looked to see his brother climbing onto the canvass. Lee splayed himself out—Ulysses returned from war. The boy crawled through the window to join his brother who stared blankly into the night sky.

"What happened?" Rebel whispered.

"Books," Lee had said.

"Books? Whatcha mean, books?"

The older boy rolled over to face the dirt road he'd just walked. "I stripped that car to the bone. Whole damn thang. Nothin'. No pot. No guns...no severed heads."

Rebel studied his brother's back, frustrated by what amounted to incoherent babbling.

"Just books." Lee said softly. "Locked up in the trunk like they was fuckin' gold in Fort Knox."

"You mean Playboys and stuff?" Rebel asked earnestly.

"Naw. Real books. Utopia. Invisible Man—but not the kind of invisible man yer thinkin'. Grapes of Fuckin' Wrath... Poe-Thoreau bullshit. All stuffed up under where his spare tire's supposed to be. Ever'one of the damn thangs was marked up... like he's been scribblin' in 'em forever."

And in that moment, in the silence there under the stars, the boy watched his brother give up.

CHAPTER 8

Father and Ferret

By late afternoon, most of the day's heat had ebbed, its warmth bottled up in the dirt and trees. Rebel's tires hit the dirt road leading to the trailer right at Pony Time and he slowed to prolong the ride. He'd wedged the six-pack just so, between the handlebars and his crotch. He was careful to miss the larger rocks and holes so as to not spill the beer or himself. Taking in the stretch ahead, Rebel imagined the trailer a lonely matchbox, tossed aside by someone aloof, abandoned from boredom. Around the boy, all was brightened by a weightless umber, such that much of the dirt melded into an organic gold, compelling the child to consider if by luck he'd transmuted to Oz.

Entering the trailer, Rebel found his mother balled up on the couch in the space usually occupied by Tab, feet tucked securely beneath her. Dennis was aligned next to her, his long arm wreathed around her. Charleen looked worse for wear, her hair frayed and greasy from tears. The day's despair had been greedy, leaving every hard-earned wrinkle on full display. Even so, the boy found her beautiful. Charleen looked up and wiped a smudge of mascara from her cheek as she forced a smile.

"Come here, baby," she whimpered, extending hands toward her son. Rebel obliged, the six-pack still tucked under his arm. "You okay?" she asked.

"Yes, ma'am," the boy responded, finally making eye contact with Dennis. The man rose to relieve the child of the beer, extracting two cans from the box before depositing the rest in the fridge.

"'Preciate the run, lil' man," he said, puncturing the lid of each can. "And tell your guy I said thanks." This reminded Rebel of the leftover money and he dug to retrieve it.

"No, no, no," Dennis protested, reclaiming his spot beside Charleen. "I told you that's yours to keep."

Charleen stroked the back of Dennis' hair, casting the boy a glance. *Wasn't that sweet?* the look said. *Isn't he thoughtful and generous and kind.*

Rebel knew something odd was happening with his own mouth. His lip had curled involuntarily and he made efforts to relax.

"Listen, Reb...I asked Dennis if he wouldn't mind stayin' with us tonight," Charleen suggested sheepishly.

"Why?" Rebel shot back, surprised by how quickly this escaped.

"Well, just to make sure we're okay. With what happen and all...be nice to have a man here, you know, just to keep..." her voice trailed.

For the boy, the room was collapsing, borders of a vintage photo burning slowly, edging closer and closer to its center. He stared at the woman on the couch, bewildered, as hate ratcheted through his intestines like pigweed.

"We're fine," Rebel choked out.

"I know, baby. I know...we gon be aw'ight."

"No, I mean now. Right now. We're fine." The boy felt warmth form under his eye, then slide over his cheek to settle at the corner of his mouth. Charleen's expression changed and she sat forward on the couch.

"Hey," she said softly, "forget I said that. He don't have to stay, okay?"

"You're the man of this house, son," Dennis said rising from the couch. "I was just keeping your mom company 'til you got home."

Charleen grabbed Dennis' hand. "It's fine," he reassured her.

"You don't have to go right this second," she said, rising to meet him.

Yes, the boy thought. *You do have to go, you connivin' son of a bitch. Get yer lanky fuckin' ass outta our house and never come back. And take that shitty rat growin' on yer lip with ya.*

Dennis took another beer from the refrigerator before moving to the door. Charleen followed the man onto the porch, pulling the door closed behind her. Rebel could make out blotchy silhouettes from the other side, could see them move close to one another. The boy listened to the muffled voices as he looked at the couch where they'd just sat. The corner spot was a scoop of flattened foam covered in an over-worn material, curved deep with indention from years of television and cigarettes.

Standing there, Rebel wondered if he could manage just as well on his own. He wondered, if his mother had followed Dennis from the porch and into his truck, never to be seen or heard from again, would he be okay? Certainly there was precedent. The boy tried recalling every child abandonment story he'd ever heard.

One such instance had the baby deposited at a fire station, only to see the child adopted by a wealthy family. The kid would go on to attend Harvard and ultimately helm a successful law practice in upstate New York.

Rebel had witnessed Lee run away so many times it had become laughable. Shock of his brother's absence faded with frequency. The first time it ever happened Lee was eleven, and Charleen all but tore her clothes in public lament. A clan of worried neighbors assembled sometime after 10 p.m. and proceeded to comb a five-mile radius well into the 3 a.m. hour. At some point a neighbor walked Charleen back to her trailer for a coffee refill and the pair found Lee digging through the fridge. Charleen rushed to embrace her son, only to have Lee shove her away. "I went off and left without any fuckin' bologna. I ain't stayin', so don't even start," Lee had grumbled.

Later in his room, Rebel traced the patterns of the paper-thin paneling, imagining how harshly one of his Hot Wheels would have to take some of the turns on the elaborate track. The boy kept the room immaculately clean while the rest of the trailer maintained a perpetual state of disarray. Rebel stretched long on the twin mattress, tightly covered by a faded bedspread. Charleen found the comforter at a thrift store and her son loved it almost as much as his comics.

The expanse of the universe and all its constellations were displayed on the material from corner to corner. The ultramarine of space had bleached grey. Rebel observed Neptune for the thousandth time, warped and oblong from washings. Saturn's rings were nearly imperceptible. The boy wondered how many other kids had marveled at this same Neptune back when it still held its shape.

When he opened his eyes, the only light he could see was the moon's. He had no idea what time it was, only that he was hungry. Sliding quietly down the hallway to the kitchen, he surveyed the countertops, settling on a half-eaten blueberry muffin. The boy placed his mouth under the faucet, gulping enough water to allow the muffin to pass. As he drank, he noticed the stove clock: 3:17 a.m.

Rebel stood straight, water dripping chin to chest. He'd never been awake during this particular window of night. His grandfather had woken him and Lee on multiple occasions within the 4 a.m. hour, nudging the boys from sleep for an early hunt. But this was 3 a.m., and as far as the boy was concerned, cause for high alert, if not panic.

Lee's favorite thing to do in all the world, besides sex with "any skank whore who'd have him," as Tab liked to say, was watching horror movies. This involved elaborate schemes at the cineplex: precision-taping torn stubs back together for re-tearing, slipping in and out of bathrooms between showings, and timing re-entry to coincide with theater cleanings. Between the *Friday the 13th* and *Nightmare on Elm Street* franchises, Rebel guessed his brother had watched the films at least a hundred times, enough to quote every movie line for line. Lee's most recent fixation, however, had been possession.

Somehow, lost in the barrage of slasher gore and chainsaw wielding madmen, Lee had missed *The Exorcist*. But once he saw Linda Blair's grey, pot-marked head spin three-sixty on her shoulders, his obsession was absolute. As his fascination grew, he learned that within possession lore, 3 a.m. was, indeed, the witching hour—the time when the devil and his cohorts were most active.

More than once, Lee had begged, then threatened his little brother to stay awake with him to see if there was anything to the mythology. Rebel refused, of course, sometimes at the cost of a beating, but he never regretted his decision. He'd heard Pastor Barnett warn time and again against "giving the devil a foothold" and "flirting with the occult." Whereas Lee was hellbent to taste and see the dark arts, the boy was easy to faith and the admonitions of obedience.

But now, here he was, caught squarely in the crosshairs of the witching hour, and fear engulfed him. The boy turned to face the round kitchen table, fully expecting to see at least two, maybe three of Satan's horde starring at him hungrily, daring him to flinch. Instead, four empty chairs. Rebel forced himself into the living room which seemed surprisingly spacious. Too much open air for spirits to move about as they pleased, he reckoned. And then the boy considered his mother's quarters. Certainly he should muster the courage to check on her, ensure that Mephistopheles hadn't already plowed whetted black claws into the softness of Charleen's neck.

Rebel stepped forward in the silence, half-expecting to see any number of grotesque, violent acts on display; his mother's blood the paint for a demon's canvas. The boy opened the door to the bedroom as slowly and carefully as possible, so as not to stir the dead. Inside, as his eyes rightly adjusted to the dark, there was only stillness. Two forms lay side by side, breathing in time, rhythmic and serene as a metronome. Rebel knew instantly the larger form, so long its feet had slipped well past the covers and hung over the bed's edge.

The Tourist.

For a moment, the boy felt time had sluggishly suspended. The air in the room had coagulated into plasma, and Rebel figured if he grasped the space in front of him he would very well have clenched something as finite as moon rock. That was the first moment. The second was an unmistakable realization that he was not surprised. Rebel questioned if he had clairvoyance in knowing this is what he would see even before turning the door's handle. Perhaps he knew from the moment Charleen had mentioned The Tourist would not stay over. He couldn't be sure. None of that mattered now as the boy considered what to do next.

"Motherfuckin' asshole."

These words, ones he thought had formed in his own head, were spoken aloud. Rebel recognized the breathing pattern and turned to see Lee at the foot of the bed.

"What the fuck is this?" Lee snorted.

Rebel turned back to observe the two lumps, no more surprised that his brother was in the room than seeing this strange man lying next to his mother. Lee flipped the rope around his neck onto his back, the same way Isaac would his tie when sitting for a meal at formal occasions.

"You okay wi' this shit?" Lee whispered furiously.

"No," Rebel replied as he watched Lee pace, his brother's face contorting through phases of disgust.

"Well, what are you gon do?"

"What do ya mean?"

"I mean this sumbitch rolled up in our mama's bed like he lives here."

"I told her we was fine and don't need nobody," Rebel said in a defensive hush.

"Well, that's just great. 'Cause you and me both know Charleen always chooses her boys over dick."

Rebel felt the hardness of the dead boy's cheek against his palm, the inside of his hand afire from the wallop. For an instant, Lee marveled at his little brother's instinct and grinned. This gave way to a seething contempt as he reached into his back pocket and brandished his butterfly knife. He flipped it open in a flurry of movement, back and forth and around again with the deftness of a sous chef. He approached the boy, close enough for Rebel to see the part of Lee's cheek he'd just smacked, raised and discolored even in the dark. Lee yanked Rebel's hand toward the knife, slamming the handle against the boy's palm. He closed his little brother's fingers tight around the grip.

"You got balls enough to swing on me, but you just gon stand there seein' this and not do shit?"

Lee pressed Rebel's fist that held the blade flush against his little brother's chest. The boy pushed him away, and Lee seemed to vanish into a ribbon of ebony on the other side of the window. Rebel moved alongside the bed then, past the enormous, naked feet of the longer form, coming finally to Dennis' head. The boy watched the two of them for a while as they slept. Mockingly still and content. He expected tuffs of Dennis' mustache to lift and fall in cadence with his breath, but not a single hair had moved.

This had a rage-fuel effect on the boy, and heat flushed his cheeks through from the inside out. He lowered his fist, the knife at his hip. Rebel was closer now to the stranger than he ever intended to be. He looked to his mother, her shoulder bare, her torso open toward the man. Rebel followed the run of her arm down to her hand which lay securely against the stranger's midsection. The man was on his back, flat and static. With Dennis' pronounced cheek bones and blockish forehead—along with the goatee—the boy envisioned him a pioneer corpse. Stiff against open pine, just like he'd seen the Dalton Gang displayed in an overdue library book he checked out last year.

Rebel leaned closer, following the rim of the man's nose until the strong Greek arch came to an abrupt halt. He noticed the slits of Dennis' eyes, cracked wider than he expected, and watched two sable discs slide slowly toward the knife in his hand. A new heat now, quick and plumb to Rebel's neck, as he realized the man was very much awake. Rebel glanced to the corner where Lee had been to see the emptiness of shadow. A ruffling sound pulled the boy's attention to the bed where he watched Dennis cross his hands behind his head, positioning himself as if absorbing rays beachside.

The air changed again. The darkness of the room, tinged grey by moonlight, seemed expansive. Rebel marveled how the space between he and The Tourist suddenly felt like a vacuum. The boy suspected movement by either party would be streamlined within this void.

"Well?" Dennis purred in a honeyed bass.

Rebel was instantly self-aware and the knife in his hand heavy. It was hot in his palm, and he found his body swaying though he hadn't meant to. The boy looked down at his fist. The blade that seemed so impressive moments ago now appeared Lilliputian.

"She gotta' name?" Dennis whispered.

"What?"

"The butterfly?"

"Oh...naw," Rebel mused, looking again to the dark corner. "I don't thank so."

Dennis eased himself upright and extended his hand toward the blade. "Lemme see," the man said. Rebel surveyed his mother, undisturbed throughout. He offered the knife to The Tourist. The man turned the blade over in his hand, running his thumb over the handle's worn faux wood. Dennis stood, his white legs elongated from the floor until they disappeared into a snug pair of Fruit of the Loom underwear. Dark as the room was, Rebel could make out the man's bulge, floppy and sinking within the undergarment and the child winced.

"Where'd you get it?" Dennis asked as he moved toward the living room. Rebel followed, watching him flip the blade open and shut again.

"It's my brother's," Rebel said quietly.

Dennis retrieved a beer from the refrigerator and used the knife to pop the top of the bottle.

"Was," the man said.

"What?"

"Was. The knife *was* your brother's," Dennis said, propping his long pasty form against the kitchen counter.

"I mean...yeah. It's mine now." Rebel shifted.

"Wrong again. It ain't yours either," said The Tourist.

The boy looked over his shoulder toward the room where his mother slept, for backup from someone he trusted. Someone he knew. There was nothing. The Tourist was an angular statue painted Confederate gray against the cheap vinyl. "How you fig'er?" Rebel forced himself to ask, knowing this would lead to an undoing.

"Well, your brother's dead. So he don't have no use for it." Dennis measured the boy's expression. "And you're obviously too much of a pussy to use it yourself. But most of all 'cause it's in my hand now."

Rebel expected the breadth of what was being unearthed. Maybe not exactly like this. He certainly hadn't foreseen it involving his brother's knife. That seemed random. He was surprised, however, that Dennis was allowing the mask to slip so soon. This was brazen. Amateurish.

"Unless you want to come take it from me," the man said. "Is that what you wanna do, pussy?" said The Tourist, extending the knife out in an open palm. "Come on. Come get it."

"I ain't no pussy," the boy said, the bottom of his eyelids

welling. Rebel stretched his face long, making oval his mouth, trying with all his might to keep a single tear from betraying him. *Don't you give this asshole the satisfaction*, the child said to himself.

Dennis pushed from the counter, extending his palm further. "Go ahead. If it's yours then take it."

Rebel could see The Tourist's face clearly now, his outsized cheekbones framed hard within moonlight. The sallowness on the sides of his mouth, dueling below a thinning widow's peak, proffered the man as a first-rate pirate. In the boy's estimation he only lacked the eye-patch. The scar cratered within his eyebrow completed the look.

Rebel remembered the same invitation being offered once to a young Kung-Fu pupil he'd seen on television. An ancient Chinese master sat cross-legged and solemn, wizened with years, stroking an unreasonably long white beard. Palm outstretched, the master had presented a single piece of rice to his pupil, a boy not much older than himself. This, of course, was a litmus test of the pupil's training: could he snatch the rice from his master's hand before the old man clenched it shut?

But standing at the kitchen's edge, on the tail-end of the witching hour and staring into the eyes of a patch-less pirate, Rebel could not for the life of him remember if the pupil had succeeded. A flurry of movement disrupted this thought and the boy realized Dennis had flipped the knife closed, teasing safety. The child stepped closer, widening his stance like a gunslinger. Rebel thrust his fingers toward the man's palm and Dennis yanked back his fist, knife firmly in hand. The man's grin faded. He sighed and extended the knife a second time, already bored with the game.

Rebel eyed him cautiously, then shot his hand forward and grabbed the knife as Dennis offered no resistance. The boy stepped back, having snatched the last scrap of bone from an unfamiliar dog. The Tourist simply looked down at his enormous feet. He massaged his eyes with those mallet-sized palms.

"My old man...when I was about your age, had this ferret," Dennis said. "This fuckin' ferret," The Tourist chuckled to himself. "Mean as hell and it hated the shit outta me."

Rebel began to uncoil.

"Pop lived on the road. Booze'n and whore'n wherever he went. He always left me in charge of taking care of that little fur snake. Hated that goddamn thing. Anyway...he's gone once for... hell, I don't know. Two, three months. When he finally decides to show up, the first thing he does, of course, is go lookin' for his rat. But I'm a kid and by this time I'm gettin' into all kinds'a shit myself...dope and fights and finger fuckin' any bitch who'd let me."

Dennis glanced at the boy and smirked, registering the child's disgust. "Oh, don't worry, kid. You'll be itchin' to dip your little prick in some pink any day now." Any sense of ease evaporated, and Rebel averted his eyes. The boy made himself study the empty couch, illuminated by a gunmetal sheen in surprising detail.

"So he gets home—I can smell his drunk ass before he hits the porch. And I know all hell's about to break loose 'cause I forgot to feed the damn thing for two or three days. I didn't even know where it was. Pop's throwin' shit around, kickin' chairs, yellin' out for it. More pissed by the second. He finally finds the little fucker, curled up under some dirty clothes, skinny as hell." Dennis laughed. Rebel watched the man slide his index finger up through the divot in his eyebrow.

"He's holding the ferret in one hand like a slinky and backhands the shit outta me with the other. Lays this wide open. Did it with this ring right here," Dennis said, turning the largest ring on his fingers over and over. "Turns out this thing cuts like a damn razor 'cause it's chipped on one edge. See?" Dennis extended his hand for examination. "You can't really see it in the dark, but anyway...I'm bleedin' all over the goddamn carpet which makes him even madder, and he drags me over to the closet and says, 'Hit him.'"

Dennis read consternation on the boy's face.

"I know!" Dennis laughed, "I thought the same thing. *'What in the hell are you talkin' about?'* But he says it again, 'Hit him.' He holds the thing out in front of me by the neck and starts shakin' it at me, 'Hit him! Hit him goddammit!'

"So I hauled off and slapped the shit outta that ferret, and this fuckin' thing starts hissin' at me like a cobra. My old man goes, 'Again!' So I do it again. I end up smackin' the damn thing four or five times. And it's flailin' all over the place, madder'n hell. Then all of a sudden, Pops opens the door to the closet, pushes me in, throws the ferret right in my lap and wham! Slams the door. It's pitch-black, but I can hear him wedging a chair up underneath the door handle."

Transfixed, Rebel feverishly followed the chronology of the story. "What happened?" the boy asked.

"What the hell you think?" Dennis laughed. "Goddamn thing went apeshit. Bitin' and clawin' me all over the place. I'm slappin' at it, tryin' to stomp on it, but I can't see shit so we're like two hornets goin' at it in the dark."

Rebel giggled, incredulous. Then the boy watched the smile drift from the man's mouth as Dennis traced the outline of the divot with the flat of his forefinger.

"How'd ya get out?"

"Huh? Oh. By the time I caught it I was done bein' scared. Couldn't see nothin', but I knew I was bleedin'. And all those bites and scratches hurt like a motherfucker, so I was pissed. Once I got hold of it, I bit that fuckin' thing right back—took a chunk out of its neck. But it was all neck. Gross as hell. Fur caught in my teeth. After a couple minutes it quit squirmin'."

The boy stood aghast, astonished that the mouth he was watching speak not only clenched down upon but ripped out some unknown section of ferret. A sense of awed admiration took hold of the child. Rebel was suddenly aware of his surroundings: the lateness of time, the oddity of standing there with the stranger. Could the story really have happened? Was it true? The boy figured he had no real reason to doubt The Tourist, sensing no strain of embellishment as Dennis spoke. He wondered then what prompted the man to recall his father and the ferret.

"Guess I'm gon go to sleep," Rebel said, sliding through the kitchen.

"Yeah," Dennis mumbled, not looking up.

The carpet of the hallway felt thick beneath the boy's feet. Before turning into his room, a searing pain erupted at the back of his head, followed by a deep thud, the sound of his cheek crashing against the corner of the doorframe. Any adjustment to nightshade vanished as the child's vision gave way to black. Consciousness escaping him. A moored throbbing brought the boy to, with pain pushing concentrically from the back of his head to his eyes; a leaden pressure he did not know. Deep in his eardrum came a low garble of rhythmic of sound.

Rebel was rising through the air. His view rushed up and away from the carpet and the room whirled until he saw only The Tourist. The man slammed the boy hard against the wall of his bedroom, and the child made out a recognizable sound—the crack of wood as his shoulder crushed into the paneling. His eyesight settled, and a new pressure at his throat was the man's hand. The boy tried measuring the expression on Dennis' face. Disgust? Perhaps disappointment. Disappointment seemed likely.

Rebel's efforts were distracted by a warm sensation running the length of his neck. He reached behind with a hand and placed it on that warmth, retracting it to see his fingers bathed in crimson. Dennis let go his grip and leaned against the chest of drawers behind him. The Tourist gestured to the boy's bloody hand, then pointed to the massive ring he'd rotated moments earlier.

"You see!" Dennis said, satisfied. "I told you this thing was a son-of-a-bitch!" The man laughed and Rebel reached out to steady himself on furniture that that was just beyond his reach. "Easy now," Dennis said, helping Rebel sit on the bed. The Tourist assumed a seat next to the boy, lifting the ring up just so.

"See. That chipped part I was tellin' you about, on the edge. Right there," Dennis instructed, pointing to a tiny piece of flayed metal at the corner of the ring. "If you turn it just right before you let loose, you might as well have a fuckin' spike for a finger." The man adjusted the boy's body forward, fishing the butterfly knife from Rebel's back pocket. The Tourist held the blade up beside the ring: exhibit A and B.

"So with this—yeah. You flip it out, whirl it around, lookin' all cool and shit...but by the time the show's done the son-of-a-bitch standin' across from you's already knocked you the fuck out. You're already stabbed, shot, whatever."

Dennis used his thumb to tap the ring of the same hand. "But with this...it's always on you, see. You don't have to conceal shit. Sits right there in plain sight, whenever you need it."

Rebel felt a tinge of nausea at the top of his stomach and closed his eyes to slow the rushing inside his head.

"This? This is bullshit," The Tourist said, whipping the

butterfly back and forth. "It'll get you killed before it ever helps you out of a jam." Dennis slipped the closed knife under the waistband of his underwear. "Remember that."

The man reached out and took the boy's hand, clasping it solidly around his own. Rebel observed his small hand dwarfed by the larger one, both dressed now in the boy's blood. Dennis tilted Rebel's head down to survey the wound.

"You'll be alright," he mused. "But listen, you can't go to sleep for a little bit." Rebel could see the man lower his head with the droop of his own eyelids, trying to maintain eye contact. "Hey," Dennis said, firmly slapping the boy's cheek, "you hear what I'm sayin'? You can't go to sleep yet 'cause you might not wake up, you little shit. Your mom would be a mess losin' two back-to-back. Here..."

The Tourist helped the boy stand and led him down the hallway to the front door. "Go on," Dennis said, opening the screen. "Walk around outside for a little bit and wake the hell up. Then come back in and take a shower."

Rebel could tell his feet were descending steps though he'd not ordered them to move.

"Last thing your mom needs is more shit to worry about after your brother, right?" Dennis watched as the boy ambled to the center of the yard, slowly coming to a stop. "Right?" The Tourist asked from the porch. Rebel shuffled around to face the misplaced blur speaking from the porch.

"Yeah," the child's voice faltered.

"'Ere we go," the man said, tapping the porch rail with approval. The Tourist disappeared.

Rebel reached once more to feel the back of his head. The spot was already hardening from hair and blood congealing into a waxy goop. The boy shuffled out a few steps more and strained to see the barn in the distance. Within the bay, an elfin fire. And the shadow of what he knew was his brother.

The dead boy stood over a flame, shiftless, warming his hands like a Great Plains cowboy.

CHAPTER 9

Black Blood

Rebel crested the last step of the loft, his head genuflect, having already played out the ensuing conversation. Lee stood with his arms folded in front of the bay.

"Where the fire go?" the boy ventured as he moved closer.

The floor at his brother's feet was only dust and pine. "What the fuck you talkin' 'bout?" Lee snapped.

Rebel surveyed the room. "I saw you standin' by the fire a minute ago...from in front of the house."

Lee's face twisted as he turned back to the open air. The boy knew this look, not unlike the one Dennis expressed after the wallop. Lee was a master of setting an unseen bar of approval for others, having himself done nothing to garner the respect that demanded such approval. Nevertheless, it was there.

Rebel had noticed this with others as well. People seemed to innately want to impress his brother, and this had baffled the boy to no end. He'd watched his own mother bend to this intangible tension. Perhaps it was the snubbing nonchalance he seemed to radiate. Lee simply did not care what anyone else thought of him, and this was no showy effort belying puerile insecurity. Rebel never detected a hint of doubt when it came to Lee's self-appraisal, and the younger had envied the older in this.

Much of Rebel's young life had been spent trying to win his brother's approval, all in an effort to have Lee deem him worthy—brave enough to fight when he had to, smart enough to lie when needed, man enough to fuck when he wanted.

"What t'hell you talkin' about, Rebel?" Lee was pacing now. "Why would I have a fire up here'n the middle of the gotdamn summer?

"I don't know."

"You know this place is a box a fuckin' kindlin' wait'n to go up any second!" Lee growled.

Rebel watched a charcoal vein lift within his brother's neck, pulsating with what the boy could only imagine was black blood. *Surely the dead all have black blood. Iron in the dirt or somethin' makes it turn black. Gotta be some science somewhere to make sense of it...gotta be.* Somehow the word "oxidation" was pulled from the caverns of his memory, uttered in the voice of a forgotten science teacher.

Lee pulled at the rope around his neck like a too-tight-tie although by now the noose hung limp at all times. "Give it back," the dead boy demanded, extending his hand.

"What?"

"You know gotdamn well what. Come on."

Rebel looked anywhere but the crystal daggers that were his brother's eyes.

"You let him keep it, didn't ya?" Lee mocked.

"I ain't let him do nothin'," Rebel fired back. "He damn near knocked me unconscious, Lee. What t'hell was I s'posed to do, huh?!"

"Not let that long-neck fucker keep my gotdamn knife is what!" Lee exploded, pushing the boy to the ground.

Rebel was up like a spring, enraged, and rushed toward his brother, throwing every inch of his weight into the dead boy. Lee hurtled backwards, his heel catching the edge of a lifted floorboard. This propelled his body over the edge of the bay.

Rebel was breathless, staring blankly at the empty window. He forced himself forward, pop-eyed, to see if he'd brought about a second death. The boy extended his arms, securing his palms against the base of the frame and leaned out, peering over the rim of a gulch of unknowable depth. The ground, some thirty feet below, was a hushed mass of overgrowth. Drowsy and undisturbed. Beyond, the moon seemed to lose faculty as the stretch to the trailer lay enfolded by an umbra of pines.

An indistinct snap echoed behind him, pulling the boy back into the room. In the center of the loft Lee warmed himself again, palms hovering above the same fire the boy had seen from a distance. Rebel approached his brother, flummoxed by Lee's indifference. He came to stand beside the dead boy, marveling at this fire that burned but did not consume. Smoke eddied toward the ceiling, steady and genteel, but the boards beneath remained unchanged. No charring sprawl or run of flame. Lee rubbed chalky hands together and blew into them, as if this spot in the loft in the dead of summer was home to the best ice-fishing in all of Anchorage.

"Whatcha doin'?" Rebel asked.

Lee glanced at the boy, annoyed. "What's it look like?"

Rebel went back and peered over the edge of the bay. Nothing. "You aw'ight?" the boy asked, walking over to place one of his hands near the flames to test authenticity.

"Y'know...'at there's ya problem, Rebel. Always worried about ever gotdamn body. Wantin' to make sure ever'body's happy and gettin' along and shit."

The boy jerked his hand from the fire, his fingertips red with heat.

"But the fuckin' problem wi'that, little brother, is this world ain't meant for peace. And the longer you keep thinkin' it is, the longer you gon keep gettin' ya ass handed to ya."

Lee shook his head and looked into the fire. Rebel recognized this as Lee's default whenever he'd hoped for the best but knew the worst was inevitable. "I'm tellin' ya...you wouldn't believe."

"What?" the boy asked.

Lee jabbed one of the logs with his sneaker, awakening the fire momentarily. Sparks trickled to the trusses above. "The shit I seen...since the time I been gone, I mean." He motioned to Rebel's watch. "How long's it been?"

Rebel examined his wrist, mentally walking through the timeline. "Friday makes two days."

"Aw'ight. Two days. But it ain't been two days on my side, see."

"Whatcha mean?"

"Aw'ight, ya know when ya smoke pot? What am I sayin', course ya don't. Why wouldn't ya ever smoke a joint wi'me when I give it to ya?"

"I did."

"No hell you didn't. Don't lie to me, Rebel. I know. And I ain't have to fuckin' cross over to know either. So damn obvious... wobblin' around after takin' a fake ass drag. That's how ya act when ya drunk, dumbass, not high."

"Whatever," Rebel mumbled.

"Anyway, when ya high, time slows down. Like, you know that ya sittin' inside a minute, but the minute feels like it's stretched the hell out. I don't know how to explain it just right, but...ever'thang on my side is fluid and streamlined. Like divin' through water real hard but goin' slow at the same time.

Rebel looked down at the miracle fire, and as runnels of sweat streamed down his neck, he began warming his hands as well.

"Who's all over there?" the boy asked.

"You 'member James Strickland?"

"Yeah."

"Blew half his damn face off huntin' with his cousin?" Lee grinned.

"Uh-huh."

"Well, he's still a dick."

"He get his face back?" Rebel asked.

"Hell naw. And it's disgustin' as hell. Like ya talkin' to a damn half-eat piece a hamburger."

Rebel laughed and Lee grinned at his little brother.

"Ain't nobody wont t'see 'at shit," Lee chuckled.

Rebel wheezed, his gut cramping with laughter. Lee moved to stand underneath what was left of the rope he'd hung himself with. He jumped up and swatted at it lazily like a piñata. Rebel's smile faded as he allowed his fingers to dip and rise in and out of the hole at the back of his head.

"Well...I'm still here," the boy said bitterly. "Glad you can show up whenever ya want to, see all kinds a cool stuff in the spirit world. While I'm stuck on this side dealin' wi..."

"Well, it ain't a damn free-for-all. They's rules on whatcha can and cain't do." Lee said.

"I don't care, Lee!" the boy shouted, his chin wriggling. "You hear me?! I don't fuckin' care!" Rebel kicked the fire, releasing a flurry sparking smoke toward the ceiling. "Right when…" he tried gathering his breath as tears formed against his will. Lee perched himself in the corner of the bay, bobbing one leg over the ledge.

"Right when this man shows up…that's when you decide to leave," the boy said crying. Lee peeled a fragment of dead wood from the ledge and hurled it through the air.

"I oughta come over and push yer ass through 'at window again. But you'd just pop up somewhere else," Rebel said. Lee looked away so the boy could not see the grin that was forming. "So I'm gon handle it myself," the child exclaimed. "'Cause it's just me."

Lee swatted at a mosquito. The boy had noticed more of them even within the last few minutes. Flies and gnats mostly, drawn inevitably to the exposed parts of the dead boy's ripening flesh. In life, Lee would abide the occasional insect, especially granddaddy long legs. Rebel guessed it was because the spiders were wiry in the same way his brother was. Lee had told the boy many times how vemonous these spiders were, rendered harmless only because their fangs were neither long nor strong enough to penetrate human skin. Rebel's new theory, however, taking shape in this very moment, was that Lee simply loved teasing peril. Get as close to death as possible in order to feel alive, then tell it to go fuck itself.

"The Tourist ain't stayin'," the boy said, mostly to himself, "That's fer damn sure."

Lee hopped from the ledge and ran, jumping in time to grab hold of the bottom of his death-rope, swinging out toward Rebel like a deft chimp. "Whelp," Lee grunted, thrusting his legs for altitude. "He ain't some limp-dick fucker like the others Charleen's taken up with."

Rebel watched his brother swing higher as Lee tried touching the tip of his shoe to the adjacent truss beyond. The boy inched to the side, making way for the dead boy's sloppy gymnastics. Rebel followed the wrenching sound of the rope, watching as it grated against the beam. "I got a plan," the boy said, his eyes swinging in time with Lee's momentum.

"You do?" the dead boy huffed, almost horizontal with the floorboards below.

A firecracker pop, and the rope snapped free from the truss. Lee flailed through the air, a fluster of lurching knees and elbows. The dead boy crashed onto the floorboards with a thunderclap, bouncing once then rolling directly over and beyond the fire that was still very much alive. Rebel watched as flames leeched onto his brother. Lee swatted to extinguish his hair and smother the burning noose around his neck.

"Yeah," Rebel said. The spirit-flames grew low and quiet once more. "I got a plan."

CHAPTER 10

The Quarry

Rebel had by now mapped the entirety of the Riverchase subdivision. Every dead-end cul-de-sac, every pallet of sod waiting to be laid. His greatest discovery within the neighborhood, however, could be found just behind the new girl's house. Past the tall line of Emerald Greens buttressing the family's privacy fence was a stretch of woods filled with congested brush and stalwart pines. This dense labyrinth provided an additional layer of seclusion for the neighborhood, insinuating isolation for what appeared to be tens of miles.

But the boy knew better. In navigating the far reaches of the new community, Rebel had stumbled upon a sprawling, cavernous kingdom of rolling dirt hills and enclaves carved from earth movers. Extensive excavation had left a quarry some hundred yards in length and nearly half as wide, leading Rebel to wonder if planners intended on this being the site of a manmade lake. A communal pond, perhaps, busy with ducks you weren't supposed to shoot and shiftless frogs. All cushioned by a pristine, cement walking path that would encircle the perimeter. Rebel could see it, and figured if this wasn't their intention it certainly should be.

A handful of sleeping bulldozers and dormant backhoes anchored points across the bowl; war machines resting from battle. This was the holding area for vast loads of soil, sand, and gravel. Property of the company tasked with constructing the development. For the imagination of a twelve-year-old boy: wonderland eternal.

However, Rebel knew the oasis would be short-lived. It would most likely be chipped away, bit by bit, as the war machines were called back to the battle lines day after day. Earthen pyramids had already begun to be overtaken by indigenous plants and grass, presenting an ideal moss-laden habitation. The boy was well aware that the largest of these pyramids was home to a Cherokee witch-queen named Nilahasi Tayyi. She and Rebel had come close to war more than once, deterred only by some obscure bit of political ideology they happen to agree upon.

All of this had been well-documented by the Rekishi Lords, sightless scriveners who emerged snake-like from the gravel mounds every crescent moon. They hovered, inches above the earth, gliding to the center of the basin and leaving behind leather strips with The Quarry's volatile history inscribed. The earth would swallow the bindings wholesale, securing them in a clay coffer like a mother hen, only to be unearthed by a new boy, in a new development, some hundred years from now.

Those dwellings, and the undulating, granular hills that constituted the White Lands—full of buried Sand Giants, hibernating and raised from birth by the Alzahrion people—all would succumb to civilization in a matter of months. And yet, for every off-shoot trail and curvature of soil, Rebel had conjured full, fleshed out backstories—this nation's history and that race's mythology, the political machinations of barbarous warlords and the distinct ethos of cultures.

He would enjoy it while it lasted, but not alone. From the second he laid eyes on this treasure, one thought had consumed him—showing Kip.

The boy found this happening at near constant pace since he'd met the new girl and he was astonished, if not annoyed, at the law of occupancy at work within his young mind. Whereas before, his musings ranged from recollections of his brother—ones he thought long lost—to how much bologna was left in the fridge. Now everything seemed to sift through an alternate template. Present reflections for the young man fluctuated as follows:

I wonder if she loves PB&Js much as I do.

I bet she'd hate The Tourist...of course she would. Would she like Lee or hate him right away?

I wonder how many boys she's kissed.

He realized he couldn't stop the trend if he tried.

The boy worked at cutting a trail from The Quarry's edge to the back of Kip's house for most of the day. Using Lee's old machete, he'd hacked briar and brushwood until blisters covered most of his palms, two having burst. In actuality, the distance from The Quarry to the row of Emerald Greens couldn't have been more than fifty yards, but the density of woods created a chasmic separation of worlds. His plan had been to start early enough so that just before dusk he could show his friend, retracing the fresh-cut path for the first time with the Indian Princess in tow. Presenting The Quarry with a revelation as pretty as Kip (especially to Nilahasi Tayyi, who was prone to new and shiny things) would surely earn him further favor within the kingdom.

As soon as he saw the Emeralds his heart quickened, and

in spite of the burning of his palms, he whacked at the brush with renewed vigor. Rebel slid between two of the large trees and slumped against the unfinished wood of the privacy fence, catching more than a few splinters in his back as he went. He winced and sucked air abruptly, surprised by the pain. He began the task of contorting his arm behind his body, fishing out shards of cedar. Rebel yanked his shirt off and wrung it through as sweat showered the ground, then he used it to dry himself. He rested, allowing his chin to find home at the bottom of his neck, and watched tributaries of perspiration descend his heaving stomach.

He was thirsty. Any moisture he'd started the day with was long spent on the work of the trail. Droplets had leapt from his eyebrows and nose, eager cliff-divers splattering the leaves and stalks of grass as he pushed ever forward. He considered bringing water from home but had refused, largely because Lee had so often mocked the very concept of preparation. With his brother, the journey was survival, and survival was the journey. Bringing supplies or preparing in advance was only for "pussies and queers."

"Anythang we need, God done give it to us in nature," Lee had preached.

"But nature don't always wanna give up what God give it," Rebel countered.

"Well, that's when ya find out what t'hell ya made of, ain't it?"

That was usually the end of the conversation. Because what rebuttal was there? For Lee also had the uncanny ability to turn practically any topic of discussion, much less debate, into a sweeping examination of manhood. Manhood that for him was defined by the amount of pain one could endure or self-reliance one might insist upon. This was a difficult recipe for the boy, who by nature was prone to hugs rather than punches. Lee had identified this early on in his little brother as an insufferable weakness. An infantile softness that might well lead to homosexuality or worse. For every passing cuddle Charlene might insist on from her sweet one, Lee made sure to offset with hard, blunt edges.

The crawl of ants near his hands reminded Rebel of the mission and he pushed himself upright. The boy had prepped entry days before, having pulled just hard enough at the bottom of two fence boards to free them from the base stud. He'd oiled the top nails sufficiently with a rusty can of WD-40 so that the boards swung apart like the curtains of a window. His goal was to make the trip as effortless as possible for his new friend.

Rebel slipped through the opening and jogged his way to the back of the pecan tree where he shinnied up the ladder. He laid down on the floorboards of the loft to catch his breath, feeling the thickness of the white paint, dense as rubber beneath his fingers and elbows. Rebel cranked his head to make sure the stash was there, and, sure enough, the corner still held the small pile of pecans Lee had snacked on a week before.

The boy fired a pecan side-arm through the opening and watched as the nut fell short, failing to bounce even once in the thick grass. He found one with more girth and threw harder this time, nearly clipping the top of the opening. The nut smacked onto the deck and rolled all the way to the back door, finding home on a rug Rebel thought too fancy to be outside.

Moments later the boy spied a brown ponytail cresting the bottom of window frames in succession. Kip flung the screen door open and scooped up the pecan for inspection. He watched her smile before looking up at the treehouse. She waved inconspicuously from her hip, scanning to make sure she wasn't being watched.

The Princess bounded from the deck, sneakers lost in the dense Bermuda. Watching her run, Rebel noticed for the first time the shape and tone of her legs, tanned and proportioned to perfection. Something stirred in him that hadn't before—an arousal that was decidedly sexual, scary, and exhilarating at once. Topping the last rung of the ladder, Kip grinned as she threw the pecan back at the boy. The nut fell dead against Rebel's damp tee.

"Hey," she said.

"Hey." Rebel's eye caught a glisten of moisture gathering at the base of the girl's neck and he looked away.

"What?"

"Nothin'," Rebel dodged.

"What is it? Why are you acting weird?"

"I ain't actin' no way," he said, throwing the closest pecan he could find toward the Emeralds behind them. And now the boy caught himself looking at her shorts, white and snug and unsullied, not yet loosened from a long day of play.

"So what is it?" the girl plied.

Feeling found out, Rebel squirmed, certain the dynamic between them had instantly changed although he hadn't wanted it to.

"What do you have to show me?" she asked.

"Oh!" Rebel said, relieved. "You gon love it. Come on." He scurried down the ladder and rushed to the fence opening, holding the boards wide. The pieces of wood swung without a sound and the boy felt proud. On the ground, Kip glanced back at the house one last time before darting under his arm. He tried registering her expression as she passed. She was exhilarated.

It was beginning to settle onto him that the girl loved adventure. As he slid past her to take the lead, this realization took shape. The way she ran across the street to meet the strange new boy who wrecked and spilled onto the ground. Secretly offering her bike, and later stealing away with him to secure beer for The

Tourist. Even now, as she swatted the branches that reached out to touch her face with no idea of where the boy was taking her, there was no hesitation.

Farther along the trail, Rebel looked back to ascertain her level of enjoyment and surveyed his workmanship. Had he made the path wide enough? In certain spots it should have been wider, he was convinced. None of that mattered now, because every over-the-shoulder glance reassured him that the commitment of the Indian Princess was resolute. Her delight was complete.

Up ahead, Rebel could see the tree he'd marked. A strip of red bandana tied to a branch reminding him to stop. "Okay," the boy said, unable to hide the excitement in his voice, "from here on I gotta blindfold ya."

"For real?"

"Come on…I told ya it was a surprise."

Rebel retrieved the remainder of the bandana from his back pocket, having kept it as clean as he could. He rolled it into a proper blindfold and prepared to wrap it around her head. The boy gently tucked the girl's hair behind her ears and his heart gained speed. This extraneous business was risky; she might see through it, recognizing it for the poorly masked effort to touch her that it was. In truth, Rebel had already envisioned how the blindfold process would go earlier that morning, having decided that if the day was going well and she was enjoying herself, he would be forward enough to curl her hair behind her perfect little ears.

The gesture felt akin to touching the most sensitive area of some exotic cougar. Enjoying his hands beside her face, he tried reading her expression. The slightest grin came at the corner of the girl's mouth, and she inhaled deeply, letting the breath leave her with measured satisfaction. Rebel imagined standing there much longer. She would remain still, and his hands would not leave her until the sun yawned for sleep and benevolent shadows had gathered around them.

He took her hand, warm and secure in his own, and continued on. The trail grew wider, reminding Rebel of how he had started his work that morning at full strength. As the day passed, the trail narrowed. But the child's workmanship was standing up, and as far as he could tell not so much as a dandelion whisker had grazed the ankle of his friend. Reaching the trailhead, Rebel moved Kip into position, just feet from a ledge that offered a sweeping view of the quarry.

"K...ready?"

"Yep."

Rebel sighed deeply and removed the blind, watching as Kip squinted. The girl let her eyes adjust and finally registered the scope of the small canyon. She drew in a quick breath.

"Be careful," Rebel said, motioning to her feet.

"Oh my gosh!" Kip bleated, grabbing hold of the boy's arm as she stepped back. "That's so steep!"

Rebel smiled as he supported the small behind her back. "It's aw'ight," Rebel said. "I gotcha." The boy admired the landscape as well, hopeful she would find it as fascinating as he did. "So... whatcha thank?" he asked.

Kip's eyes followed the thick row of pines along the ridge where they stood. Across the bowl on the other side, she established lush, unruly growth. There, select weedlings had stubbornly ballooned into small trees as kudzu clamored for every inch of open space, layering everything in a sea of virescent heart-shaped petals. That side of the quarry was veritable jungle, and Kip half expected to see a troop of gorillas amble underneath a canopy of elephant ears for shade.

"Oh my gosh…" she marveled, slowly releasing his arm. The Princess moved to take in the fullness of the bowl's belly, shocked by its length and depth. "I can't…I can't believe this is so close to my house," she said finally, and looked at her friend. Rebel studied her eyes, round and full and grateful.

"Ya like it?" he asked.

"Rebel, this is incredible!" she said. "How'd you find it?"

"Just ridin' around," the boy said as he moved toward the pine row. "Come on. I made us a way to git down over here."

Kip followed, gazing as she went, mindful of the steep edge. Rebel descended the steps he'd roughed in days before. This had been the first project he set himself to—creating steps from the quarry depths up to the pine row. He took into consideration the shortest distance from Kip's house to the ridge line and designated the trailhead accordingly. He'd even chiseled around various roots from the side of the raw earth to serve as handrails for the most dangerous sections of the descent.

Reaching the quarry floor, he took her hand, and they ran to the epicenter. The boy turned The Princess around to face the trailhead high above them, elongating her sense of awe from the opposite vantage point. Kip laughed with pleasure, and Rebel noticed that her hand remained in his.

"This is like a mini–Grand Canyon," she said.

"Yeah. It's fer sure the biggest quarry I ever seen."

The boy made his way to the jungle side, toward a sturdy sapling the war machines had failed to touch. The small tree stood just feet from the dense overgrowth beyond, pleasantly isolated. Having gleaned the lion's share of rain and sun, it reached higher than those farther out, with budding, flexible branches fanning out like a tropical parasol. It was as if the dozer operator had been struck by some unexpected bout of nostalgic appreciation, recognizing the youngling's undeniable virility.

Days before, Rebel had also found another tree, this one felled and dismembered. With no small effort the boy had rolled one of the logs into place beneath the sapling to form a bench. This had been the second project after the earthen staircase. He waved Kip over. His final presentation.

Rebel sat near the most comfortable spot on the log. The boy had noticed a natural dip in the log when dragging it into place and had gone to work shaving away what knobs and protrusions he could find. He'd envisioned The Princess sitting in the spot even as he worked on it. And now, here she was, in the flesh, about to settle into this small throne.

"Here ya go," Rebel offered, patting the fashioned seat. The girl looked down to see a carving embedded into the meatiest part of the wood. It read: R+K.

Kip smiled, blushing. She slid into the dip, the curve of the wood meeting her bottom. "Wow. You made this?"

"Yeah," the boy said.

She relaxed into her chair, admiring its fit.

"This is perfect," Kip beamed, and for the first time she noticed just how intently Rebel was focused on her enjoyment. "Like it was made just for me."

"It was!" Rebel said, unable to hold himself.

"Thank you. The Grand Canyon makes you feel small like this place does," Kip said, glancing across the quarry's stomach.

The boy perked. "You actually been there?"

"Yeah," she smiled. "My parents took us there a couple years ago. That's the last big vacation we took, and it was amazing. You feel super small and immediately start thinking about how in the world something like that got there. At least I did."

He watched her remember, contemplating if he should share

The Quarry's origin story. "What's yer theory?" the boy asked.

Kip shifted forward on her throne. "Well, they say it was carved out from millions of years of ice when glaciers plowed through. But I like to think aliens."

"What?!" Rebel laughed, and the girl did too.

"For real!" Kip shot back, pushing him sideways on the log. "Why not? If they expect us to believe the entire universe fell perfectly into place when a bunch of atoms crashed together then why can't I believe the Grand Canyon happened when some aliens crash-landed?"

"Crash-landin' aliens, huh?"

"Yeah," Kip said confidently. "It's sure a lot more fun to think about that than ice taking a gazillion years for ice to nudge its way through some dirt."

"That's fer sure," the boy said, convinced he could never love someone more in a single moment than he did right then. Rebel felt his chest race and an odd pressure pushed toward his throat. A lightheaded euphoria would have had him sway right off the back of the log if his hands were not anchoring him to it.

Kip was still smiling as she looked straight ahead, imagining the shape and girth of a space vessel big enough to carve a trench so wide as the Grand Canyon. Rebel vacillated in a punch-drunk fog, until instinct got the best of him. He leaned toward the girl until his lips found home, gently, at the corner of her mouth. He easily could have landed on the swell of her cheek, had Kip not turned her head at the last second.

Just as Rebel decided to release the pressure of his face against hers, he could feel her adjust, so that their lips might press flush together. He remembered Lee's orders to close his eyes and did so, and he could feel The Princess lift her head and extend her neck—want commensurate with his. Rebel paused on the softness of her lips, as sublime as he'd imagined, and wondered if she would be the first to pull away. The thought had no sooner occurred to him when they both leaned back, searching the eyes of the other.

Rebel faltered in holding his share of the stare, letting his gaze drop to the log beneath them. When he did look up, Kip's face was toward the fading sun, suspended by an insuperable grin. Addressing what just happened would be madness, the boy figured, and instead he blurted out what moments ago he wouldn't have dared.

"I gotta tell ya what this place really is."

The girl faced him, curious, as Rebel watched the last of her flustered smile hang on. He stood, surveying the breadth of the bowl. Emboldened by Kip's Grand Canyon confession, the boy unveiled The Quarry's true history: when an ancient Sand Giant, the first of his kind, decided to make a bed for himself. And so, having dug the length of his enormous body, and deep enough so the wind might pass over him like a blanket, he lay down in hibernation. The chunks of earth he'd tossed aside from the dig had become the hills of Chilton County over the years, spread apart by miles. However, the sound of such violent excavation had drawn attention, and it wasn't long before creatures and tribes of every kind sent scouts for discovery. What they found was a Sand Giant who did not consist of sand at all. In fact, this colossal being turned out to be more closely related to humankind than troll or ogre. And keenly shy. As more eyes fell upon his bedchamber, the Great Giant felt violated. In a fit of rage, he cursed the spies with an eternity of strife, so that if The Quarry ever did reach some tenuous balance of peace, it was doomed to be short-lived.

But what the ancient man had inadvertently done was create an enviable valley rich for settlement. Soon came the Rekishi Lords, brought in by various chieftains to exorcise the Great

Giant's curse. They failed in fantastic fashion, and instead took to becoming The Quarry's resident historians. The arrival of Nilahasi Tayyi and her Cherokee brethren, however, had changed the entire political landscape. Her lust for power was executed in savage, mercurial ways to the detriment of the greater order.

The Princess listened all the while, captivated. The boy moved and talked, explaining the strategic moves of kings and departures of fed-up peoples, the affairs of princes and escapes of maidens. All of this flowed from the child as an unfettered stream.

He finished as Pony Time descended upon the long crater and made himself sit down beside her. He was nervous. Expectant. Kip's countenance had vacillated between shock and utter delight as she listened to the boy's yarns. Rebel's suspicion was that she was thoroughly invested, as if she herself was the newest member of a community she'd only just come to know. The girl took a deep breath, allowing all of the color and heat and love and loss she just experienced to settle onto her. Rebel watched her eyes drift to the farthest reach of the small canyon.

"Whatever happened to the Sand Giant who wasn't actually a sand giant?"

"Whelp," Rebel sighed, standing again, "they say he struck out northeast from here. 'Bout fifty miles. And settled near Childersburg...but this time he burrowed way down deep. Made sure to git away from ever'body. So he made hisself a cave. 'Ey call it DeSoto Caverns now. I been there. Our class did a field trip there once."

"Wow," Kip said sincerely. "They should have left the poor guy alone."

Rebel picked up a rock and smiled, skipping the stone across the flattest part of earth he could find. "Yeah," the boy said as the rock vanished into a mound of sand. "He was the best of us."

CHAPTER 11

The Walrus & the Vampire

This early in the morning, *Grayson's* appeared more ramshackle garage than convenient store. Rebel made sure to get there before sunrise, knowing the old man preferred to open before the rooster crowed. The boy sat near the door on a concrete car block, cracked and crumbling at both ends. He tried tracing the outline of The Quarry with his finger in the gravel, pausing to listen to the sounds of morning. Crickets hummed in sync in the woods behind the shop, and there was the snap of pine from the leap of a squirrel. The boy had always felt the morning was sacred. In so much as the witching hour welcomed the demonic, he knew this duration of lifting shadow was set apart for the movement of angels.

Just as light began cresting the tar beyond the gas pumps, Rebel could hear the old man's approach. His '65 pickup gurgled pleasantly enough, despite the fade of its turquoise. The boy loved the truck since the first time he'd visited *Grayson's* years ago with

Isaac. He would watch his grandfather sidle up to the farthest red-speckled stool similar to Eastwood in *High Planes Drifter*. His upper body fusing with the countertop. Grayson and Isaac had grown up together as childhood friends since grade school. But Rebel would not discover this until later, when he listened to Grayson share words at his grandfather's funeral.

The boy accounted for the warm, effortless conversation they shared as the way all old men must talk to one another. Short and certain. The two men used their words like framing studs, precise and worthy of bearing weight. Rebel figured this kind of talk would come naturally to him as well when he got old. The boy remembered Isaac seemed to genuinely enjoy Grayson's anecdotes, trying and failing to match his friend's storytelling prowess.

Now, as Grayson circled behind the store in order to park facing the road, Rebel reaffirmed his affection for the pick-up. The older it got the better it looked.

"Now, I know you ain't a early-bird," the old man grunted through the window as he parked the truck. Grayson grabbed his sack-lunch from the seat of the cab.

The child stood, dusting dirt from his bottom. "Naw'sir. I don' like gittin' up early too much," Rebel said.

"Isaac used to say you'd ruther sleep 'til noon than drop a buck by dawn." The old man smiled as he walked.

"That's about right," the boy grinned.

"Well?"

"I was gon ask ya fer a job."

The old man paused, feigning surprise. "A job, huh?"

"Yessir. I's gon help Mama out so she ain't gotta be at *Larry's* all time."

"I see," Grayson wrestled keys into the storefront. "Well, I ain't really busy much these days. But I might have some odds'n ends you can help me with."

"Yessir," Rebel said, "I'll take whatever ya got." Inside, the old man settled in while the boy surveyed the store anew, not as a customer seeking treasure, but as an employee, wondering what tasks his grandfather's friend might ask of him.

"Okee-dokee," Grayson exhaled. "Let's see. First off let's talk wage. Whatchu got in mind?"

"Oh," the boy faltered, "I didn't even thank about that. I mean...I guess whatever the work's worth to ya."

Grayson grinned, pushing thin wire spectacles further up his enormous nose. "Now that... is exactly sump'm yer grandaddy would say." He arranged his newspaper and slid onto his stool behind the counter. "Aw'ight, Johnny Reb. Here's what...first I want ya to cut back all that's growed up around the shed and dumpster out back. Let's gitcha goin' on 'at 'fore it gits too hot. 'At should take ya all way to lunch."

"Yessir," Rebel replied dutifully, moving toward the door.

"Ever'thang you need to cut with'll be in the shed."

The boy shoved his head back inside to say, "I 'preciate it, Mr. Grayson."

The old man waved him off. "Just 'Grayson' from here on. "And hey—grab ya a Gatorade from the 'frigerator but don't bust the damn thang against the glass like last time."

"Yessir," said the boy.

Within minutes Rebel was excising strains of stubborn kudzu from behind the shed. In addition to some deficient hedge cutters and a primeval hoe, the boy had unearthed a rotted pair of work gloves from inside the small wooden building. He made short work of a thick run of briar strangling the perimeter of the property. Pulling the length of the rogue weed was more than the old man had asked of him, but Rebel was intent on making a good impression. This work reminded him of cutting the trail from The Quarry to Kip's house earlier that week. The thought of actually getting paid now for his labor was invigorating.

By 10 a.m. the boy had worked up a generous lather, having paused intermittently only to admire his efforts and hydrate. He suspected he would have the whole of the property cut back and cleared within the hour and felt thoroughly satisfied with himself. Along the way, Rebel had gathered anything he considered trash and placed it in the dumpster, while anything he thought the old man might want to keep, he organized within the shed. Out of sight and tidy as cloistered dominoes. Discarded car parts, crumpled mechanic rags, empty gas cans; all found their place within the building.

The shed was in worse shape than it appeared, and the boy spent the last of his time repairing what he could: re-nailing fallen boards, clearing clutter, and removing excess tools from a worktable that it might be usable again. This table was built in as part of the back wall, notched and battered from years of hammering and tossed tools. At its center was a cast of rich scarlet from a bygone staining job.

The boy was affixing tools to the long nails he'd driven as hangers when he heard the creak of the backdoor. He rushed from the shed, eager to see the old man's expression.

"Good Lord," Grayson whispered to himself, his mouth agape. Rebel watched the old man crane his neck in disbelief, starting at the far end of the lot where the woods began, past the dumpster, finally arriving at the shed itself. Rebel's goal had been to make a formal demarcation of Grayson's property from the woods beyond. What before looked like an unbroken rash of wilderness now appeared to be a proper backyard.

"You gotta be kiddin'," the man coughed in disbelief.

"Lotta that brush come out easier'n I 'spected," the boy said.

"Well, easy or hard, I certainly didn't expect all this, son." Grayson walked to the center of the lot and turned a slow circle. "Top notch work, Rebel James," the old man smiled. "Where'd ever'thang go?"

"I put a lot of stuff in the shed for ya."

Grayson moved past the boy to peer into the little building and let out a howl. "No way I'm seein' this!" Grayson snorted.

The old man laughed until he lost wind, coughing his way to a raspy stop. Rebel laughed with him, beaming with pride at a job well done.

"This old heap ain't look this good since it was first built," the old man said slapping the boy on the shoulder.

"Well, it's usable again."

"That it is, my boy. That it is." Grayson shuffled to the craggy worktable and allowed a puffy, sun-spotted hand to run the length of it. "Whelp," the old man said, turning to the boy, "you did good, son. Damn good work. Come on." Grayson patted Rebel on the shoulder as he passed.

Inside the store, sweat chilled a filmy ice layer on the child's skin. By the time he climbed atop his grandfather's favorite stool at the end of the counter he was cold. Grayson slid a bottle of Yoo-hoo and a bag of sour cream-n-onion chips in front of the boy and said, "'Ere ya go."

"I'll pay ya back. Or you can take it outta my pay," Rebel said, shaking the drink to purity.

"Bullshit!" the old man shouted. "You asked me to pay ya what the job's worth. Well, I ain't got enough for whatcha done out there but I'll do my best."

Rebel tilted the bottle up, allowing the cold chocolate to slide down his throat in torrents. The rush of sugar livened his posture and he stopped only to breathe, nearly finishing the drink in one go. "I sure 'preciate it," the boy said.

"So," Grayson murmured through admiration, "ya tryin' to git yer momma outta that bar so she can be home, huh?"

Rebel nudged the empty bottle aside, making way for the chips. "Not just to be home wi'me so much as she don't feel like she has to make all the money by herself."

"Y'all up against it?" the old man plumbed.

"Naw'sir. I mean, no more'n usual. I just won't to git it so she ain't gotta depend on nobody else." The boy pulled the chip bag apart and dug in with a dirty paw.

Grayson shuffled his newspaper. "I see," he said, measuring the child's face.

"He don't see shit," said a voice from the candy aisle.

"'Ol' fucker's 'bout half blind."

Rebel turned to see his brother molesting a bag of barbecue chips. The boy spun to see if Grayson had detected this disturbance as well. He had not.

"Why you tellin' this asshole our business any-gotdamn-way?" Lee swung the bag of chips like a fly swatter at his brother's head and Rebel dodged. "I tell ya what ya can tell that ol' fart... tell 'em this store's gone to shit since he stopped carryin' Playboy."

Rebel smirked and returned to his snack.

"Go on! Tell 'em!" Lee shoved his little brother, subsequently dislodging a family of flies previously at rest on the edge of his noose. The dead boy had certainly looked better.

The pencil-thin lines constituting lips were decidedly purple now. His skin seemed to curl and retreat at the edges of the ears, fingernails, and eyelids. Rebel could see his brother losing color, as if his epidermis had acquiesced to defeat, disavowing hope for rejuvenation. Moreover, the smell of decay did not mix well with sour cream-n-onion, and Rebel pushed his chips to the side.

"Hey!" Lee clapped, demanding Grayson's attention. "Hey, ol' man," snapping his fingers, "look here." Lee leaned in, gesturing as if he were talking to a child hard of hearing. "Reason nobody comes to this shithole anymore is 'cause you done away with all the titties." Lee relaxed in a huff, dismissing the old man as a lost cause.

"My brother used t'come in here a lot," Rebel said. Grayson shifted on his chair, allowing his wrinkled brow to furrow deeper still.

"That he did. Listen, I heard about what happen. I'm real, real sorry for y'all, Rebel."

The boy offered a small smile. "I 'preciate that."

"Terrible thang," the old man ruminated. "Terrible."

Rebel looked to his brother, who was sucking the remnants of barbecue dust from corroded fingertips.

"Nosy ass fucker. Don't tell him shit," Lee snapped.

"There's this man my mama's taken up with," the boy said. Lee shoved himself from the counter in a snit and retreated to the beverage aisle, cursing his brother along the way. Rebel continued, "He owns a car dealership or sump'm and a'course Mama thanks his shit don't stink."

"Most people's don't, first off," Grayson said.

"Yeah. Well, I see 'em for what he is. But Mama don't." The boy folded the chip bag closed and re-capped the empty bottle of chocolate. "She never does."

"Where's all the fuckin' beer?!" Lee screamed from the back. "Gyat dammit! 'Ere used to be beer stacked floor to ceilin' back here! Now they's just a buncha damn Gatorades and fruity-ass shit."

Rebel craned his neck in Lee's direction, then addressed the old man. "Why'd you stop carryin' beer and stuff?"

"You plannin' to git sauced on the job?" Grayson grinned.

"Naw'sir! Naw. I just 'member when I come in wi'grandeddy you used to carry some."

"Yeah," Grayson sighed, his tired eyes canvassing the store like a museum of uncommon relics. "I used to sell a lotta stuff that I don't no more. I figure what's got me in trouble don't need to be a stumblin' block for nobody else."

"'At makes sense," the boy admitted.

"So you thankin' if you can make enough money here then ya mama won't need to keep this new fella around?"

"Yessir. I mean... my best friend says she thanks it ain't just about money fer Mama. She thanks she wonts comp'ny and somebody her own age to talk to."

"Well, that's some good wisdom. You do good to keep that friend around," Grayson smiled.

"Yessir. She's real smart. But she don't know 'em like I do."

"No. She don't. She sure as hell fuckin' don't," Lee hissed, climbing back onto a stool at the counter. He wiped sweat from a Dr. Pepper. "She don't know he's a fuckin' phony. Or that 'eez been beatin' yer ass on the side."

"Just once," Rebel corrected.

"What's that?" Grayson asked.

The boy glanced between Lee and his boss, wondering for a moment if the two could suddenly hear one another. "Just once I wish she'd let it just be us... and be aw'ight with that," Rebel said studying the countertop.

"Well, that's understandable," the old man mumbled as he fished for something below the counter. "Here." Grayson reappeared with the sack lunch he'd pulled from the cab of his truck. He took a puny steak knife from a junk drawer and unfolded a square of foil from the brown bag—a thick layer of ham and cheese layered between two pieces of white bread. The old man went about dissecting the sandwich diagonally with the small knife and pushed the foil in front of the boy. "Eat up."

"'At's yer lunch, Mr. Grayson, I cain't…"

"I ain't gon hear it, now. I got more in this bag than just that. I'm fine. But'chu cain't work a full day on chips and chocolate. So go on." Rebel started to pick up the sandwich but paused, torn between the kindness of the gesture and manners. "Go on now!" Grayson commanded, and the boy obeyed.

Lee finished a gulp of soda, and streams of brown overflowed to run the corners of his mouth. Some fell on the hangman's noose. Intermingling with the sepia of the rope, a rich black collar now clung to the dead boy's neck, and Rebel couldn't envision his brother looking any more like an honest-to-god vampire. He was proud.

"Well, since you and the ol' man are fuck buddies now ya might as well tell 'em how we gon do it," The Vampire growled.

Rebel choked on a mouthful of ham, coughing his way through a laugh. Lee moved around the counter to stand beside Grayson. "So, we got several ideas, and a'course mine are better… but whatever." The dead boy gesticulated as if blocking out a scene.

"Now…next time that piece a'shit crawls in the bed with our mama, we gon already be under there."

Lee paused to acknowledge his disappointment in his little brother. "Not just stand there like a fuckin' scarecrow 'til the man wakes up," he said rolling his eyes. The Vampire resumed the roleplay and picked up the knife Grayson used to cut the sandwich. "Like I said, Reb's gon be under the bed like Jason's mama in *Friday the 13th*. Long-Dick-Silver's gon be layin' there, havin' finished his business...takin' his after-fuck smoke just like Kevin Bacon..."

Lee slid behind the old man, shaking out his hands as a pianist would readying to manifest Liszt. Rebel's expression changed and he straightened, tracking his brother's intentions. The boy's brow hardened and he shook his head, grunting a garbled, *"No,"* through a mouthful of sandwich. The Vampire grinned, lowering the knife to the old man's throat.

"What?" Lee mocked. "I ain't gon hurt this ol' bastard!" Lee's lip curled as he examined the old man. "I couldn't git this flimsy-ass shit through 'em anyway," the dead boy snarled, wagging the plastic knife in Rebel's direction. "Neck's like a gotdamn turtle shell. Buncha fuckin' wrinkled cowhide back here."

Rebel noticed something overcome his brother then. A fiery, caustic resentment he'd not seen since the last time Charleen mentioned the name of their father. Lee slid from behind the old man and glared at the boy. An encroaching, brutish seethe that unnerved the child.

Lee moved to Rebel's side of the counter, dragging the knife through the uneaten half of Grayson's donated sandwich. He leaned close to his brother's ear. Breath the boy expected to be warm with rage was polar instead—a brassy current against the hairs of his ear canal. The child shivered as he shrunk away from the dead boy.

"You thank," Lee whispered, "this old fat fuckin' walrus is gon help us?" A fly leapt from Lee's eyebrow and circled those words, each landing with grim, sticky certitude.

This sudden cower was not lost on The Walrus, and the old man observed the boy anew. Swishing what little coffee remained in his mug into a small tornado, Grayson peered down, considering if the answer to whether he should prod on or stay silent lie within the dregs. Lee began walking the aisles of the store.

"You know, we never really got to talk about what happen last time you was here..."

"Yessir," Rebel responded, "I'm really sorry about that. That bottle slipped right outta my hand. I meant to come back and clean up ever'thang but I forgot. I 'pologize. Sorry I left a mess for you to have to clean up."

"Well," Grayson muttered, downing the last of the coffee, "I wasn't ever any good at science, but gravity says if that bottle slipped then it should'a fell straight to the ground. Meanin' the mess should'a been all over the floor." The old man motioned toward the scene of the crime. "As it was, Yoo-hoo was all over that door like it come out of a shotgun."

"Yessir," the boy squirmed, "I'm really, really..."

"Stop 'pologizin', son. Shit. I ain't mad. But I *would* like to know why you threw that bottle. 'Cause it weren't dropped."

Rebel started to speak.

"And listen," The Walrus pulled himself a little straighter on his stool, "before you get dodgy, you need to know I can smell horseshit a mile away."

The boy's shoulders deflated. With the zombie vampire behind and the leather walrus before, the child was properly caged.

"I thought I seen sump'm in the door. I mean...reflected on the glass or sump'm 'nother." Rebel searched the old man's face. "It just scared me's all. I'm real..."

Grayson raised his hand, forcing the boy to leave that last sorry unsaid. The old man breathed deeply, and a sorrowfulness like regret became his face. Rebel could only recall seeing this kind of fixed gaze once before, when Isaac had returned from looking for a missing child.

A six-year-old black girl had gone missing in West End, and

what was initially reported as a kidnapping among family turned out to be homicide. The little girl's body was found piecemeal, strewn about an abandoned landfill by the killer or by animal or both. At first, the crime had united the county in a way no one anticipated. The most forward-thinking Baptist church in Clanton called an all-hands-on-deck meeting where the pastor rallied his congregation into a twenty-four-hour prayer vigil for little Markeesha Tremble. The women would stay at the church and pray while the men loaded up in more than a dozen pickups and caravanned to West End, aiding in the search.

Although not members of this particular church, Isaac had famously said that his family would "join the search or be damned," and so they did. Ray Mims, Lee and Rebel's father, had recently returned from work out of town and insisted only he and Isaac go when the boys begged to join. Loaded in Ray's truck with hunting spotlights and rifles on the rack, Isaac and his son-in-law departed just after dusk.

When Ray's truck pulled back into the drive the next morning just before 5 a.m., only Isaac walked through the door. The old man was visibly shaken and seemed to have aged years within those hours. Having only ever seen their grandfather as an unremitting oak of strength, the boys were terrified. Isaac refused details, saying only that they'd found the girl and she was, in fact, dead. Ray was apparently so upset by the discovery he'd insisted on walking home to clear his head. Isaac asserted wearily that Ray should be home within the hour. Lee and Rebel would never see their father again.

As the boy studied the old man now, the cavernous lines of Grayson's face looked similar to those of his grandfather that early morning. Overwrought and solemn. Grayson allowed the bulk of his upper body to lurch forward as he came to rest on two meaty forearms.

"You know, when I come back from overseas, I'd see thangs from time to time that weren't there," the old man said. "Lotta boys I served with did."

"Like what?" Rebel asked.

"Aww...thangs a person don't like to talk about. Thangs that ain't fit for daylight."

Rebel looked to see Lee tipping chips and candy from the top of shelves, item after item dropping to the floor as he walked. The boy turned back to the old man, having acquired an odd spark of resolve. "I see my brother," Rebel admitted. He searched Grayson's face. For what, he didn't know. Empathy? Disgust? Disbelief? "I mean, that's what I saw—who I saw... in the glass back 'ere."

"I see," The Walrus said quietly. "That the only time you seen 'em?"

"I mean," the boy relaxed, "he comes and goes really. Just like he did when he was alive. You know how Lee is."

"Oh yeah. I was givin' that rascal dranks and candy long before you come along." Grayson grinned to himself. "He was partial to Dr. Pepper and BBQ chips...always wanted sump'm with some bite. Sump'm spicy. Which was the damnedest thang 'cause the boy was fair as a haint."

The old man looked at the aisle where he stocked his more peppery fare and smiled at The Vampire he was staring at but could not see. "Always tryin' to prove he was tough with sump'm spicy. But the whole time he's sweatin' like a whore in church. Me and Isaac would laugh 'til we cried," Grayson chortled.

And the boy realized, watching the old man laugh himself into another coughing fit, that Lee had experienced an entire relationship with The Walrus before Rebel even knew Grayson existed. A relationship the boy knew nothing about. His brother had always talked poorly of the old man, but with no more or less reproach than any other authority figure Lee despised. But now it dawned on him that he was merely second in line. This intimate, wink-if-you-know friendship the boy shared with Grayson was anything but unique. Lee had been here before—known the old man before—and Rebel found himself pushing his body from the counter.

He didn't realize he was in motion until he felt gridded metal at his back. Rebel turned and saw he was pressed against a rack of Moon Pies. He examined The Walrus anew with contempt, and could swear this fleshy, bulbous mass before him smelled of brine and guano. The child moved to the aisle closest to the glass door. Directly across from him, just three aisles over, was The Vampire. Lee had settled upon the jerky section, and currently had the biggest piece of sausage he could find in his hand, allowing it to bob and lift at his zipper like an enormous flaccid penis.

Again The Walrus, and the boy could feel the back of his jaw grow tight as heat gathered at the base of his neck. The eyes within the mass seemed perplexed, observing the child's movements with shameful sympathy. Rebel could not break his gaze with the beast and reached out to touch whatever his hand might find— the rubbery slick of magazines. He pulled at them and they fell, splashing to the ground in folds.

The Vampire and his beef jerky cock grew still, taken aback by this action. The boy continued to claw, pawing at the magazines until the entire top rack crashed to the ground. The dead boy dropped his plaything and smirked, lifting onto his toes to get a better view of this magical thing that was happening. Lee lazily grazed his own top shelf, clearing a row of pretzels with one swipe.

The old man rose and cut his eyes hard at the boy, then The Vampire. Grayson placed his hands firmly on the counter and arched his torso; a silver back establishing dominion. Rebel looked at Lee, and the two shared a grin. The kind of leer only blood can share: consciousnesses intertwined by some slapdash marriage of biology and fate.

And so they commenced—throwing, ripping, and tearing apart everything in sight. Soda cans exploded across the room, ricocheting off walls and windows. Aisle after aisle, the brothers thrashed about in a hysterical, senseless mania. Unbound circle jerks swinging and launching items violently, pushing entire racks so they toppled onto one another. Within moments, the store's interior had become a canvas for blind anarchy.

And then they stopped—coated, The Brothers Mims, in sugar and pop and chocolate and salt. Fingers raw and bloodied and trembling from the mauling and punching of immovable things. A ringing now in the boy's ears, like the whisper of sea lost in a shell. And that shell lost in an eternity of sand. All now lost to the world. Rebel could hear the swell, in the same way his chest heaved within the milky saccharine shirt that clung to him now.

"Sir?" said the boy.

The old man leaned from counter, his forehead cresting and folding with consternation. "I said next time you see ya brother let me know."

Rebel looked down to find himself unmoored. He sat plainly on the stool as he had before. The second half of the donated sandwich lay before him as well. Untouched. The child swung to see the havoc he and The Vampire had wrought, but the aisles and rows remained orderly and right as a regiment. The boy stood, stepping onto the bar's foot-ledge to raise himself higher. He peered out, searching for signs of toppled racks and exploded soda. Crushed magazines. Traces of madness. Mostly, he looked for The Vampire.

Nothing.

Rebel slouched onto the stool and looked at the old man. Grayson appeared less walrus than ever. The boy could surmise, beyond the weight of folds and the punishment of time, a rich softness beneath eyes now clouded by the yellow haze of glaucoma.

"If Lee ain't much for talkin', you can always come to me, aw'ight?" Grayson said.

"Yessir."

CHAPTER 12

Innocentia

Rebel felt confident the two weeks that followed were the best of his life. He would wake early, galvanizing himself with chocolate Pop-Tarts and whatever other sugary provisions he might scrounge from the trailer's kitchen. Charleen would remain fast asleep until she wasn't, then spent the rest of her time preparing for another endless shift. He saw Tab only at night when she would make sure the boy had something in his stomach before her aunt clocked out.

The Tourist sightings were practically nonexistent, causing Rebel to wonder if Dennis had been reckless enough to confess details of their most recent conflict to Charleen. On the other hand, the boy figured the man smart enough to do just that—get ahead of Rebel's own reveal, making sure to weave in enough superfluous explanation to soften the harshness of the encounter. If Dennis had the forethought to be this proactive, the boy suspected this would translate to time and distance between the lovers. Dust would need to settle on Charleen's anger.

What he was certain of was the boundless freedom he was enjoying with Kip each day, invariably spent together at The Quarry. The two convened promptly at 10 a.m., their rendezvous point the swing-and-hinge opening of the backyard fence. The boy provided drinks in the way of employee-discount Yoo-hoos, while Kip supplied lunch: pigs-in-a-blanket with mustard one day, ham and cheese sandwiches the next. Once Laura sent with her daughter the leftovers from her weekly book club meeting: chicken salad on croissant. On this day, Rebel insisted they pretend his Aunt Lou had joined them at the jungle side of The Quarry on the log bench, beneath the sapling the war machines had missed.

"She gotta join us when the food's this fancy," the boy had said, and proceeded to explain the oddities of his mother's aunt, the opulent old woman from Mountain Brook by way of Homewood. The Princess played along sweetly without missing a beat, even suggesting they leave her throne seat empty for their guest. And so, the two sat, opposite that empty hand carved space, talking over and across Aunt Lou, laughing and apologizing intermittently for the inconsideration.

Kip had convinced her mother the leftovers were going to a good cause: her daughter's auspicious, budding relationship with a nice new girl down the street. The nice new girl did not exist, of course. But The Princess knew Laura would vehemently disapprove of days spent alone with the likes of "that Mims boy." Rebel, aware of the ruse, was not offended in the least. He warmed at the idea of Kip conjuring phantoms for the sake of time with him.

Moments with The Princess, the boy resolved, sanctioned or otherwise, were sacrosanct.

CHAPTER 13

Pickle Jar Parley

The boy woke to the sweet smell of honey-cured bacon. It was Saturday, and Rebel's wristwatch read 9:47a.m. He and Kip had agreed to take the day off from The Quarry. Laura's suspicions were beginning to peak regarding the nice new girl she'd yet to meet who never came over. Kip recommended they each do a family day to assuage parental demands. Rebel had agreed, with no expectation of what the day might hold for himself.

The Princess explained that every so often, her mother would urgently, if not forcefully, demand their family spend time together doing something traditionally wholesome. "Worthy of a *Better Homes & Gardens* spread," Kip had said. For Laura, this meant everyone dressing far more formally than the occasion required to participate in an activity that was boring as far as The Princess was concerned. An ornate brunch on the back porch resulting in enough uneaten food to embarrass the Pope. Or a visit to the public library where each person checked out a book, then to a park where they would all read. Quiet as souls, for hours on end.

But now, as the aroma of grease and sugar called to him, a singular thought occurred to the boy, perhaps for the first time ever: he was glad he was not rich. The lives of the wealthy were obviously more comfortable. There were more toys, bigger houses, nicer things. Ample choices. But as he lay there, motionless in his bed and stretching long against the timeworn sheets, the child felt utterly content.

The trailer only smelled this way, only echoed the sounds the boy was hearing, when his mother was up and cooking a robust breakfast. Saturdays like these were glorious in the Mims home. They meant Charleen was off work (at least during the day) and in particularly good spirits.

Charleen poured another blob of pancake batter onto the griddle, peppering in chocolate chips. The boy loved his mother's cooking, a skill which Larry had nearly sequestered her for until he realized how good she was on the floor. Rebel slid next to his mother, cocooning himself around her. Charleen smiled, gripping him warmly as she flipped another cake.

"Well, hey there," Charleen said through a kiss. She ran fingers through the cowlick that served as the gateway to the boy's caramel hair. "How'd ya sleep?" she asked, watching him glance toward her bedroom. "He ain't here, Rebel James. I told ya that was a one-time thang."

The boy resumed work on his latest drawing at the kitchen bar, manufacturing shadow for a muscled figure at the center of the page. A gentle drag of the thumb across a line of charcoal and it was done. "Where's he been at? I ain't seen 'em much," the boy spoke into the page.

"He's been off at some trade shows...one of 'em all the way out in Las Vegas," Charleen cooed. "And you ain't gon believe what he told me."

"What?" Rebel asked, invoking as little interest as possible.

"He said one of his goals while he's gone was to find a certain somebody a truck. And have it ready for them by a certain birthday."

The boy recognized the lilt. An inflated pitch she took when she was consummately euphoric. Charleen turned from the griddle, searching his face. Rebel cracked and let slip a grin which he thoroughly regretted.

"Ahh!" Charleen laughed, rushing over to gouge at the boy's ribs.

"Stop!" Rebel yelled through a broken smirk, trying to stifle any shred of joy escaping him now. "Quit, Mama!" he giggled. "You gon let the pancakes burn!"

"Uh-huh," Charleen said. "I thought that'd gitcha attention."

Rebel adjusted back onto his seat, straightening the sketch pad and realigning pencils from the tussle. He studied the figure once again, long and sinewy. The protagonist stood in the bosom of what appeared to be a vast caldron made of stone, lionhearted against a foe who, as of yet, existed only within the cusp of the boy's imagination. Continuing at his work, Rebel realized, as he rendered foliage from crags within rocks, that he'd subconsciously recreated The Quarry.

This version appeared more brutal than the real one. Harsh and unfeeling. He second-guessed himself for a moment, but after sketching several saplings into the background for scale, it was obvious. Stone had replaced the dirt of the bowl's belly and the pines on the cliff edge had become rows of Romanesque columns.

The hero held a barbarian's sword at his side, blood-soaked

and blunted against a rippled, vascular thigh. Rebel had decided him battle-weary, drawn so that the warrior's long hair covered much of his expression. But now, brushing precisely with the angled edge of his eraser, the boy cleared space for a visage.

He put efforts toward a mouth. First there were pursed lips that held within them a primal scream, and the history of loves and battles lost. Then came a set of clenched teeth braced for an impending charge.

Nothing suitable.

And so, bands of serried brindle grew again in the space between the champion's nose and chin.

"You know, I don't need a truck no time soon," Rebel said. He acquiesced that the eyes of the warrior would have to be enough to tell his story for now.

"A'course you don't, baby. But that ain't the point. The point is Dennis is thoughtful enough to thank aboutcha." And here, the boy could tell, where the first statement had an empathetic softness baked within, the second did not. Charleen scooped the last cake from the griddle and lumped it onto the existing stack with more aggression than Rebel would have liked.

"Not ever'body's the boogeyman, Rebel."

"I didn't say he was."

"You didn't have to," she said, shoving the plate of cakes farther down the counter.

"Ya ain't gotta get mad, Mama," Rebel soothed, watching the woman's shoulders deflate.

"I ain't mad. I'm..." Charleen searched for words while looking for a dish rag. She threw the closest one she could find over the food to conserve warmth. "I'm tired, son." She grew quiet, the last piece of bacon popping loud in the skillet. She'd not so much as adjusted bodyweight on her feet, and the boy could tell she was weeping. No feint bounce of the shoulders or jolting sniffle. Only a breathy stillness. On cue, a swelling guilt pulled at Rebel's gut.

He pushed from the counter and disappeared from the kitchen, only to return with an old dish towel, balled and cinched at one end by a collection of frayed rubber bands. He jingled as he walked, cheeks flushed with excitement. The boy plopped himself onto a chair and nodded to the one across from him.

"Sit down fer a second," Rebel said, ensuring the bag made the loudest clank possible as he hoisted it onto the table.

"What's that?" Charleen asked.

"Sit down and I'll show ya."

Charleen sat reluctantly, wiping her nose of wet. "I don't want it to get cold," she said, watching her son work at the bands, pulling and stretching them until they snapped, flinging wildly from the pouch. He flipped the bag on end, allowing its contents to spill onto the table: three weeks' worth of treasure.

Charleen looked at the crinkled dollar bills. Some twenties mixed in, all surrounded by dozens of coins, some still spinning their way to stillness. She surveyed the boy. Rebel beamed, toggling between his mother's reaction and catching coins eager to roll off the table's edge. He pooled the booty together.

"This is for you. I mean, for us. As a family," the child said.

"Where'd you get all this?" his mother asked.

"I worked for it," the boy said proudly. "I been workin' for it for a while now. Couple weeks. Longer'n that prolly."

"Where?"

"Down 'ere at Grayson's," Rebel said. "I asked 'em if he needed any work done and he hired me right on the spot." He was pushing the pile of money toward his mother.

"Rebel James...this is great, Reb," Charleen said, piecing together her son's meaning. "I told ya if ya needed money for anythang you just need to ask me."

"I know. But this ain't for me. It's for our family."

"Baby, 'is money is yers. You worked for it."

"I know, Mama, but you ain't listenin'," The boy's pitch rose. "I got 'is job so you don't have to work as much. But even if ya did, that's a'ight. 'Cause if we start addin' this to what you make ever month then we won't need help from nobody else." The consternation on her face fueled the child's frustration.

"What do you mean, 'help from nobody else,' baby? We don't git help from nowhere else," Charleen said.

"Him, dammit!" Rebel snapped, smacking the table hard enough to wake most of the coins from sleep.

"You better calm down and watch yer mouth," his mother warned, her eyes narrowing.

"I'm talkin' about him and anybody else like 'em! You know who I'm talkin' about. We don't need nobody comin' around, actin' like we need savin'. Or like 'ey live here or belong here 'cause they don't! Don't nobody live in 'is house but me and you and Lee." Moisture rose from the bottom of the boy's eyes. "Why cain't it just be us?"

"It is just us, baby."

Rebel shot from the chair. "Stop callin' me baby, goddammit!"

As quickly as he stood, his mother's palm met his cheek, clapping hard against the boy's jaw. Rebel froze, instinctively moving his hand to the point of contact, cradling the side of his face. Charleen's countenance retained its rage, daring the boy to flare up again. Rebel smashed his hands into the pile of coins and loose bills, sending money flying in every direction across the kitchen.

"Pick it up!" she yelled, pointing to the ground.

"No!" Rebel shouted and stormed to his room. He slammed

the door with what he was certain had to have been superhuman strength. A pee-wee league baseball plaque fell to the ground as several He-Man figures toppled from a shelf. Rebel's chest swelled and lowered, his cheek now fully ablaze. He moved to the tiny mirror above his dresser to assess the damage and could hear a muted version of his mother, screaming for him to return and clean up the mess. The boy pushed onto his toes, tilting his head to make out the raised, puffy outline of his mother's hand.

He turned in search, ultimately finding the worn duffle bag he'd inherited from Lee. His brother had received the vintage piece from Isaac's time as an Army grunt. The boy flung the thing onto his bed and spread it wide, allowing legions of dust particles opportunity for escape. Millions of fine silvery bits danced in a band of sunlight spilling through the window. For an instant, the child's anger gave way to wonder.

Rebel combed through drawers and other hiding spots he'd created, collecting clothes and various essentials for the journey ahead. He thought first of the barn, of course, but that would be too obvious. Not to mention proximity. He would need a true escape. Somewhere far enough to impress adults should he be found and hidden enough to elicit shock from the cops.

The Quarry.

The boy nestled his favorite comics into a corner inside the duffle. There was a tap at the door, but he would only allow himself to consider the infinite worlds living within that band of dusty sun.

"Rebel," his mother said softly.

The child continued to pack, reckoning his biggest regret of the day would be missing out on the lumberjack breakfast, now lukewarm and wasted. *Damn shame*, he thought. Rebel could tell from the moment he'd entered the kitchen she had prepared enough for three from force of habit. Herself and her boys.

"Rebel," Charleen said again, more convincingly this time, yet somehow softer than before. The boy did not respond. She opened the door to find her son struggling to zip closed the duffle. A futile effort. Charleen slid quietly into the tiny room, grinning at the sight of the old bag she thought Lee had destroyed years ago.

"I'm sorry," she said.

Rebel packed harder, uselessly shoving pieces of clothing around inside the bag. The duffle was full, the job finished, but the boy continued anyway, looking for anything he might abruptly grab to cram inside.

"Where ya headed?" his mother asked.

A jingling sound drew his attention, and Rebel could see she'd collected the entirety of the spill, having confined all the crinkled bills within a paper clip and amassing the coins into a pickle jar. She moved to the bed and sat opposite the child, the duffle between them, and carefully placed the bills and jar into the bag.

"This is yers." Charleen said, tears gathering. "You earned it and it's yers to spend...or save, or whatever you want to do with it. I understand why ya worked for it too. And I really, really appreciate it." She reached to touch the red of his face, but he pulled away. "I know you just tryin' to help but we're fine. We're gon be fine, okay?"

Rebel could feel himself decompress, disgusted he couldn't hold bristle. But then again, he was never able to look at his mother without feeling a modicum of sympathy, especially when she wore this sad strain of humility.

"You don't need to worry about bringin' in money fer us, okay? 'At's my job," she said.

"I know. But this could help…"

"Listen to me." Charleen straightened. "Ain't nobody movin' in. Dennis ain't tryin' to replace anybody. And I know ya don't like 'em…but he really likes you."

Rebel retracted once again, unable to keep his mouth from contorting against the lie.

"I'm serious, Reb, I can tell. He told me as much."

"I don't care what that man thinks about me," the boy said and pulled the duffle closer. "He ain't nothin' to me."

"Rebel James. That's just ugly," his mother frowned.

"Why? Why's he s'posed to mean sump'm to me? You told me when I met 'em he was just a friend."

"He is."

"Well, Lee has all kinds'a friends you don't like. And you make it known you don't like 'em. You got friends I don't like."

Charleen sighed. She took the boy's hand. "This ain't you. And that in there," she said, nodding toward the kitchen, "that *definitely* ain't you. That's yer brother. And yer better'n that."

Rebel pulled his hand away. "Don't say that." The boy stood, swatting his hand through the thick band of sun dust sending the particles crashing into his mother's hair.

"Lee feels the same way about 'em."

Charleen's face changed then. The slow, unavoidable change that happens when a dreaded realization takes a body unawares. Her eyes moistened, quicker this time.

"All I want is for him to stay away from here. Why cain't ya just be friends with 'em when ya at Larry's?" There was pleading in the child's throat. "You don't need him to be happy, Mama. Just be happy here wi'me."

"I am happy here with you, baby" Charleen said, pushing the duffle aside to move closer. "But it's okay for adults to have adult

friends, Reb. That's a good thang. That's the way it's s'posed to be."
She watched the boy's eyes fall to the overstuffed bag. "But okay."

"Okay what?"

"Okay to ever'thang. Okay to Dennis stayin' away from here. To me seein' 'em just at work like you said."

Rebel wanted to smile but refused the pleasure, acknowledging that if in any way the pitiable tenor in his voice had moved her to such resolution, he could live with it. Brazen machismo be damned. And Lee, the boy thought, wherever the hell he was at the moment...well, he could be damned too.

"For real?" Rebel said with the threat of accountability.

His mother stood.

"I promise," she said, and hugged her son for a very long time.

CHAPTER 14

Bested By Medusa

The bulbous television sat as an anvil, wedged snuggly in the space the old man had cleared for it, between a high stack of old newspapers he refused to throw out and the cigarette rack. Rebel, meanwhile, worked at catching his breath, having carried it from Grayson's pickup to its new home. The old man twisted at the antennae hoping to clear the screen of snow and translate the crackling into intelligible voices.

By now, and in general, Grayson had run out of things for the boy to do, having had him cut, clean, and scrape everything he thought worthy of attention. Lately, the old man had resorted to having Rebel act as a service attendant, cleaning car windows and pumping gas for customers. Grayson even started having the boy ask people at the pump what they wanted from inside the store. He would take the cash, quickly returning with items and change like a backwoods concierge. The few customers that did come by found this incredulous, if not endearing, and for a short time the shop experienced an uptick in traffic, intrigued by this bit of vintage nostalgia.

"Gotta git this up and goin' so we can watch some Bama games. They kick off in a couple months and we gotta be ready," the old man said jostling the antennae once more.

"Yessir," Rebel affirmed, positioning himself on a stool and imagining the rightness of enjoying games together there in the store.

Grayson studied the boy.

"You sure are in a good mood," the old man said suspiciously. "Finally got some sugar from that little girlfriend I reckon."

"No!" Rebel laughed as he lied.

"Well, she is ya girlfriend, ain't she?"

The boy's cheeks warmed as he repositioned on the stool. "I mean…I guess. She's my best friend that's fer sure."

The old man grinned. "Lovin' a person comes easy. It's gettin' loved back that's the trick."

"Looks like my Mama's done wi'Dennis," Rebel diverted. "Said he wouldn't be comin' around the house no more."

Grayson watched the boy's shoulders relax even as he said the words, prompting the old man to turn off the set. He squared himself across from the child. "Well there ya go," Grayson said smiling. "That's whatcha been wantin' the whole time, ain't it?"

"Yeah," Rebel replied, catching the informality of leaving off his typical "Yessir." The genteel warmth in the old man's face reassured Rebel he was safe, and the boy took a moment to bask in their familiarity. "Mama said he's been off at a trade show and was lookin' for a truck for me when I turn sixteen. But I don't know 'bout all that," Rebel explained.

"I see. Beware the golden handcuff," Grayson said with a wag of his finger.

"The what?"

"Golden handcuff. When somebody gives ya sump'm or helps ya out, but ya wind up indebted to 'em."

"Oh." The boy was piecing together in his head what his heart had inferred since the first time Charleen mentioned the gesture. "Well," Rebel said, "I ain't takin' nothin' from him. I don't need nothin' from that man." He looked at his boss for affirmation and read within the yawning crease above a bushy eyebrow that he spoke rightly.

The cowbell signaled a visitor and the pair looked in unison. A line of sun bounced off the glass of the door, catching bends within a woman's blonde hair. This same light cascaded through the rest of her locks to create a seraphic lucency as she entered. Rebel knew instantly who this was from glide and posture alone, having yet registered the whole of her face.

Kip's mother paused in front of the first aisle, situating the purse strap on her shoulder. She scanned the store methodically, letting her fists come to rest on her hips. She stood, a begrudging superhero ruing her latest assignment. The woman was undeniably striking, and Rebel decided he would sooner die than give her the pleasure of allowing her to catch him in a glance of admiration.

Laura moved on through the store, stopping only to pick up a magazine from the rack. She passed judgment casually, then tossed it onto a case of root beer. "You retired the smut," Laura observed, unfurling the purse from her torso and onto the counter. She smelled otherworldly. Something delicious the boy could not name, but assumed was easily recognized among her kind. Rebel watched Grayson, unaffected, turn and begin scanning the sprawling cigarette assortment behind the counter.

"Well, you know what they say, Mrs. Tunstill...new wine fer new wineskins."

The boy was certain he detected a slight huff from Laura, who continued to survey the place with disdain. Rebel tried desperately not to look at her blouse, but it may well have had a personality all its own. Lifting and falling with the slightest movement of the woman's length, baiting and cajoling. It was made of a delicate silk unlike the boy had ever seen, sheer enough for Rebel to realize she'd made efforts in matching the color of her bra.

"Hello, Rebel," Laura said stoically. She joined them at the counter and the boy rose nervously from his stool.

"Hey, Mrs. Tunstill," Rebel said as politely as he could.

"Oh, don't get up on my account," she replied.

"Well, 'at's what a gentleman does when a lady enters the room!" Grayson blurted out, having finally found the pack of cigarettes he was looking for. The old man winked at the boy as he slid a pack of Camel's across the counter in the woman's direction.

"I quit," the woman said.

"So you say," Grayson replied, tapping the pack with his fingers. Rebel could feel himself shrink away from these two, as if his body knew what his mind did not and insisted on distance to fix these two incongruous points within the same plane.

Laura propped an elbow on the countertop, her hip cocked as he'd seen Tab do a thousand times before. Cream slacks hugged her hips and legs crisply, and the boy looked away. Rebel prided himself on the self-control he knew Lee would have scoffed at.

"My father tells me you're the best employee he's ever had," the woman said. The boy's eyes darted between Laura and the old man, realization coming to him in waves.

"A hard worker," she condescended.

"You gon catch a fly, you ain't careful," Grayson smirked.

The boy realized his mouth had parted to create a small oval. He closed his lips to swallow dry air, then said, "Sorry. I didn't know y'all was..."

"Well, she don't really claim me, son, so don't beat ya'self up about it," Grayson said. Laura's lips pursed. "Will you relax? I'm just messin' with the boy, that's all," the old man chuckled. Rebel covered his mouth momentarily, searching for a familial resemblance he could not find.

"So you know Kip?" the boy fumbled, "I mean, a'course you do."

"Oh yeah. That Injun Princess yer always goin' on about, that would be my granddaughter."

Rebel frantically tried to recall all the instances he'd mentioned Kip as she related to the old man and the store. He'd told The Princess about getting the job and why he'd done so. Kip had said it was a good idea, and a "mature way to handle the Dennis situation." He was even more convinced he'd mentioned Grayson by name; the business was his namesake after all. But as he floundered, wondering why his best friend had failed to mention such an intimate connection, his eyes drifted to Kip's mother. Any sense of affable formality had vanished, her arms now folded. Since their first encounter, Rebel noticed Laura's expression had gradually softened whenever he came around. Her glares had simmered mostly to stale regards one might offer an insect. Repugnant yet innocuous. But now the scowl was back in all its bumptious fury, making smaller by the second this trailer-trash urchin before her. She finally turned to her father and said, "I'd like to speak to you privately, please."

"I ain't movin' in," Grayson sighed. "You wastin' ya breath. And don't send Steve down here neither 'cause I'll tell him the same thang."

Laura stared down at her purse, her jaw tightening into an impossibly hard angle. This triggered a ripple through the tissue of her cheek that seemed to run all the way to her temple and for the first time the boy felt the urge to leave.

"Listen…" Laura's tone descended to an ominous hush. "Nobody enjoys this less than I do. I can promise you that. But this isn't about me, and for once, Daddy, it's not even about you. It's about your granddaughter."

"Who barely knows me, thanks to you," Grayson fired back, his jovial demeanor gone.

"Well, this is your chance."

"Then bring her to me! Bring her here. She needs to see where her people are from. How her mama was brought up. But you don't want that do ya? Don't want her to see all this, or be around me…or him," Grayson gestured to the silent boy. The old man took a labored breath. "You need to remember, I didn't ask you to move back."

"You didn't have to you arrogant son-of-a-bitch!" Laura seethed, and immediately glanced to the child. She tried to calm herself, but the pristine ivory of her neck gave way to a disloyal rush of blood. Rebel observed the woman afire and felt his chest race, for this was something new. Something raw and dangerous and unhinged. He could swear he heard her accent change. In just those few words it had devolved from something wholly sophisticated into a scorched-earth palette. Here was pitch and tone and cadence he would've expected to erupt naturally from the likes of Tab, but not this person.

Grayson looked at Rebel and nodded. "Go on, son. Yer done for the day."

Laura sniggered and smacked the countertop with her palm, sending an assemblage of lavish bracelets jangling to life. "Oh, okay. So *now* you want the kid to go? Things getting a little uncomfortable for you, Daddy?"

Grayson looked at the boy with somber sincerity and motioned to the door. "It's okay. I'll see ya tomorrow."

"No!" Laura snapped. "The boy stays."

"Laura-Beth."

"No, you stay, Rebel," the woman laughed. "Please. Stay and learn more about your boss here."

"That's enough," Grayson warned.

"Because clearly there's some sweet, grandfatherly, mentor-bonding bullshit going between you two that, personally, I'm glad I got to see," Laura continued, sliding onto the stool in front of her.

"You come in here just to show yer ass?" The old man stood.

Laura cupped her knees and leaned toward the boy, a schoolteacher at story time—Rebel the eager innocent at her feet. "He tell you he was a vicious drunk who used to beat the shit out of his wife and kids?"

The boy cut eyes to Grayson, who turned and began pouring coffee from his cup back into the stained pot. Rebel knew this signaled closing, the familiar first step in the old man's lock-up regimen.

"He probably didn't mention that," Laura said. "Did he tell you any history about this piece of shit store when he hired you? Hmm?"

The child was spellbound, caught between the feverish, sardonic smile Laura wore and the bombshell she just disclosed. The woman seemed suspended in time as an entreating marionette, and Rebel suddenly realized her question was not rhetorical. "I, um..." the boy stammered, "I know him'n my grandeddy was friends."

"Ah, yes," Laura enthused, "Good ol' Isaac Headley. Bastion of the community. You're exactly right. He and my pop were big buddies. Isn't that right, Daddy?" She dismounted the stool and reassembled the purse onto her torso. "Thick as thieves."

Grayson continued with his business as if he were alone in the store, collapsing the remnants of his lunch back into the brown crumpled sack.

"Be sure to ask your mentor about the time he and your grandfather beat a man to death. Happened just outside," she said, gesturing over the boy's shoulder, "in the shed out back. Those were good times." Laura took the boy by the shoulders with a benevolent firmness. She glanced at her father one last time, then smiled down at the child with all the maternal affection of a long-suffering abbess.

"But guess what?" she smiled. "Just a few years ago, Harris Grayson met Jesus. That's right. And that changed everything. Ol' man Grayson stopped drinking and carousing and being an all- around son-of-a-bitch and decided he was born-again! Isn't that incredible? And so what that means is, all those bad things he did—well, as a matter of fact, all the bad things he's ever done—even to his very own family...they just...go away. Just like that. Like they never happened."

A leaden, finite quiet cradled the room. Rebel sensed Grayson had stopped moving altogether, but this was only a peripheral realization, for his gaze was still held fast by the impassioned woman. There was a moment when the boy registered a transformation in her countenance. A glassy film had glazed over her eyes without warning, then an inevitable tipping point, as tears slid and sloped her cheeks. Rebel watched them descend, finding crevice in the crease of her lips.

Laura stroked the boy's hair. Her hand caressed his face sweetly, and Rebel knew the gesture was genuine. The heat in her throat was gone, and all that remained was a lonesome, delicate timber. She studied the child, and seemingly for the first time recognized an innocent beauty. Beyond the soil that raised the boy. She saw in him a swell of earnest soul set about for good things. For a moment, she saw herself as a child in the palm of her own hand.

Rebel blinked, and within that blink were surely hours, for when he opened his eyes the woman was gone. Only he and the old man remained, bested by Medusa, as Grayson was a statue behind the counter, his back still turned. The only noticeable change Rebel could discern was a greater hunch than before. Heaviness hung about the man's neck—not from age but demons come to call. The boy wondered then if any of it had happened at all. Had the striking woman actually visited them? He looked past the windows to the road beyond for measure: it was still day. Still plenty of light out. The lingering scent of the woman's perfume was all Rebel had as proof.

Grayson sighed deeply. *Proof of life*, the boy thought. And with that, he set about exiting as silently as possible, intent on not registering the face of his friend, much less endure words of frail explanation. He had no reason to believe Kip's mother was lying, just as he had no reason to believe she spoke the truth. But Rebel knew grandstanding—no actor in any movie he'd ever seen could touch the theatrical panache of his brother mid-meltdown. What transpired just now was not that.

The boy took a step toward the door and the old man said, "It's true."

Rebel stopped.

"All of it. Ever'thang she said."

The child looked at the glass of the door, the cowbell hanging lifelessly from its handle. He debated which would be more respectful: walking out without a word or remaining still until dismissed.

"It ain't none of my business," Rebel said softly.

"That's where ya wrong, see. You should know what type'a man ya workin' for," Grayson mumbled, facing the boy. The catch in the man's baritone suggested Rebel might see tears, but there were none—as if his quota had been spent years ago. Grayson took an old rag and began wiping the countertop.

"The soul's a fickle thang, Johnny Reb," The Walrus mused. "Most ever'body starts out good enough, I s'pose. Then life goes along. Thangs come at a person and they ain't got no control over it. So they end up quittin' or makin' do somehow or nother. Other times, people make choices that push 'em further and further away from the good they started out with."

And for the first time the old man met the boy's eyes. Rebel fought every instinct to look away, figuring that if this was to be a confession, and he the only person in the world to ever hear it, then the kindest gesture he could offer would be allowing the man to be seen in his entirety.

"I reckon I fit in wi'that last bunch," Grayson said, inching the rag toward a new area of the counter. "I done as much bad before I had a family as I did after...which, I guess... some people might say makes a person rotten all way through." The old man's cleaning slowed to a stop. "But I seen a purely rotten soul before." Grayson looked at the boy with something like horror. "I seen one, son. And when you see one up close, it comes clear as day whether there's any good left in ya own self or not. And they's a cup'a good soul in me still. I know it. And they was in ya grandaddy too."

The stare he held unsettled the child, and Rebel made himself speak. "Is that what she meant about Jesus?"

Grayson seemed to have escaped a long fog and a smile appeared. The first the boy had seen since Laura's visit. "Now that one there's good all way through!" the old man said loudly with a palpable sense of relief. "Ain't nothin' but good in Jesus."

Tightness loosened around the boy's shoulders.

"Yeah. That part of what Laura-Beth said's true too," Grayson continued. "Course, she don't put much stock in it. She says, 'You can clean up the outside all ya won't, but it don't change whatcha done.' And hell...she's right. Some thangs, I don't guess ya come back from this side'a glory."

Rebel felt this last statement was as much warning as confession and began thinking about the most despicable things he'd managed to do so far in his twelve years. "Pastor Barnett says Jesus can forgive anythang," the boy contested. Grayson saw yearning in the child's eyes, a desperation for that to be true and stay true as long as he was alive to believe it.

"Well, sure he can!" the old man bellowed. "He can and does and always will. And we oughta thank him ever'day that he does. Listen, Johnny Reb, all my rotten is hangin' on that cross with Jesus. But the kind of forgivin' he does—the through-n-through kind that don't keep score—it's hard for some people to accept, much less give. It's rare."

"It shouldn't be," Rebel said, his eyes falling.

Grayson smiled. "Well, here's what else I know. If a soul's fickle, then justice is unforgivin' as hell. I reckon it has to be or it's called sump'm else. And I ain't got full what I deserve yet, but when it comes, I'm due it." Grayson emptied out the day's old coffee and refilled the pot with fresh water.

"Whatcha doin'?" Rebel asked.

"I'm gon make me another pot. You go on. I need to finish up a couple thangs."

"Yessir," Rebel replied obediently. There were no things that needed finishing, the boy knew, but he made his way to the door anyway.

"Rebel," Grayson said. The boy stopped. "I'm sorry, son."

"I told ya. It ain't none of my business."

"That ain't right at all," the old man persisted. "If they's anybody I owe a apology to, it's you."

A disheartened grief encamped within the folds of the old man's face. Rebel felt an overwhelming urge to rush over and hug his friend but refrained.

"Yessir," said the boy, and left The Walrus to his coffee.

CHAPTER 15

The Essential Virtue of Man

Rebel purposefully chose the long way home. The switchbacks and cut throughs he and Lee had forged through the woods got him to the trailer in under thirty minutes. This was a feat, considering the first time he'd taken trails to the store it had taken him a full forty.

Street roads were another matter. The long way bore tedious, stagnant lengths of asphalt with inferior scenery. Closer to civilization, only foot-worn paths served as sidewalks alongside the more bustling roads, and this always left the boy feeling uninspired. He'd decided that concrete was the venom of imagination but resolved himself to the route in light of the day's events. The monotonous stretches offered plenty of time for the boy to absorb the onslaught of revelation and he welcomed the dulling.

Sun still clung to the highest hill in Manookie as shadow initiated on the farthest reach of the Mims' driveway. Gloaming always began here first, inching its way toward the trailer. Rebel could make out an unfamiliar blue in front of the house, and he heard an indistinct voice say within in his own head, *Brace yourself.* The voice was not Lee, he was certain. His brother would never warn the younger of impending danger. Lee reveled in subterfuge, more so the consequences.

Rebel watched the object take its true form the closer he got: a monstrous, pristine Chevy. The sky-blue of the pickup seemed to elevate the truck higher than its oversized mud tires already did, a contemporary wonder among the perishing hues of the trailer. Charleen seemed to appear from nowhere, bouncing down the wooden steps and running to the vehicle like a game-show hostess. She spread arms and fingers across the hood, too seductive for the boy's liking.

"Welcome home," she said, gleeful to the point of hysterics. Her mood accentuated her aesthetic, and against this new prize the boy thought she looked younger and prettier than ever. For a moment Rebel found himself unable to resist such sincere exhilaration and smiled in spite of himself.

On cue, the screen door creaked a second time and the boy knew without raising an eye who stepped through it. Dennis sauntered onto the small deck, an unvanquished gunslinger, resting his long forearms on the porch rail. The Tourist's smirk stood in contrast to his mother's warmth. A portentous acknowledgment of a nonnegotiable gift that undoubtedly read: Golden Handcuff.

"Well?!" Charleen blurted out. "Whatcha thank?"

The boy knew he was about to fail in whatever words he decided to form, but would venture nonetheless. "It's nice."

"Nice!?" his mother yelped, "Rebel James Mims. Come on now. This is incredible! Dennis got it for ya at auction, baby, just like I said he was. But what I didn't know," she said cutting Dennis an aggrandizing grin, "was that he was gon come back with sump'm this awesome!"

The boy watched his mother admire the truck, gliding her hand alongside the chrome stripe running its length. The vehicle was impressive by any standard, and Rebel imagined that if he had been asked to pick out the truck of his dreams, he could have done no better. *Damn you to hell, Dennis Cleckley*, played in the child's head.

"Well, come on and look at it!" Charleen cooed, taking her son by the arm. She dragged the boy to the truck and placed his hand on the door handle. Charleen bit her nails as she looked on, half-expecting the machine to glow; Arthur having touched Excalibur. Rebel felt infantile next to the truck, smaller even than when he was around Dennis, which made him loathe this beautiful new thing.

Charleen cut a nervous glance in The Tourist's direction, dissatisfied with her son's response. She rushed to the passenger side of the truck and hoisted herself inside, patting the driver's seat. "Hop in," she smiled, "it's as nice inside as it is out."

Rebel used the foot rail to aid his climb. The leather he sat on was blue as well, a much deeper cobalt than the exterior. The cab ensconced the two. The boy gripped the wheel, which was overlaid with a pre-fashioned foam, itself wrapped in corresponding leather to match the aesthetic. He let his fingers sink into the plush grip, wondering what other indulgences he might discover.

Charleen scooted center and slid a congratulatory arm around Rebel's shoulder. "So, a'course he's gon drive it 'til ya turn sixteen," she said, reading the grin forming on her son's mouth.

"What?"

"He's got to, Rebel. Ya can't let a vehicle just sit. It ain't good for it. Gotta keep the battery up, keep the tires from dry-rottin' and ever'thang."

She studied the child's face.

"But it's yers. And you know you gon git to drive it a lot on back roads from now 'til then. I know it seems like forever away, but it'll fly by. I promise. You'll wake up and be takin' ya driver's test before ya know it."

"K," the boy said, staring at the man on the deck.

"It'll be waitin' on ya," she sighed, admiring the smoothness of the dash. Rebel recognized the breath. This was the restful, satisfactory sigh Charleen generated whenever something was going right in her life. They were rare, and the hearing of it softened and saddened the boy's heart at once. He looked at his mother, sweet and pleasantly pleased in the afterglow of the reveal. Rebel fought back the urge to cry.

He loved her so very much, and yet it was easy to predict how all of this would end. It might run the course of days or months. It may even last a year or two. Dennis had already proven himself more adept than any of her previous suitors. But the boy knew— in the same way his narrow fingers had imprinted their form into the cushion of the steering wheel—this was fated wreckage.

"Listen," Charleen lowered her voice needlessly, "I want us to have dinner tonight, okay? Just as a way to say thank you for this and to welcome 'em back from his trip. 'At's all."

And now it was the mother's turn to decipher the breath of the son: an exhale of resigned hopelessness. His expression would have likely been rage-weighted had he not seen it all coming; The Tourist's return. The bearing of gifts. His mother's olive branch invitation. Rebel had anticipated all of it.

"I thought you said he was just..."

"He is. He's just a friend. This ain't that. We ain't together, baby, he's just back from the trip and come over to show us the truck." She rubbed the blue beneath them. "He just come by to show us what he got for ya. Least we can do is say thanks by havin' dinner with the man."

Rebel watched Dennis blow smoke off the edge of the porch. The boy wondered then if foul things sought passage from soul to soul through the molecules of foul air. "Aw'ight," the boy relented. Charleen hugged him hard and kissed his cheek harder before jumping out of the truck. He watched his mother go, bouncing her way onto the deck and into the arms of The Tourist.

The child remained fixed in the vehicle. He wore the stare of a painter on the edge of madness, at wit's end to capture the nature of a subject too foreign for his brush. He wondered: *What yearning was so irresistible, so innate, that it blinded a person from the proof of experience?* Imperishable hope in the essential virtue of man? Doubtful. The boy knew his mother well. She held fast to a keen sense for bullshit as well, much like The Walrus. If that faculty happened not to be instinctual then it was surely incubated from years of raising the likes of her firstborn. And yet, she seemed to operate on an emotional quotient that swelled or ebbed in relation to face-value gestures: This man did a kind thing so this must be a kind man.

Rebel watched Dennis raise his cigarette toward the boy in toast, then disappear into the trailer with his mother.

CHAPTER 16

Pink Flesh White Fang

Tab could be a surly cunt. This had always been the statement Lee made whenever he found his cousin's demeanor too salty for his liking. In actuality, Lee misunderstood the word as "surely." Tab could be a "surely cunt"—a genuine witch of the highest order. However, Lee's pronunciation had come out 'Shirley,' so from early on, Rebel assumed at some point in history there was born a woman named Shirley who possessed such monstrous disposition that her very name became synonymous with a particularly venomous breed of she-devil.

Now, parked safely at the end of the driveway, some forty yards away from his cousin, the phrase played on loop in the boy's mind as a precautionary bulwark of self-preservation. Tabitha lived alone in a stark, unlovely apartment building not far from the interstate exit. What the builder had lacked in artistry was saved in function, as four brown-brick units sat like enormous car batteries in a cursed and forgotten section of dirt.

A long industrial sized freight container served as the communal trash dump for all four buildings, and Rebel watched for a while as several canines wrestled over garbage clustered on the ground near it. The boy despised visiting Tab here, although he'd only been twice before in his life, and on both occasions with his brother. That last time, Rebel remembered Lee walking down the steps from Tab's apartment with one eye newly bloodshot and a busted bottom lip. He was smiling like an idiot as blood saturated the front of a faded AC/DC tee. Rebel made sure not to say a word as his brother approached, but somehow knew that would be Lee's last attempt at sex with The Gypsy.

The development was called *Indian Village*, yet every resident of every apartment in all four buildings were poor blue-collar white folk. One unit was home to a big-rig trucker who was never home, another to a single mother removed from an abusive ex. This woman seemed at all times overwhelmed by what Rebel was certain were no less than nine children but, in truth, were only four. Each sibling looked identical to the other. With the shag hair of the boys and the ever-present food and dirt stains they all wore, divining names or gender or other differentiating characteristics was impossible.

Rebel found himself standing in front of Tab's door, wrapping nervously on the dingy beige wood. A sharp, bullish bark erupted from within and the boy took a step back. *'At damn dog.* He steadied a push-off foot for retreat.

The boy could hear his cousin approach and he tried releasing what nerves might be kind enough to go. He listened to the flip of the deadbolt and watched the door ratchet open, tethered taut by four inches of old chain. Below, at the height of the child's waist, bulges of pink flesh and white fang pushed through the narrow crack. Rebel watched drool slip and stretch from the dog's teeth to the concrete below.

"Sitzen," his cousin said through a cigarette, and the pit sat, quiet and still as stone. "Back the hell up," Tab ordered, and the dog obeyed, disappearing from the slit. She removed the chain and opened the door, and Rebel immediately made efforts to locate the dog, who was busy assuming his spot on the couch. Tab had moved on to the kitchen, leaving the boy to figure out for himself if he was meant to enter or not.

The space inside was simple and sparsely furnished: a thrift-store couch whose far end was clearly the favorite spot of the pit-bull, a press-board coffee table with nothing on it. Just beyond, a small round table accompanied by a single chair. The entire place reeked of isolation. Nothing really changed since the last time he was here. As the boy observed this emptiness, he marked the beginnings of sympathy on Tab's behalf.

The only sign of life beyond the steady breathing of the beast on the couch was that of the beast in the kitchen. But as Rebel watched his cousin retrieve a beer, the loop started up again as the name *Shirley* reverberated inside his skull.

Tab popped a can and extended it to the boy.

"I'm good," Rebel said, searching for a place to sit.

"Damn, boy. You still ain't loosened up none? Even after gettin' some pussy?"

"Watch yer mouth!" Rebel yelled. The dog shot to attention, absurdly muscled, poised at the edge of the sofa and glaring at the boy.

"Frieden!" Tabitha said through a laugh, and the dog retracted into a benign sphere. "'Ere it is! Hell yeah, 'at's what I'm talkin' about. Balls *have* dropped a little. 'Bout damn time," she grinned wide. Rebel could count on one hand the times he'd seen his cousin's teeth, leading one to believe this might have been her lone physical shortcoming. The solitary detraction of an otherwise exquisite piece of art.

No.

Tab's smile, and the teeth therein, was as arresting as any other part of her. The boy's ultimate reasoning was that she simply didn't find many things in life worthy of the gesture.

But on the few occasions when he had been present to witness it, her smile seemed to introduce the world to a different person altogether. She dumped ash from the cigarette tray she was holding into the sink, then poured beer into the tray just shy of the rim.

"This calls for a toast, Roscoe," she said to the dog, and placed the ash tray at the edge of the coffee table. Tab settled next to her pet, rubbing the soft part of his head. "Our boy's finally gettin' the stick outta his ass and breathin' a little bit!" She nuzzled the dog's snout with her own.

Tab waved the boy over, patting the cushion beside her. Rebel could only stand and watch the animal drink to his bravery. "Come on," she coaxed, exhaling smoke away from the dog and toward the child. "Come 'ere." Rebel sat and Tab pulled him close, kissing his cheek with congratulatory affection.

"I wasn't tryin' to disrespect ya girlfriend, aw'ight? She's cute as hell and seems real sweet," she said, and moved some of his bangs aside with her cigarette hand. Rebel wondered if his hair might catch fire. And then he wondered if she'd ever set another human being on fire on purpose.

"How do you know about her?" Rebel asked.

"Oh, I know, Rebel James." She smiled again and slumped into the couch. "You thank I was gon let my favorite cousin start goin' with just anybody?"

"I'm yer only cousin now."

"Bullshit," Tab smirked, looking over to observe Roscoe

finish the last of his ash tray beer. She looked deeply into the boy's face and took a long, serene drag. "I know you seen 'em."

Rebel stared intently at his cousin. "Whatchu talkin' about? Why you say that?" the boy asked, hopeful.

"I just know ya have."

"Quit playin', Tab."

"I ain't playin'," she said rising. "I mean…I don' know whatcha seein' exactly. Or what the hell he looks like to ya. Just about anythang would be an improvement fer his bony ass." She slid open the screen door leading to the balcony halfway and lit another cigarette. "I see it'n yer eyes sometimes."

"What? You see what?"

"I don't know. I don't see him nes'ssarily. Just more me knowin' that *yer* seein' 'em. Listen, we ain't gotta talk about it. I ain't a damn shrink. But I do thank it's happenin' fer a reason."

"What reason?"

Tab only shrugged. She read discomfort in the child's face. "Whatcha come for anyway?" she asked.

"Dennis come back from that trip and a'course he's at the house," Rebel said. He pulled Lee's butterfly knife from his back pocket and tossed it to Tab.

"What's 'is for?" She turned it over in her hands.

"I stole it back from Dennis. He took it from me and I just need ya to keep it 'til he's gone fer good. Anyway, Mama wants to have dinner for 'em tonight. Says it's to say thankee fer a truck he bought me, but…"

"No fuckin' way—that sleazy bastard bought you a truck?"

"Hell no," Rebel insisted. "'At's what I's about to say. He bought it for hisself, but you know Mama."

"Uh-huh. Bet she was creamin' over it." Another rare smile.

"He ain't no more bought it fer me than he would'a bought it fer Lee. And I can tell he hates Lee too, even though he ain't never met 'em."

Tab smacked her hip as she moved toward the door and Roscoe was at her heel in an instant. She opened the door to let the dog out and closed it again, and Rebel wondered which of the white trash folk was about to lose their life. "Come on now," she said, "that man would hate Lee whether he knew 'em or not."

Rebel leaned forward. "I don' know why people hate Lee so much." Those words brought on an unforeseen sadness to the boy, and he looked away to the balcony to hide the quiver in his chin. "I love 'em," Rebel said through tears. "I was around 'em more than anybody else...and I seen a cup'a good soul in him too."

Tab nestled next to the boy. She held him for a moment, then gently nudged his head with her own, a commiserative mare prodding her foal. "Hey," she said softly, "a lotta people seen good in yer brother." She stroked his hair and the glass of the balcony blurred for the child as it held his gaze. Tab rubbed his back gently, then whispered, "I was just never one of 'em."

Instantly rigid, Rebel looked at her. His cousin was doing her best to suppress a laugh.

"Seriously?!" the boy said, shooting up. She let go a snorting chuckle.

"I'm kidding!"

"Yer unbelievable," Rebel said, shocked.

"Calm down, Reb, it was a joke," she said, trying to compose herself.

"Unreal!" he said furiously and started to leave.

"Rebel."

"No! I cain't believe you would be such a asshole!"

"Gotdamn, boy, I said I was kiddin'."

"You know what? I come over to ask if ya'd come to the stupid dinner Mama's makin' us have for that *other* asshole...but fergit it!"

"Well, hell, Rebel. You should'a said that at the beginnin'. I could'a saved ya some time. I wouldn't show up fer that shit if ya paid me."

"You see!" Rebel screamed murderously. "I knew it! I knew you wouldn't come!"

Tab rose to meet his fury, her good humor gone. "Why the hell should I be there?"

"To help me not be alone for it!" And he was crying again, this time from a deep, gurgling disgust.

He wished in that moment he could utter some kind of Bayou La Batre incantation that would make everything about her that was beautiful turn ugly in an instant. He would curse her with miserable plainness for all time. But all the boy could do was turn and leave and hate himself for crying in front of her.

CHAPTER 17

Civilized People

From his position in the kitchen, if he leaned back far enough in the pinchbeck chair, he could see clear to the far end of the trailer and into his mother's room. In that room, barely visible on the floor at the foot of the bed, lay a soot-gray duffle which matched the bearing of its owner.

Rebel allowed his weight to bring the chair down onto its feet, surveying a table that had not teemed with this much food in years. A monstrous, heaping pot roast bordered by potatoes and steamed carrots served as the centerpiece. The boy watched steam rise from the meat as Charleen delivered other dishes: mashed potatoes rich with butter such that Lilliputian ponds of yellow had formed in the larger divots. Bread, garlic-drenched green beans. More bread.

The sheer volume of food repulsed the boy, and he wished he could vanish into the steam of the meat. The pink of his skin blending with the orange of the carrots, the brown of his hair conjoined with the dark of the roast. Together they would rise in a rapturous funnel of wet balmy air. He would be gone. And free as well, held by nothing but the length of his own imagination, adventuring wherever his courage might afford.

The flush of the far toilet brought him back, and he listened as Dennis made the length of the trailer. Rebel eyed the food once more, his mother next to him, and the empty chair to his right. The head-of-the-table-chair remained empty awaiting its king. Dennis sat in that chair, breathing a natural, easy grunt that caused the boy to wish him dead.

Charleen beamed, sighing with pleasurable relief. "Whew!" she laughed. "That was a lotta work. But so worth it." She squeezed her son's hand, then The Tourist's, and began extending dishes to them both, encouraging helpings beyond reason. A woeful compassion stirred inside the boy for his mother. She'd worked so hard on the meal and was so clearly desperate for this to go well. Rebel decided he would not be at fault should the evening devolve into chaos.

"I 'preciate the truck," Rebel started, putting effort to sentiment. "It's real nice."

Charleen glanced at her son, never so proud. She winked, which made the boy want to grimace, but he shirked the impulse.

"Aw, you welcome, son," Dennis said, his mouth already full of the steaming dead meat.

"Rebel," Charleen corrected, playfully swatting Dennis' hand.

"Oh yeah. Rebel," Dennis said, digging his knife into another slab of roast. "Sorry," he grinned. "Like your Mom said, it'll be waitin' on you when you turn sixteen."

The boy watched The Tourist chew, grease soiling the corners of his pirate mouth and oiling his goatee to a shine.

"Baby, you mind grabbing me another beer?"

"Of course not," Charleen said rising.

The man and the boy sat, holding the other's look in silence. Charleen popped the top for the man as she sat and rubbed Rebel's shoulder warmly. "Dennis said they was enough cars at that trade show to fill a dozen football fields. Corvettes and Mercedes. You said they was even a couple monster trucks 'ere didn't ya, babe?"

The boy wrangled his glare onto the glob of potatoes he'd not yet touched. *"Babe."* He'd heard her call different men this over the years, and the sentiment seemed to lose sincerity by increments.

"Oh yeah," Dennis murmured, "You name it, they had it."

The door opened and the three of them looked to see Tab entering. She swiveled to knock the heel of her cowboy boot against the base, freeing a pinch of dirt. Rebel felt a warm rush of blood shoot down his arms and glanced at the man to see how this new guest was being received. Tab took a pull from her cigarette, sizing up the party.

"Well, hey there!" Charleen bellowed. "Come grab ya a chair, girl. We just sat down."

Tab hovered, contemplating whether to turn and walk back through the door she'd just closed. She looked at her cousin and sighed, tossing her dingy purse on top of the television.

"Aw'ight," Tab said. "But I don't wanna bust up in anythang y'all got goin' on."

"Are you kiddin' me!" Charleen called out. "You know better. Come on. We got enough fer a army. But you gotta put that cigarette out."

"I know, I know," Tab said crushing the smoke into a tray. "I ain't that hungry but I'll stay fer a minute." Tabitha assumed the empty chair between the boy and The Tourist. She scanned the surplus of food and glanced to Rebel who rolled his eyes. Dennis had not so much as exhaled in the girl's direction.

"We's just talkin' 'bout Dennis' trip. So I guess you seen Rebel's new truck outside?" Charleen smiled, chasing her last bite with sweet tea.

"Can't miss it," Tab's eyebrows peaked. "Damn fine truck, Reb. Congratulations."

"Can we talk like civilized people at the dinner table please?" Charleen admonished genially.

"Sorry," Tab said, her hands raised in guilt. "That is most certainly an exceptional means of transport which hath been gifted unto thee, Sir Rebel James of Manookie."

Charleen and Rebel laughed as Tab held a steady grin.

"Smart ass," her aunt said, pointing a fork at her niece. Dennis' stare did not move from his plate. The boy watched his mother glance at the man. Charleen's smile faded.

"That musta hurt the ol' pocketbook," Tab said as she leaned to retrieve a toothpick from the bar behind them. She treated the thin stick of wood like a surrogate cigarette, flipping it from corner to corner across her lips.

"Oh, he can handle it," Charleen said winking at The Tourist.

Shadow seemed to cling around the long man's neck and the boy's breathing quickened. Dennis moved food around on his plate in a systematic fashion, positioning his thoughts just so. "Well," Dennis said slowly, "if you wanna know the truth... it's really none of your goddamn business." The clink of forks diminished to nothing.

"Babe," Charleen said playfully and nudged his arm, clamoring for the last bit of good humor.

"No, no," The Tourist continued, "she asked a question. I'm just givin' her an answer."

"Dennis," Charleen said, cutting her eyes to her niece.

"What?" Dennis laughed. "I can't fuckin' speak? I can't respond to this...weird-ass bitch?"

Tab had not changed her grin from the joke she'd made moments before. She remained slouched in the chair.

"Well?" Dennis stiffened off of Charleen's look and turned back to The Gypsy. "What do you think, *Tab?*" he mocked. "Will that answer suffice? Hmm? 'None of your fuckin' business.' Does that work for you?"

"What are you doin'?" Charleen's voice was quivering.

"Shut up!" Dennis barked venomously. His finger had whipped within an inch of her nose and he held it there. Tab slowly slid Lee's butterfly knife from her back pocket and opened it under the table. Rebel's heartbeat was in his throat, and he watched a tear form, then release, then rush the length of his mother's cheek. Dennis glared at Tab.

"Why are you even here? I'm serious. I wanna know. Who invited you? Cause I know I sure as hell didn't. Did you?" Dennis looked at Charleen.

"Leave her alone," Rebel said.

"What the fuck did you just say to me, boy?"

"I said leave her alone, motherfucker!" Rebel shouted. As the words left his mouth so too did flesh, as Dennis shot from his chair and swung wide, backhanding the child. The boy's lip was cleaved through and he crashed to the floor. Rebel's blood splayed across Tab's face, and for the first time, a reaction: she clenched the edge of her seat with one hand, her fingers flushing white, while simultaneously shoving her pelvis hard against the seat of the chair. With the other hand she pushed the butterfly knife slowly into her thigh. Deeper, until blood soiled the denim. She spat the toothpick out and closed her eyes, making every effort to slow the swelling of her chest.

Charleen let out a shriek and pushed herself from the table, backing away in horror. She started toward her son, but not before Dennis grasped a clump of hair at the base of her skull. A second shriek.

"Sit down," he seethed, forcing her back into her seat. "This is what you wanted, right?" Dennis asked, pushing her head down toward the table until her cheek and hair submerged into one of the butter ponds of the potatoes. "Big. Nice. Family dinner. Huh? All of us together?"

Tab finally opened her eyes and looked at the boy on the floor who was feeling at his face, holding the loose part of his lip in the fingers of one hand. She closed the knife and stuffed it back into the pocket of her jeans before standing, then moved to kneel beside Rebel, her hair forming a dark curtain. "Get the fuck up," she whispered. Her voice was raspy and like hot metal on the boy's nose.

Rebel looked into her face, disoriented, his head tilted as a dog's would at high pitch. "Listen to me," she breathed. Despite the shadow cast from her hair Rebel could see her jawline ripple with tension. "You better git'cher ass up right now, you understand me? Pick yer shit up."

Beyond the darkness of his cousin came a low whimpering moan from the table. Tab stood. She walked slowly to the television and retrieved her purse with the dutiful attention of a surgeon's assistant—and left.

CHAPTER 18

The Mark

Wind clotted the cut into a rock-ribbed glob of petrified crimson. Adrenaline still numbed any pain, so his bottom lip simply felt weighted, as if a bulbous growth had sprouted suddenly, intent on squatting for good. Gravity created a small window for air to rush to the back of his throat and curl around his molars. All Rebel could hear was the snap and splinter of bicycle tires slicing through the dry dirt. The wind pressed against his face as warmth escaped through his hair.

The boy heard the door close. And with his cousin went the faint smell of marijuana. Feet from where he sat huddled on the floor, a man held the side of his mother's face to a pulpy mound of potatoes.

As it grew darker, Rebel made sure to avoid the worst of the potholes, having memorized their positions in the road. He took a trailhead as soon as he could, easier through the wooded paths. He still managed to get bits of air from the jumps he and Lee had sculpted. Pleasure for pain.

The man was back in his chair, having returned to his meal as if all wrongs had been righted. He carved at bands of stringy roast with unbothered concentration as the woman wiped clumps of white puree from her ear canal.

The store was covered mostly in shadow save a few interior lights. This gave the boy hope the owner might still be there. From outside, the word *Grayson's* still cast a measure of dim light onto the gas pumps. Rebel leaned Kip's bike against his normal spot. Through the windows there was the low-level hum of machines tasked with refrigeration. The boy looked for the old man inside but did not see him.

The boy remained moored to the linoleum, smearing the worst of the blood covering his fingers onto his jeans.

"Grayson!" Rebel called out, and with the yell came the cracking of the crimson at his mouth. An agonizing pain now that he very much could feel. A fresh torrent of blood. The boy instinctively tried to catch it as it spilled, but the best he could do was shuffle around the counter and hold one of Grayson's dingy rags to his mouth. He was familiar with the old man's junk drawer and fished from it a handful of aged Band-Aids. He set about trying to dam the breach.

What an odd, funny scene, the boy thought: among a table of wasted food and spilled drinks, the woman smiled. A disheveled mess of destroyed make-up and crushed potato. The grease of melted butter slicked her cheek, and she whispered, "Go." There was a pitiful urgency within bloodshot eyes.

Rebel heard a falling clang from outside. He stilled himself until all he could hear was the beat of his own heart in his ears. His pulse in his lip. There it was again, this time accompanied by other sounds: a louder racket, and then the intermittent rise and fall of a muffled song. Its mournfulness reached the inside of the store. Suddenly the crack of shotgun powder, loud as canon, and the boy clamored through the store and out the back door, onto grass he'd cut not two weeks prior.

"It's okay," she whispered again, and her hands trembled in her lap like that of a very old lady. "Go on, baby…please," said the lady with trembling hands.

"Boom!" the old man howled, laughing himself hoarse and into a proper coughing fit. Rebel ducked as Grayson swung the shotgun his direction. "Johnny Reb!" his boss shouted. "Hot damn, son, get out here!" Standing yards away, Rebel could smell the ripe stench of whiskey, hard and jarring to the senses even from that distance.

"Come take ya a shot," Grayson said, disappearing into the shed. Rebel scanned the area and remembered how far they were from the closest house. If the shot was heard, even at this time of night, no one would think anything of it. *Runnin' coons or possum out from garbage*, they'd say.

The old man reappeared with several ancient whiskey bottles, all of them empty—ones the boy remembered stacking neatly. A bottle fell from Grayson's arms just as he took his next step, and he inadvertently punted the thing a full ten yards ahead of him.

The old man reacted as if a panther had been loosed and dropped the other bottles as well. He swung wildly with the gun, fumbling his way into a shooting position.

"Stay back!" Grayson slurred. "I got 'em, Johnny Reb. Don't you worry none."

The man lowered the gun to measure distance from himself to the bottle, then aimed and pulled the trigger. The explosion made Rebel wince and he took a step back, reminded of how much he despised the deafening sound of gunshot. The bottle that was the man's target sat peacefully.

"Did I git it?" Grayson asked as he tried picking up the bottles he dropped.

"Naw," the boy replied, and made himself move toward the man. "Why don't ya put that gun down for a minute."

"You don't wanna shoot?" Grayson said holding up the gun and bottles in disappointment.

"Naw, I'm aw'ight," Rebel said, resentful of not knowing how to act around this version of his friend. The boy's eyes continued to adjust to the night as he walked, and he noticed the sky was pregnant with stars, such that all the grass around the old man appeared ashen.

"What t'hell's on ya face?" Grayson asked, leaning toward the boy and squinting, then stumbling.

"Dennis."

Grayson laughed. "Well, I hope ya give 'em more hell'n you got! Come on," he waved sloppily, "come 'ere and lemme git a better look at'cha."

Rebel followed the old man into the shed, which felt surprisingly inviting. Grayson had secured oil-lit lanterns on opposing walls, hung on nails the boy had purposed for tools. The man slumped onto a seat he'd created from stacked crates.

Taking one of the lanterns from the wall, he waved Rebel over as he lurched for a bottle of Jack Daniels.

"Demons...'ey always come back 'round, Reb. Remember that. You can only run from 'em fer so long. Or pretend 'ey don't exist. Or that they ain't set a mark on ya."

The bottle of Jack and another just like it were the only new containers in the shed. The boy watched the man drink from the bottle and noticed its twin was empty.

"Once that mark's made," he swayed, using the bottle as a pointer, "those sum'bitches come t'collect." Another swig. "'Ey come at a man like 'ey come at Job!" He suddenly grew loud. "Takin' 'eez house. An' wife. 'Eez family. Took mine...took yern. 'Ey keep takin' and takin'. Ow down'a line. Family after family, down through generations. 'Til somebody..." He looked at the boy, wide-eyed. "'Til somebody decides t'break the curse." The old man pointed at the boy with his bottle-hand. He teetered there, raising a finger that slowly pressed against wet lips.

"Lean over," Grayson said holding out the lantern. The boy obeyed. "Good Lord, son! 'At's the worst patch job I ever seen!" He pulled together more crates, fashioning a seat for the child. "You put anythang on it?"

"Whatcha mean?" the boy asked.

"Salve. Blue Star, peroxide? Vaseline? Hell. Motor oil? Anythang?"

"Nuh-uh," the boy answered.

"Well, the bad news is all that shit'chu taped on gotta come off and it's gon hurt like'a sum'bitch." He coughed hard before taking another swig. "Good news is—you ain't gon feel nothin' 'bout thirty seconds from now."

Rebel realized his fingers had gone to his lip as the old man spoke, in protection from something he knew was coming. The old man reached out without warning and yanked the Band-Aids from the boy's mouth and Rebel yelped.

"Hey now!" Grayson chuckled through coughs. And for the third time in as many hours the lip gushed. The old man grabbed the boy by the back of the neck and held him at an angle, dousing the wound with whiskey. Rebel shrieked, and Grayson shook the boy's neck too hard. "'Ere we go!" he bellowed. "'Ere we go, son! Cleansed the wound, now we cleanse the mind. Here," he said holding out the bottle.

"I don't..." Rebel choked through tears and blood, "I don't want none."

"Drink the fucking whiskey boy!" the old man snarled violently and smashed the empty bottle of Jack against the wall.

The boy shuddered from the outburst, forcing liquor down his throat in torrents. Rebel knew then that he was seeing Laura's hurt. This was the man she knew as a little girl. One to be feared. If the woman and the boy never spoke again Rebel reasoned that he would share something with her forever, knowing her in a way no one else ever could.

Grayson looked as if he'd seen Mephistopheles reflected in the eyes of the child and slouched against the rough pine of the shed. He stared at the boy. Smelled his fear. Observed his impulse to run from the small space that was now a prison. The man's head dropped and he stared into his lap, dragging the bottle close to his chest. He began to sway. A low, woeful sound came from deep inside of him as he closed his eyes. He sang, "Well they ain't no graaaave... gonna hold 'dis body down...they ain't no grave..." The song lost in tears. "She stood right outside that door," the old man said, staring at the opening of the shed, transfixed.

Rebel looked at the doorway too.

"'Daddy!'" Grayson barked, and the boy jumped again.

"'Daddy, stop!' she was screamin', 'Stop it!'"

In the child's gut there was a flutter of nausea, and his cheeks grew hot. Grayson coughed violently then, and a small eruption of blood spurt from his mouth, causing Rebel to gasp. The old man dragged a paw across his chest and continued, "I turned to ya grandeddy n'says...'We cain't do this, Isaac.'" Grayson stood over the center of the worktable. A wrinkled hand came to rest on the scarlet stain Rebel remembered seeing on his first day of work. "Laura-Beth...she was bangin' away on 'at damn door just as hard as she could," he wept. "She knew..."

"What?" the boy asked against better instincts. But the liquor was having its effect.

Grayson rubbed his palm across the stained area of the table, as if some bit of old blood might lift from the crags of the wood.

"You know 'ey found that little girl's body all over that landfill. Like somebody took pieces and thowed 'em far as 'ey could in ever direction. Folks said it was dogs. Or coyote. But it weren't."

Grayson turned from the table, forcing himself to look at the drunk boy.

"What was it?" Rebel said in spite of the burn in his belly. "What done it?"

"I tried to git Isaac to stop after a while. 'That's enough, dammit!' I kept yellin'. 'Those boys need a deddy! We gon...'" Grayson trailed.

"Gon what?" Rebel shifted on the crate, and as he did, a bridge of bloody spit swung from his lip to the floor. His face was numb. "We gon what?"

"If you... if you'd a been at that landfill," Grayson said covering his mouth, "and seen what we seen. You'd understand, son..."

"Stop callin' me son!" Rebel screamed as he wobbled to stand. "I ain't yer damn son!" The boy paced, shaking his head in defiance as hot tears rushed to his chin. "What'd y'all do to 'em?" he cried.

"What was done to 'at lil' girl weren't human."

"Shut up!" Rebel growled. "I don't wanna hear about the girl, I wanna hear about the man in this room! What'd y'all do to my deddy..."

"We seen evil..."

"I said shut the fuck up!" The boy grabbed the crate he'd sat on and hurled it across the small room. The wooden box exploded to pieces above the old man's head. More destruction, as the boy lurched for whatever he could find, swinging and throwing and punishing. He kicked through the wall of the shed on one side, and moonlight mixed with the yellow of the lanterns. The child turned finally, heaving with drunk exhaustion, and paused to observe The Walrus.

The old man sat as he had before, no longer the sobbing confessor. Only a slothful lech balanced atop dusty crates. Blood and whiskey had married at the corner of his mouth, drizzling onto his massive stomach. Rebel watched him cough more blood and the bottle fell from his hand to the ground. The head of The Walrus bobbed once, then again, then his eyes rolled back in his head. The old man spilled over, his mass crashing onto the floorboards in a leaden heap.

The boy watched the blob on the ground squirm and twitch as more liquid spurt from its mouth. Rebel felt fury leave him as quickly as it had taken him up, and he shook the old man violently. "Grayson!" he yelled, hoping but expecting nothing in return. "Wake up!" He shoved at the man's body. Rebel ran outside and turned every direction for help that was not there.

He rushed back into the shed and tried sitting the old man upright. Futility. The boy felt his heart race as it had at the dinner table. He rifled through every pocket of the old man's clothes, slapping Grayson's face intermittently.

Inside the store, Rebel scoured behind the counter until he found the truck keys. And then he was driving, pushing pedals he could only reach by scooting to the seat's edge. His face was still hot from whiskey as the vehicle careened down dark roads. These were roads he knew, but not in this way. Not going this fast, in a machine that seemed more in control than he was.

The old pick-up screeched to a halt just short of Kip's house—some brush and a few saplings its only victims. Rebel spilled from the vehicle and his knee slammed hard against the curb. He cried out, rolling back and forth as his hands cradled the leg. Several exterior lights shown bright, and the boy could hear the door of Kip's house open, a flurry of female voices growing louder. The Princess stood over him, the same eager tenderness she expressed the first time they met—again to rescue the spilled boy.

"Oh my gosh!" Kip gasped and tried helping him up. Rebel wailed and she jumped. "I'm sorry! Oh my gosh, Mom, look at his face!"

"Go back inside," Laura said standing over the boy.

"What?!" Kip blurted out, "No!"

"Right now, Kip" the woman said, and knelt down beside the child. Rebel was groaning, doing his best to sit upright.

"Mom, he's hurt..."

"I know he's fucking hurt! Now go back inside!" Laura screamed, and Kip teared instantly, observing her mother as a strange new person she did not know. The girl disappeared.

"Yer deddy," Rebel winced.

"What happened?" There was fear in her voice.

"He passed out," the boy said, "they was blood...in the shed behind the store."

She was gone. The boy's head throbbed and he forced himself

to stand, testing the knee with a grimace. Laura reappeared, this time with Steve. The two split off and Laura hurried to the garage as Steve jogged on to the boy.

"Hey, champ," the rich man said, more casually than Rebel thought appropriate. "You okay?"

"Yeah, I'm aw'ight."

"He do that to you?" Steve said, motioning to the boy's mouth.

"No!" Rebel said more harshly than he intended, causing the lip to bleed.

"Was he breathing when you left?" Steve asked, needlessly slicking back dark hair that might as well have been set in plaster. Laura was backing out of the driveway in a white Mercedes.

"I thank so."

"Okay. We're headed over there now." Steve nodded to the truck. "You leave the keys in it?"

"Yeah."

Laura thumped onto the road, scraping the bumper on the gutter. "Damn it, Laura! You can't help the man if you get yourself killed on the way there!" Steve said, bending to examine the bumper. Laura slammed the vehicle into drive and lurched forward, screeching to a stop next to her husband and the boy. The windows were down and Rebel could see the clench of her teeth.

"You better not be here when we get back," she said, staring at the boy.

"Are you fucking kidding me?" Steve snapped. Rebel was silent.

"He smells like a distillery," Laura said coldly.

"Go!" Steve pointed, and Laura squealed off. The man sighed, shaking his head. "Don't listen to her. She's just scared. I want you to stay. Kip doesn't need to be alone and she can get some ice on that knee. One of us'll be back soon and we can take you home, okay?" He placed his hand on the boy's shoulder. For Rebel, the touch was as soothing as a tranquil rain. And the only thing keeping him from tears.

"Yessir," the boy replied, hoping the man would leave right away, or else he would surely cry. Steve hopped into the truck and fired it up. Rebel noticed Kip's father appeared more athletic than he'd let on, and tried imagining him forty pounds lighter, with a head full of that same dark hair. Yes, in his prime Steve had been formidably handsome, and his pairing with Laura felt far more reasonable. Rebel watched him glance over his shoulder through the truck window at the vegetation destroyed on entry.

"We'll work on your parking," Steve grinned, "but you did the right thing coming here, Rebel." And he drove away. The boy's name coming from the man's mouth seemed like Rebel was hearing it himself for the first time. He'd always been 'kid' or 'champ,' or some other vaguely assigned designation that may as well have been 'friend of daughter.' A cheery pride rose in his heart.

Kip walked toward him with an ice bag and towel in hand. "Are you okay? Let's go call your mom," she said.

"Naw, I don't wanna call her," Rebel said. Kip lifted his arm and placed it around her shoulder to help him walk. The fall from the truck had killed the last of any buzz that was left, and Rebel was grateful to have his arm around his best friend. "Let's just sit here," he said, slumping onto the porch steps. He could feel her staring at his mouth. "Why didn't ya tell me you was kin to Grayson?" he asked, applying the ice.

"Seriously?" Kip shot back, pushing him hard enough for the ice to fall from his leg. "That's what you're worried about? Tell me what happened!"

"I don't know!" Rebel said loudly, as frightened by her outburst as he was angered by the pain in his knee. "When I come up on 'em he was drunk."

Kip suddenly began to cry, burying her face in her hands.

"Hey," the boy said softly, "what'd I...what's wrong?"

He placed his hand on her shoulder and felt like crying too, but only at the sight of her upset. Kip composed herself, wiping at cheeks Rebel wanted desperately to kiss if the moment weren't so inappropriate.

"He's an alcoholic," the girl said, trying to stifle emotion. "But he stopped drinking a long time ago. Doctors told him he was going to drink himself to death if he didn't stop. But he says the only reason he was able to quit is because Jesus helped him."

Rebel brushed a mosquito away from her arm, then swatted at another seeking food from his lip. The porch lights were drawing insects in hordes. "Come on," the boy said, pushing from the steps, "so we don't git eat up." Kip helped him toward the street, and the two settled on the curb. It occurred to Rebel this was the first night that didn't feel as hot as the day, and this enlivened the child in spite of the day's events.

"The main reason we moved here was because of him. My mom actually hates it here—swore she'd never come back. But she found out how bad his health was and finally decided I needed to meet my grandfather."

Rebel leaned away, trying to digest. "Are you sayin' you never laid eyes on yer own grandeddy?"

"Yeah," she said, and the boy watched her chin begin to tremble. "I mean, I've talked to him on the phone a bunch of times, but that's it. That's why I didn't say anything about us being related... it's just super weird because I don't really know him. Mom's been trying to get him to move in with us since we got here so we can take care of him. And so he and I can actually get to know each other before his health gets even worse. But he's really stubborn."

"He's just old and set in his ways, 'at's all," Rebel said.

"That's pretty much the definition of stubborn," Kip snapped. "My other grandparents are dead. I would beg and beg my mom for us to come visit so I could meet him. But she always had some stupid excuse of why we couldn't. At some point she realized I wasn't going to stop asking... she finally told me it was because he wasn't safe to be around. That he used to drink and when he got drunk..."

"He's fine to be around," Rebel exclaimed, and then, "he's a good man."

"How do you know?" Kip asked. The earnest, pressuring nature of the question unsettled the boy.

"'Cause..." he started.

"'Cause what? 'Cause nothing—you don't know. You don't know anything about him. Not really."

"Yes I do." Rebel stiffened.

"No you don't! You've worked for him for like, not even a whole month and you act like you guys are big buddies."

"Well, he's good to me."

"What about before? What about way before, when my mom was growing up? She's told me stuff you don't know anything about. And you don't keep somebody away from their family like that unless they did something to deserve it." The girl's tears ran angry.

"Whatever he done, he's sorry for. And y'all should forgive 'em," Rebel said, and wished he hadn't.

"What?! Are you for real?" She stood with a look of disgust. "You don't know if he's sorry—you don't know anything about him. You're just a dumb redneck kid who thinks he's your family but he's not! He's *my* family! Why don't you leave and go home to your own." Kip stormed toward the house.

Rebel watched her go and could tell she was crying though he could not hear the cries. The door slammed and he turned back to the street, gripped by an overwhelming sadness unlike he'd ever known. He looked out across the fresh pavement to the darkness beyond. The dark seemed to invite the boy, but Rebel knew there would be nothing for him there. Lee would not be there. Nor Tab or his mother. Only wisps of tall grass, light and airy and stinging against a throbbing knee. In the belly of that darkness would be so many unspoiled trees, and the songs of ten thousand crickets unseen. Raucous and cajoling as in defiance of a looming threat. Jokesters all.

CHAPTER 19

Wasted Breath

Slats of the ivory canopy spindled around the trunk of the pecan tree. Rebel lay flat against the floor of the treehouse, staring up at its grandeur. His gaze drifted between the separation of each board and the whole of it becoming a giant cloud of white fixed within black sky. He imagined what The Princess might be doing inside: crying in her room upstairs, curled into a ball on her bed. Or perhaps busying herself in the kitchen to take her mind off the unknown. The latter could not be possible, he decided, since he could see into the kitchen from his vantage point. Only the stark white of Laura's faultless palette. He made sure to stay low and out of sight.

The boy recalled Lee meeting him there in the treehouse. Rebel envisioned his brother again in the rocker, worming at the stuck pecan with his grey tongue. He wondered then if he'd seen the last of The Vampire. The last time was at *Grayson's*, when both had set about the wreckage of all The Walrus held dear. *Screw you,*

Lee. Yer advice was always shit anyway, the boy thought. *Just stay on that side...searchin' for somebody you ain't never gon find.*

A sharp light pierced the slats behind his head and Rebel flipped onto his belly to see a car pulling into the drive. It was difficult to make out the vehicle with headlights shining directly at him, but then a figure crossed in front of those lights. The long silhouette told the boy it was Laura.

Rebel army-crawled backwards and down the tree's ladder, skirting behind the tall shrubs. He watched Kip run out to meet her, burying her face in her mother's chest. The two stood there for a moment, then Laura guided her to the car.

The boy looked around in panic. They were leaving and he had no means to follow. He thought of chasing the car on foot, but his knee was still throbbing. Leaning against the storage building, a thought occurred to him. Inside, Rebel realized the space was much bigger than he previously thought, with so many of the moving boxes gone. The boy easily identified what he was searching for.

Kip's other bike was parked in the exact same spot it had been the first time he saw it. Rebel jumped on the banana seat and was down the driveway before Laura made the first turn from their neighborhood. He jumped a curb to take a trail he'd made himself, one that cut straight through the meandering streets of unfinished houses.

The car was still in sight and from the turn Laura took leaving the neighborhood he knew where they were headed. The hospital was west, and the only logical place they might be going in the opposite direction would be the store itself. Rebel lowered his head, leaning hard into what appeared to be a solid wall of shrubbery, but he knew where the break was in the line—and vanished.

On the other side the boy was gliding—up and down dirt mounds and around the sides of gravel stacks. This was land in the infancy of development. He was aware he would not beat them to the hospital, but he wouldn't be far behind. They would be delayed by signs and lights and turns while the child pedaled as the crow flies. His thoughts turned to what might have happened. They would take a dead body straight to the morgue for autopsy—at least that's what they'd done with Lee. Myriad scenarios flashed before him as he rode, each less probable than the last.

At the hospital, the boy could see the Mercedes, empty and parked underneath the *Emergency* sign canopy. *He's gotta be alive*, Rebel said to himself, *no need for that kind'a rush otherwise*. He propped the bike carefully against a tree, well out of sight, and eased close to the building.

Navigating its perimeter, he hoped the family might be in one of the outlying rooms with curtains open enough to offer visibility. His luck had been good spying on Tab this way. All he saw were drawn blinds and the glow of television sets, room after room. Within the few into which he could see, ancient humans peered back at him. Mummified tomcats, tethered by tubes and machines. Their mouths were agape, as if beyond the pane the boy were a nightcrawler who meant them harm. But the ancients were unafraid.

Rebel slinked back into the brush and squatted to think about his next move. His knee refused the angle, so he pushed himself up and began walking toward the entrance of the building. The Chilton County Hospital was anything but impressive—a spartan structure relative to the population and laid out as though two lowercase t's had decided to touch feet. It was here the boy paused to vomit from the whiskey and waited until the acid taste left his mouth.

Inside, he made straight for the paltry gift shop on the right. This was his only chance of avoiding the clerk at the information desk: a huge black woman with a sour disposition.

Rebel remembered the gift shop from when he and Charleen had visited Isaac in his last days. During those visits the boy sat for as long as he could in the staleness of the lobby, deciding ultimately to wander the aisles of the gift shop out of boredom. Anything but the tiresome anchoring of the cold and sterile.

"Can I help you?" the sour fat woman said.

Rebel froze just before clearing the door of the gift shop and caught a glimpse of himself in the glass. He was a mess. The visage mirrored back was swollen and disheveled, the lip as if it had given up hope altogether, having turned into a globulous purple ball. The fat sour one cleared her throat, demanding the boy's attention. Rebel made himself turn to face her.

"Sign in here an' have a seat," she said. Her eyelids drooped to cover half of each orb. At any moment she looked as if she might fall fully asleep.

"I'm just here to see somebody," Rebel said.

A sigh escaped the woman. She leaned back in her chair. "Who you come t'see?"

"The old man. His family just brought 'em in," the boy said through the swelling in his mouth.

"He yo family?"

"Naw," the boy shuffled.

"'Den I cain't let'chu back, baby."

"He's my boss," Rebel said, and suddenly his emotions sat at the top of his throat.

"Don't mattuh. He ain't kin, you cain't go back."

Her sleepy eyes dropped to the desk and she began thumbing through a magazine. As Rebel fought to keep tears from spilling, he considered his options. He could run for it, sprinting the corridors and calling out until he found them. The clerk most likely wouldn't bother giving chase. But then he would only be a rat in a maze—albeit a simple one—ambling about, disturbing the ancients.

He turned to the glass of the gift shop once again. If he cried, at least the woman would not bear witness. And then, next to his own reflection, the boy saw Laura walk by, digging furiously through her purse. Rebel followed her in the glass until the automatic door opened wide. Outside, he watched as she leaned against the Mercedes, cigarette in hand, spiraling grey plumes into the night air.

"He aw'ight?" the boy asked.

Laura started to turn in the direction of the voice, then aborted the gesture. "Of course it's you," she laughed.

Rebel considered leaving until he noticed her face, puffy and tear-streaked. Now, more than ever, he could see the resemblance. Whenever Kip cried her face had settled into a similar posture. Aside from the woman's blonde hair they appeared to be the same person, only aged apart. Tears had flushed much of the makeup from Laura's face and she looked much younger. Innocent. The bristly, domineering air she seemed to always carry all but vanished. Rebel could envision clearly the girl who stood outside the door of her father's shed so long ago, battering against it as she pleaded for the violence on the other side to stop.

"You know," Laura said, "I knew your mom. I was a couple years older than her in school. But we cheered together. She was really good. Got everything on the first try, never afraid to go up." Smoke slid from the corner of the woman's mouth. She watched it rise, waiting to see which way the air would take it. "We weren't friends or anything. Not like our dads were. She thought I was stuck up. I thought she was white trash. No love lost either way, trust me."

Rebel quietly lowered himself to the curb.

"Anyway, she got pregnant with your brother...wasn't going to tell anyone. But I knew. I knew the look. That feeling. And she came to me..." Laura took a long drag, now addressing the drifting smoke before her. "I don't know why me—I guess because our dads were so close. Maybe that made her feel like she could trust me. Maybe she knew that I knew—I don't know.

"She asked me what she should do. Scared shitless. We both were. Just kids. She knew I had some money from working at my dad's store—just like you." Laura looked at the boy and offered a slight smile. "Of course, I was saving up to get the hell out of here the second I graduated. And she..." Laura pointed with the cigarette as if Charleen stood in front of her. "She resented me for that. Everyone did. And looking back, I get it. It looked like I thought I was better than everyone else...but they didn't know..." Her voice trailed into the smoke. "They didn't know that I was just trying to survive him."

She brushed a tear with her shirtsleeve.

"So Charleen asks me one day if we could talk. Tells me the situation...then asks if she could borrow some money to have it taken care of. And I convinced her not to. 'Just imagine,' I said, 'imagine holding that little baby in your arms. This brand-new person that *you* made...that you can raise up differently from how you were raised. Safe and kind... gentle.'" Her voice quivered to nothing.

Steve suddenly appeared, leaning through the entrance. "Honey, you better get in here," he said with sober urgency.

Laura dropped her cigarette and ran inside. Rebel paced, watching as the two disappeared around a corner. He noticed the woman's discarded cigarette and gathered it up. Returning to his spot on the curb, he held it in his fingers the way he'd seen Lee do a thousand times before. He smoked what he could, coughing as he went, tasting the sweetness of Laura's lipstick on the filter.

Lee had always said he smoked to relax, but the boy knew his brother only did it to look cool. Certainly nothing about it eased the child's nerves now. He found himself rocking slightly, rushing puffs he would have otherwise tried to savor. He reached the butt, and the gradation of pungency on his tongue made him nauseous again. He spit out the remnants, but bitterness seemed to have sealed within his tastebuds.

Movement drew his attention and Rebel could see Kip and Laura make the corner of the corridor with Steve. Her mother's arm was wrapped around her, and the girl was heaving as she wept. The boy cried instantly, without noise or fuss, prompted only by what this scene surely meant.

He moved closer to the entrance and watched them sit in the lobby. The room was empty save the family and the sour clerk, who remained buried within the magazine. Rebel tried to study Kip but Laura blocked his view. He knew only that she was in pain and that he wanted to hold her, to hug her the same way her mother was now, and yet the distance from the boy to The Princess felt like the stretch of eternity.

He turned away, his thoughts settling on what had transpired inside one of those rooms, down one of the corridors he was not allowed to enter. His breath fell short, then shorter still, until he was heaving himself—a foreign, desperate panic gripping at the meat of his soul. He heard then the rushing clicks of heels on pavement and looked up to see Kip's mother.

"Did she git to talk to 'em?" the boy said through breaths he could not catch. "Was he awake to talk to her and give her a hug?"

The child's eyes darted frantically and he was pacing again—the hurt too rich to hold straight on. Laura turned the boy by the shoulders so he faced her directly.

"You listen to me," she said leaning down. Her voice was hushed. "I don't want to ever see you again. Do you understand? Don't come over to our house, and don't ever speak to my daughter again. I don't want to see…" Laura clenched the boy's cheeks hard, fingernails burying into his skin as tears streamed down her pretty face. Rebel's mouth sat pursed within the woman's hand and blood escaped his lip for the final time.

Laura jerked away as if she'd engaged a leper, her hand covered in the blood of the child. The boy did not care. He could not feel pain now. Nor could he hear the rest of her words as she flung blood from her hand onto the pavement in disgust. He watched her begin to walk away, pause, then turn back. Her mouth moved, and Rebel could tell the words that flowed from it were meant to hurt. A reckless torrent steeped in years, designed to seal him off from the world like the bitterness at the end of the woman's cigarette. The sound of those words slowly became coherent, pushing through the child's subconscious defense.

He heard the woman say: "I wasted my breath on your mother. That boy was doomed to die early."

CHAPTER 20

The Trellis

Rebel paced the loft until his adrenaline ebbed. The day was the longest the boy had ever lived, and seemed as if it had no intention of ending. Moon-glow cast its light through the bay window of the barn as it always did, with only the farthest corners of the loft clinging selfishly to shadow. The boy plopped down in the center of the space, crossing his legs and staring intently through the opening.

He would make him appear.

He would remain fixed—Sitting Bull petrified—until the dead boy showed himself. There was a conversation to be had and answers the living boy would demand, and by god The Vampire would reveal himself or the child would camp until the jeans withered from his legs and his skin grew into the fissures of the pine. He held this position. And then his thoughts turned to Kip.

They'd never shared a cross word until tonight. Their last interaction had left a curdling discomfort in the base of the child's stomach that pestered him even now. This affliction eventually reached his brain causing his head to throb. Damn the world's disappointment, but never hers. Rebel yearned for her affection unreasonably. And now her mother had decreed exile. The boy let his head fall into his hands and he scrubbed at his eyes with grubby palms. He felt sure his temples pulsed visibly and tried massaging the pain with his fingers.

Grayson suddenly appeared in the child's mind and Rebel winced. The lasting vision now imprinted was the plunging of his hands against the largeness of The Walrus, pushing into folds of flesh as he slapped at the old man's face. Useless. He had not said goodbye. Had not been able to thank his boss one last time for hiring him for work that didn't need doing, or the money he was paid that the old man didn't have. For counsel or friendship or revelation about things the boy never had the courage to let himself consider regarding his father. Rebel had questions for The Walrus too.

He craned his head, looking up to find the place where Lee's rope had hung. It was easy enough to spot. The jerk and twitch of his brother's convulsions had caused the rope to grate against the old truss, raking free ancient dust from the beam to reveal cleaner wood beneath. He traced the outline of where the rope had been with his finger and moved to stand beneath it. A breeze, almost imperceptible, touched him through the bay and he glared at the openness there.

For Rebel, the frame of it was the trellis between worlds. On the child's side: all things finite and measurable. This came to him through the pounding at the sides of his skull and the heaviness of the abused lip. Darkness on the other side of The Trellis seemed to taunt him now. Lee lived there. Free to wheel and wreck and liquify from one plane to another, injecting himself wantonly into the mess of people's lives—into Rebel's life—at will. The boy's heart began to rush once more and he swatted at the pain in his temples.

He rushed to the bay window and thrust his chest through it screaming, "You fuckin' coward!" He screamed this until the cords of his throat burned. The warmth of fresh tears sat on his cheeks, and he clenched his eyes shut as tightly as he could. The distance from The Trellis to the ground would only break bones, he figured. And as far as the boy was concerned, the damage inflicted on his face and knee was enough. He looked around the loft. There was no rope.

A rustling in the high weed below drew the boy to the bay, and he tried locating the disturbance. An exasperated grousing and raspy curses the boy recognized. Lee stamped into the clearing in front of the barn, yanking his foot free from the last of pestering vines. Draped around his neck like a fur yoke was a limp coyote. Lee held a pair of its coppery feet in each hand, the head of the thing bouncing in time with the dead boy's steps.

"Is 'at what it takes for you to show yer sorry ass? Me tellin' you what'chu really are?" Rebel snarled down at the dead things.

Lee stopped to stare up at his brother. "Pull yer fuckin' skirt up, Rebel. I had shit to do, aw'ight."

Rebel laughed, incredulous. "Oh, you had shit to do?"

"Yeah," Lee said flatly.

"You. Had shit to do. I gotcha." The boy nodded his head, surveying the field and woods beyond. "He had shit to do, ever'body!" he yelled into the void.

Lee turned in the direction Rebel was looking, the head of the coyote swinging rhythmically along. "What's crawled up yer ass?" Lee asked, shifting the weight of the animal around on his shoulders. Rebel's eyes saucered, an unfamiliar breed of rage rising in his face.

"I...can you...can you not see what's happenin' on this side when yer over there doin' whatever the hell it is yer doin'?!"

"Well gotdamn, Rebel. I cain't be everwhere at once—I ain't God—who, by the way, is real as this coyote on my back." Lee bounced the animal on his shoulders in reference. "Don't let nobody try to tell ya different."

"Then where's he at when I fuckin' need 'em!" Rebel cried.

"Well, first of all," Lee fired back, showing his annoyance, "He ain't sittin' around waitin' to be needed by yer little bitch ass! He's got shit to do too, and his shit is bigger'n everybody else's shit. He's got 'eez hands in ever damn thang all the time. You'll know what I'm talkin' 'bout when ya cross."

"So, you tellin' me you made it to Heaven?"

Lee raised the paws of the coyote above him. "Does it look like I fuckin' made it?"

"Yer a shit-ass brother, you know that," Rebel fumed. "You always was. Actin' tough, like you was so hard. But'chu ain't. Yer just a coward."

"Oh, *I'm* a coward?" Lee bristled.

"Did I stutter?," Rebel yelled back, and spit down at the dead boy.

"Motherfucker!" Lee said, dodging the slime. "I'll beat'cher fuckin' ass!"

"Come on!" Rebel screamed.

Lee stormed into the barn, wrangling the coyote as he went.

The boy wheeled, fists balled for battle. Rebel's chest was heaving, and he moved toward the steps, bracing. He heard the smack of Lee's sneakers against the stairs and decided he would simply swing as many times as he could before his brother cleared the final step. Certainly that was the only advantage he would have. That, and an untamed recklessness that had gripped him at the sight of Lee stumbling from the overgrowth.

Suddenly there were no sounds...of sneakers on wood or of mouse or mosquito. Not even the rush of his own labored breath.

"Hey, faggot."

The voice was behind him, and Rebel whipped around to see Lee holding the coyote like a baseball bat. The Vampire swung the animal hard and struck the boy squarely in the face with its snout, knocking him to the ground. One of the creature's teeth managed to graze the child and new blood came from Rebel's cheek. The boy gathered his bearings, feeling for the cut on his face as he made efforts to place Lee in the dark. The Vampire slouched onto a hip, casting most of his body into shadow by the light of the bay.

"You just got bitch-slapped by a dead coyote," Lee grinned.

Rebel sprung from the floorboards and rushed his brother, hurtling his body into The Vampire. The small wolf dislodged from the dead boy's hands and Lee stumbled. The boy pressed, shoving until his brother crashed against a beam. Rebel swung wildly, connecting with the bottom of Lee's chin. Skin slipped clean from the corner of the dead boy's face like rice paper, revealing cracked bone and the ooze of black blood mingled with puss.

Rebel gasped and yanked his fist back, rubbing his hand against his jeans to cleanse it of discharge as Lee cupped his face. On the floor, feet from where they stood, was the section of lost flesh. It lay rumpled and glued against the boards.

"What the hell's wrong wi'you?! You cain't do 'at, Rebel! Cain't you see my shit's fallin' apart?!" Lee was furious. He lowered his hands enough to reveal the damage. Rebel tried to swallow but his throat would not allow it.

The corner of Lee's chin dangled free, a section of bone

dislodged from the rest of its frame. He tried pushing it back into place as if it were a puzzle piece, but too many shards of it had joined the slice of moldy skin on the ground. He fumbled with the stray piece of his face, unmanageable and slippery.

"Gyat...dammit!" Lee hissed. "You see what'chu done?!" The angrier he got the more it appeared his face might dislodge altogether, tearing from the edges and crumbling from his brain stem.

"Sorry," the boy offered sincerely.

"Don't fuckin' say that! Gyatdamn, boy. You still don't git it, do ya? They ain't nothin' to be sorry about if they's a fight needs to be had. Quit apologizin' for ever gotdamn thang. Shit."

And with that, Lee yanked the loose section of face clean from his jaw, freeing himself of the nuisance. He side armed the piece through the bay window and into the overgrowth from which he came. "Piece a shit," Lee said of the rotted flesh. He paced, finally glancing at his little brother. "You don't look much better'n me, be honest wi'ya."

Rebel slid down to squat against the beam he'd slammed Lee into. The boy smudged blood from his cheek. "I'm aw'ight." He surveyed The Vampire, who tried in vain to slather loose skin over the section of missing chin.

"Just leave it, Lee. Damn."

"'At's easy for you to fuckin' say, ain't it?!"

"Well, it ain't like it's gon kill ya! Yer already dead. Or alive-dead...or reanimated. Whatever the hell you are."

Lee sighed in resignation. He motioned to the small wolf on the ground. "You ain't gon ask me what I'm doin' luggin' a gotdamn coyote around wi'me?"

"I figured you was gon tell me," the boy said, grazing his finger across the bulge on his lip.

"You 'member when Grandeddy got all 'em rabbits for Easter 'at time?"

"Yeah."

"And they all got eat t'hell?"

"Coyotes. Yeah. Mama cried for three days."

"And you 'member me layin' all those traps?"

"That never worked," Rebel said.

"Well, it wasn't no pack, like Grandeddy kept sayin'. It was just one really smart motherfucker who know'd not to come around for a while after 'at first run—and he sure as hell was too smart to take bait. So, I spent a week scoutin'. Got downwind. Tried callin' 'em in…"

Rebel looked over at the animal resting on the floorboards, much larger up close than it appeared in the clearing below.

"Then I finally realized…I wasn't really huntin' 'em. I was just waitin' on the damn thang.

And all the while it was gettin' more comfortable with comin' and goin', more confident in what it could git away with. And then it hit me…I had to just go fuckin' git it." Lee took the animal by its hind legs and drug it to the bay window. "Had to seek 'at motherfucker out. Make it uncomfortable."

Lee slit the throat of the coyote, tilting its neck at an angle so he could direct blood where he wished. The Vampire commenced painting the frame of The Trellis with the blood of the small wolf. The bottom he layered thick with the sudden rush, then the sides, and finally the top until he was pleased. Rebel was standing now, watching his brother work with bemused fascination. By job's end Lee was covered in most of the animal's innards. Standing there in the center of the bay, the dead boy looked like a macabre Choctaw war chief, bathed in the glint of moon blood. Lee held the floppy body out toward his brother.

"Here," The Vampire offered.

Rebel approached, unsure of the offering's meaning. The boy took the small wolf in his hands. It was lighter than he expected relative to its size, the result of wet-dressing The Trellis. He squished rolls of fur between his fingers, letting its flesh spill in and out of his hands. Lee stepped aside, making way for his brother. Rebel allowed his eyes to trace the pattern Lee had painted. He looked through The Trellis then, into an infinite night. Nothing had changed. The high weed swayed in the first winds as wild grass meandered into dense woods on either side of the barn. Farther out lay the trailer. The tin box which held his mother. And The Tourist. Home.

"Go ahead," Lee said.

"What?" Rebel asked.

"Toss it."

The boy looked at his brother. Lee had become something else. A phantom wraith of failing patch-work skin and brittle bone, sallow and anemic. The wreckage of something once alive but now poorly stitched, indelibly marked by the putrid, inexhaustible odor of decay. The child felt sorry for him.

"Go on," Lee said.

But the boy's body had gone rigid. He could feel every muscle within his small frame constrict beyond his own capabilities. He tried moving his hands which held the animal toward The Trellis but could not—the small wolf was an anvil, his arms stone. Rebel glanced at his brother for help. The Vampire offered none. He watched the dead boy lean casually against the barn wall, as if none of the present mechanisms acting against the child were surprising.

"I'm tryin'," Rebel whispered, fearful this paralysis would consume his ability to speak at any moment.

Lee lowered his head, his concave chest rising and falling with a sigh of disappointment.

"Ya asked me a minute ago... 'Is 'at what it takes for me to show up'" Lee said, staring into the floor. Then the dead boy raised his head, and for the first time Rebel could see life in his brother's eyes, lusterless grey eclipsed now with a penetrating sapphire. "What's it gon take for you, little brother?"

The boy looked down at his feet. His toes squirmed and fought for movement while his feet remained moored in the dust. Everything in the child willed motion, yet he remained prisoner of the loft. Subject to The Trellis.

"Look at me," Lee said sternly.

The boy began to cry.

"Look at me, goddammit," Lee whispered.

Rebel lifted his head and was face to face with his brother, but no longer in front of the bay. The two now teetered on opposite edges of the same crate in the center of the loft—the crate Lee had used months before. The boy felt an itchy roughness at his neck and realized a noose scrubbed beneath his jawline. Rebel gripped onto his brother's arms for balance. He tried to slow his breathing, but it was no use. His eyes tracked the rope leading from his neck to the truss above, following it over and down the other side to Lee, neck-wrapped same as he.

They wobbled there, The Brothers Mims, the older sturdier than the younger. The same rope noosed them both, appearing to have no beginning and no end.

"What's happening," Rebel choked through a distressed whisper.

"The end of it," replied the dead boy.

"Why are you doin' this to me?" the living boy pleaded.

"You put yourself on this box, little brother." The crate

emitted a loud crack as Rebel's foot slipped and he clung fiercely to his brother.

"Let go," Lee said calmly.

"I cain't," the boy cried, and felt within his arms just how frail-framed Lee was.

"Ever'body crosses alone, Reb."

"I don't want to," the child said, soaking the dead boy's chest with tears.

"Then let go," Lee said.

"I don't want to."

"You got to, Rebel James."

The boy leaned his face from his brother, a trail of snot the bridge between them. Rebel steeled himself, releasing his grip from his brother. Tension instantly brought the child up and onto his tiptoes as a surge of pressure filled the boy's eyes and flooded his cheeks. Consciousness squeezed thin, Rebel could still make out his brother's expression in spite of his head being cranked at an angle.

Lee was grinning.

Then suddenly the grin vanished, and The Vampire shoved the boy from the crate.

CHAPTER 21

Prodigal

Mid-day sun heated the boy's shoulders. The distance from the barn to the trailer was easily enough to work up a lather, and by the time Rebel reached the bottom step of the porch the whole of him was aglow. For the first time since Laura had walked into the store, Rebel could smell himself. Sweat and blood and dirt and whatever other unnamable odors the body might produce under intense stress. The boy wore these now like a second skin.

The child felt no rush of adrenaline as he made the first step. Perhaps he'd run out of the stuff. Surely the body could only produce so much. But with each creak of redwood beneath his sneakers, there was no heaving of the chest for fear of what was about to happen. No anxiety thick in the throat. A knowing resolve had affixed itself to the boy's expression, and all that was left was what had to be done.

Rebel opened the front door to find The Tourist slouched

comfortably on the couch, beer in hand, watching television. The man barely acknowledged the disturbance. The boy closed the door behind him and surveyed the trailer, half-expecting the entirety of it to have been altered but all was the same.

"The prodigal returns," Dennis said, tilting his beer in Rebel's direction. "Hey, babe!" the man called out, "he's back!" He grinned at the child. "I told her to quit worryin'. Told her you'd be back after you licked your wounds. But don't feel bad—happens to the best of us. Come in, sit down," he waved. The boy could hear the shower in his mother's room shut off. Dennis winced. "Good god, kid, you smell like horseshit. Go shower and clean up before your mom sees you. You had her worried sick, you know."

"Git out," the boy said evenly.

Dennis' brow furrowed as he smiled. "Come again?"

"I said git out. Git yer shit and leave. And don't come back."

Dennis laughed. He took a drink. "Listen, son-"

"Do it now. Git up, git'cher shit, and leave right now."

Dennis examined the boy. "You know what...I don't think I will. I think I like it right where I am." The long man eased farther into the sofa, allowing his arm to run the length of it.

"I mean it," Rebel said.

Before the boy could react, Dennis' beer bottle crashed against the wall, exploding beside Rebel's head. The child flinched, instantly covered in the suds and foam of stale Budweiser. "And I mean what I said, motherfucker!" Dennis raged from the edge of the couch.

Just then Charleen appeared, pulling closed an old robe drenched wet from her rush from the shower. "Stop it!" the woman screamed. She tugged frantically at the robe to cover a grotesque, multicolored bruise on her shoulder. The boy tried to examine her as he wiped beer from his eyebrows.

"Please! Baby...please don't," Charleen begged The Tourist.

The child could see now. The woman's movements were frenetic, and the whole of her seemed to quiver. A swath of hair, blackened from wet, covered much of her face. She pushed it aside that she might plead more earnestly with the man on the couch, and Rebel saw the fullness of harm done. Her nose had grown a hump in his absence and it bulged red. The eye uncovered from hair was purple beneath and swollen fat with blood. Charleen looked at her son and tried forcing a smile but faltered.

A dense pressure filled the boy's ears then. An odd rush of blood in the hands. He was on top of the man and swinging wildly, his small fists landing furiously wherever they might. One of the punches found home on the corner of Dennis' mouth—enough to elicit blood—and for a moment The Tourist was forced to cover up like a boxer cornered, shielding his face until he could push himself from the couch.

Once upright, the man unleashed a vehement violence upon the child: hoisting the boy by the throat and pinning him to the wall. Slaps came at Rebel's face and head, again and again—thunderous, damning claps. He tried turning his face away from the blows, but his head remained vice-gripped against the paneling. Charleen injected herself as best she could, tugging at the long man's arms as she tried shielding her son, only to be shoved aside each time.

The woman rushed to the telephone until she witnessed Rebel's face flushing red. She dropped the phone with a scream and ran, jumping onto Dennis' back. The man bobbled as he released the child, who fell to the carpet like a bag of bricks. The boy's body twitched—efforts at consciousness, his eyelids dipping up and down again.

Dennis flipped Charleen violently over his shoulders and into the living room wall, cracking the paneling into the shape of the woman's back. Her body crumpled onto the couch as pictures crashed around her. The entire trailer seemed to sway from the blow. She lay there, curled into a wet shivering ball, whimpering into the folds of the couch cushions.

Dennis saw the telephone and smirked. He yanked it clean from the wall and towered over Charleen. "You need to make a call?" he heaved, catching his breath. "Here...let me help you." Dennis paced as he held the dead receiver to his ear. "Hello, officer? Yeah, I'd like to report a domestic disturbance at 6565 Middle of Fuckin' Nowhere Street," he said, "Bumfuck, Alabama," and he kicked the thin front door hard, smashing it from its hinges.

The broken phone cord trailed after The Tourist. "That's right," he continued, "I was in this piece of shit trailer, minding my own goddamned business when I was attacked by a fuckin' little...Tasmanian devil." Dennis kicked the unconscious boy on the ground. "And then his cunt mother got in on it!" Dennis screamed and slammed the phone down onto Charleen's body. He slumped onto the couch next to the balled-up woman, exhausted. The man ran swollen fingers through his thin hair, regaining composure.

The kick from The Tourist was enough to pull Rebel from sleep, and the boy craned his head to find them. He saw his mother and the man on the couch. Another strange scene, Rebel thought as he coughed up a little blood. In another time and another place...perhaps on the far side of The Trellis, the boy might have deciphered what he was witnessing now as endearing. His mother curled on the couch next to a man she loved, his body open and relaxed. All suggestive of a warm kind of security that comes from strong, tender masculinity.

But the child had not yet crossed through the blood frame.

And as he lay there on the floor, all he could hear were the words of his cousin. *Pick yer shit up.* Rebel pushed himself upright and teetered there, gathering enough strength to stand. With some effort he rose to his feet. "Git out," the boy coughed. More blood. "Now."

Dennis stared at the child, who tried earnestly to stay himself from swaying. Rebel's ambition was to appear more solid than he was, ready for another round if need be. But a small ocean swirled inside his head, and he thought at any second that he might succumb to a swallowing darkness. The Tourist took in the curled, quivering woman next to him, then again to the child.

Dennis saw something in the boy's face then, and a disheartening malaise draped itself onto the man's countenance. He discerned within this gamy, bloodied mess before him, an inevitability. And try as he might to escape it, the soul of the thing would visit him in perpetuity and the man knew this would be so. He sighed.

"Fuck this," Dennis said, shoving from the couch and disappearing into Charleen's bedroom. Rebel stumbled to his mother and tried to move her, but she only whimpered. The boy looked up to see Dennis walk back through, duffle in tow. He went to the fridge, wrangled several beers into his arms, and walked out the busted door.

For a moment, Rebel sat beside his mother. Dumbstruck. The rumble of the Chevy coming to life had him hobbling to the porch where he looked out. Dennis was pulling away, chased by tunnels of dust that furled from the oversized tires.

CHAPTER 22

Valkyrie

Dennis parked near the back of the gravel lot, facing the truck toward *Larry's*. People-watching always seemed to calm The Tourist, and he lit the first of many cigarettes. Oftentimes at the car lot, and on some occasions even in the midst of a sale, he would drift, imagining alternate lives for the tedious people he was forced to interact with.

He would abide Joe Tackert's ramblings long enough to convince the rich retiree he was listening, nodding periodically regarding the customer's thoughts on the necessity of v-8 engines. The long man made sure to insert some innocuous verbal affirmation here and there when needed. But sooner or later the drift would take over, and Dennis Cleckley gave in to the temptation of enriching the fat bastard with a made-up backstory worth the effort of imagination. Tackert's aw-shucks demeanor was bullshit. Dennis knew that Joe had actually traded double-breasted Armanis for overalls on purpose, having turned state's evidence on some vicious mob cohorts back in Jersey. Joey Salvator Trumonti, via wit-pro, was now good ol' Joe Tackert. He was nailing the hick accent though, and this impressed The Tourist. *Sure, Joe. I'm sure you need a brand-new F-150 for your huntin' camp*, Dennis would think.

This was his custom with most of his customers. Lisa Bridgeport and her swarm of toddlers were "looking for something with a little more room" but, in reality, The Lady Bridgeport needed space for her prize-fighting Rottweilers. The Wilsons sought to trade in their Crown Vic not because it suddenly stopped meeting their geriatric needs, but because Old Man Wilson needed quick cash. His wife had suggested a penis implant and was the picture of eager anticipation.

Dennis slid comfortably into the plushness of the seat and stared out. Nightfall had arrived and most of the bar's older clientele were trickling out, making way for the younger crowd. Dennis ran his game of pretend: this patron stealing away with that one, that woman brutally betraying this man, and so on, until he grew lazy. Two cigarettes shy of retiring a pack, he decided he was calm enough to drink, and made the gravel lot to the bar.

Inside, the place was busier than usual. Larry could be seen in his office, shoving papers this way and that while barking into a telephone. Dennis slid onto a stool, initiating the first of several rounds. A younger waitress made the mistake of swapping Haggard for Tom Petty, which drew a gaggle of middle-aged women onto the pitiful wedge of a dance floor next to the bar. Dennis watched the women move, fixating on the most attractive one in the bunch as he tossed back more whiskey.

Within an hour he'd joined them, grinding in time against the skintight Levi's of a bleached blonde. He made sloppy efforts of not spilling his drink, his head bobbing loosely atop of his long neck. Hair he normally wore slicked back, showcasing a receding widow's peak, now fell to the man's cheeks, swinging forward and back. The interior of the building lived always in a lumbering amber, and the bodies of those dancing were as worms wriggling through a thick honey.

Tab entered the bar and took a short case of stairs to an elevated dining area. She weaved through the tables and chairs, filled mostly with folks in the midst of over-eating or drinking. Leaning against the railing of the lofted space, she scanned the length of the room. She identified Dennis dancing in the far corner and moved that direction, but not before speaking to Larry.

"Hey!" Tab yelled over the music. Larry was on another call, balanced in his chair with feet up. On seeing the girl, he ended the call and moved laboriously from behind the desk.

"Hey," Larry said through furrowed brow. "Where the hell's Charleen? She missed two shifts and won't answer the damn phone."

"Hospital," Tab said through the noise.

"What? What happened?"

Tab only looked at the man. His expression changed as his eyes flared through the room, landing finally on Dennis.

"That son-of-a-bitch," Larry growled, retreating to his office. He was back in an instant with a worn baseball bat in hand. Tab waved him off. "Nuh-uh," she said. "You need to go see Charleen. She's in the ER."

"Where's Rebel?"

"He's there too. They both gon need a ride home and I told her you was comin'," she said.

Larry shook his head in frustration. He set about digging car keys from the mess of his desk. Tab watched him go until the beat-up Firebird was onto the pavement and making the curve toward town. She sat on the farthest stool and waited.

At the back of the building, down a short hallway, were the bathrooms. And just beyond, the back door exit. After a time, Marvin emerged wearing the same old grease-stained apron he always did. His dark skin melded with shadow, and it appeared as if a faint grey pinafore dangled alone back there in space.

Stepping beneath the glow of the restroom sign, Marvin found Tab on the other side of the building. The two shared a look, and the floating apron disappeared.

The Tourist's movements had slowed to a drunken, rhythmic sway from one hip to the other. Most of the gaggle had dispersed, and Dennis towered on the tiny dance floor as a crane among swallows. A hand slid onto his waist, and farther to the bottom of his large oval-shaped belt buckle. The man felt a body pressing against him from behind, fleshy breasts that imprinted themselves firmly beneath his shoulder blades.

A whip of sable flashed onto his long arm, and something told him who this was before he followed that trail of hair. He turned his body slowly, unwilling to disengage from the form.

Dennis stared down to see Tab looking into his face. Maddening beauty, with a sweaty lick of desire hovering above the rim of her lips.

A swell in his jeans, and the man lowered his hips, pulling the front of the girl hard against his body by the small of her back. They danced within the remnant of other women. Her against the wet of his cowboy shirt. Him against the heat of her young skin. The crane swayed over the swallow as the two moved together, music orchestrating the long man's lust.

Tab lifted onto her toes and pushed close to the man's ear. "Take me," she said in a raspy hush. She leaned away, allowing her hand to run the length of his arm, pulling him toward her. Dennis lumbered in tow, bumping tables as he went. The air was cooler away from the dance floor, and The Tourist could smell the grease from the food and the cheapness of the liquor from behind the bar. He felt nauseated. His eyes buoyed as he tried to train them on the girl's ass, but it proved elusive in the dark and he gave up.

The whole of the girl suddenly became visible under the glow of the restroom sign, then vanished. Dennis could hear the creak of hinges and realized she was leading him through the bathroom door. With his free hand he began working to unfasten the huge buckle.

Outside the bathroom, Marvin had resumed his position beneath the sign, aligning two orange construction cones at the start of the hallway. Re-aligning his do-rag, Marvin began stretching yellow Caution tape across the hall opening in the shape of a giant 'X'.

"I gotta piss," an older burly man huffed.

"Bafroom's closed fuh now. Busted pipes. Sorry," Marvin said, loud enough for the old man to hear.

Inside, the bathroom was reasonably lit, and Dennis squinted as his eyes tried to adjust. Tab slid onto the countertop next to the sink. She pulled the man close and clasped his throat with her hand. Squeezing. She shoved him away hard, causing Dennis to stumble backwards through the door of a bathroom stall. He toppled over the toilet, his long sides ricocheting against the walls of the small space. The Tourist laughed there on the sticky floor, wedged firmly between the toilet and a graffitied wall.

"Of course," Dennis smirked, "I shoulda known." He pulled himself upright and managed to stand. "You like it rough," he slurred. The man clambered from the stall sloppily and slapped the girl hard.

Tab's head snapped sideways as blood from her nose splayed across the mirror behind. Dennis laughed harder. "'Errrre we go! Is 'at...is 'at what you like...you twisted fuckin' whore?" The man was cackling now, craning at the waist from laughter.

Tab took deep breaths. She smudged her hand through the blood on the mirror and tasted it with her fingers. Reaching to the back of her jeans, she slid Lee's butterfly knife free, releasing its clasp from behind her back. She opened the blade smoothly, peeling it back and meeting the handles.

"I said take me," Tab whispered, and spread her legs as far as her jeans would allow.

Dennis' laugh faded and he lurched closer, shoving his pants down as he went and wrangling his cock into his hand. A thumping at his side then. Odd, like the tugging of a mother's coat in the fist of a child. Or the brush of a stranger in a crowded street. Many. The man felt them at his ribs and then at his back. Again and again. Pestering thumps that he imagined would bruise.

The Tourist's eyes bobbed up to see the face of the girl jostling from movement. He thought he was inside of her, the bounce of her cheeks the result of his thrusts against the countertop. Then he looked down and realized he was not moving at all, his shrinking penis still in hand. Dennis lifted his head to see a smile take form on the beautiful face, and watched it lick blood from the grin.

Dennis leaned away, observing as Tab's hand throttled his torso like the darting beak of a woodpecker. Jutting, plowing stabs that slipped deep into his pale liquor-soaked skin. Blood flowed, and the man could feel it pooling inside of his boots, first at the heels. Tab was standing now, slowly orbiting, stabbing all the while. Dennis' legs weakened and he slammed his palms onto the edge of the countertop for support.

Dropping to his knees, The Tourist watched his reflection spill blood from the corners of his mouth. The man's head came well above the girl's waist, and Tab leaned down to speak.

"You gotta see this," she whispered.

The Gypsy clenched a loose wad of thin hair into one hand and yanked his head up straight so he could see himself clearly in the mirror. She plunged the butterfly deep into the side of his neck, the blade disappearing to the handle. A suffocating gurgle swirled at the base of the man's throat, and his last panicked effort at sight flashed to the girl.

His eyes beheld the reckoning. And the Valkyrie that was sent upon him.

CHAPTER 23

Molecular Density

Tab stepped into the farthest stall and retrieved a folded tarpaulin resting on top of the toilet. She went to work unfurling it; ripped in places and blotched with globs of old grout and paint. Fishing Dennis' truck keys from his jeans, she rolled the man onto the tarp and wrapped him in it tightly.

A moment then to catch her breath, she closed the knife and returned it to her back pocket. The girl cracked the bathroom door enough to give Marvin a nod, who checked a final time that no one was coming. He left his post momentarily to help Tab drag the tarped body through the exit, then returned to place an *Out of Order* sign on the bathroom door. Marvin slipped inside the bathroom, locking it from within. He entered the tarpaulin stall where he grabbed a bucket and mop. The tall boy flung wide every spigot of every sink, allowing water to fill the bowls and overflow onto the tiles. And so he began his cleaning, mopping the worst of the blood into the floor drain at the center of the room.

• ◆ •

Only the rhythmic hum and chirp of hospital machinery at first—one monitored pulse and heart rate, another oxygen. Rebel slowly opened his eyes and the room took shape: white and cold and blank. A blink for bearings, and the boy could see his mother beyond the thin blue curtain that separated them. Her bed was identical to his, yet she seemed to require more machines.

"She's going to be okay."

The voice was beside him, and Rebel turned to see Laura.

The woman sat upright in a boxy chair, as put together as ever. The twist of his head made Rebel aware of the weight on his mouth, and he raised a hand to feel at the mass of gauze affixed to his bottom lip.

"They say she's going to be fine," Laura smiled, shifting to the edge of the chair. "And so are you."

Rebel closed his eyes only to blink. He tried desperately to reopen them, but it was no use, and he disappeared into a deep darkness.

• ◆ •

The exit door of *Larry's* flung wide to reveal Rodrick. He sat on the rear bumper of his idling Buick, the trunk lid open behind him. Roddy pushed from the edge of the car and took over, tossing the length of The Tourist over his shoulder. Tab disrobed as she walked, down to panties and bra. She hopped in the car and lit a fresh cigarette, relishing it as if it were some rare Belgian chocolate. Roddy closed the trunk and the Buick crept around the dumpster behind the building. Tab snatched a bag full of clean clothes from the backseat.

They drove alongside the cheap cars belonging to the waitresses and cooks, then on to the main graveled parking lot out front. Rodrick rolled easily toward The Tourist's truck until Tab lifted a hand. She got out and adjusted her black tank, then finished hiking a fresh pair of cut-offs onto her hips. Scanning the lot, she enjoyed a long drag as Rodrick pulled away and onto the main road.

He was gone. The Gypsy walked casually to the Chevy, unlocked the truck and got in. The engine fired with a buttery rumble and the girl took a deep breath.

◆ ◆ ◆

Laura tucked a band of blonde behind a jeweled ear. "How do you feel?" Her face was earnest, her eyes searching.

"Pretty good," the boy coughed. Constriction caused the child to wince, and the woman cringed in kind.

"That's your ribs," Laura said as she stood. "Three of them are broken. But the doctor said they're going to heal up just fine." Another smile.

Rebel looked again to his mother. Charleen was bandaged thoroughly, unrecognizable if not for the faint smell of country-fried steak. When he turned back, Laura was in tears, with both hands gripping tightly to the bedrail as if to steady her nerve. Her lips, outlined to perfection in a modest cardinal, quivered as she made efforts at words.

"Rebel, I'm so sorry." This was whispered with a hushed urgency, as if waiting to say it for another moment would have forfeited the opportunity altogether. "I'm so...I should have never treated you the way I did. You didn't deserve it. And I'm ashamed..." tears muted speech and she inhaled suddenly, covering her mouth with her hand.

The boy placed his hand on top of hers and this caused the

woman to cry harder.

"It's okay," Rebel said, and felt a tear leave the corner of his eye, trailing its way to the pillow beneath him.

"When I first saw you in the kitchen that night," Laura said, gathering herself, "I'd made up my mind about you before I even walked in. The same way people used to make up their minds about me when I was a kid. All based on...where you live, who your people are." She wiped at the corners of her eyes. "And I always hated that. So, I tried to run away from everything that made me, me. But you know what...it doesn't work," she laughed.

Rebel could tell the woman was looking now at his mother. "Because our people are our people, and we have to take care of them." She looked down at the boy, feathering his bangs gently to one side. "Like you tried to help my daddy." New tears formed around her blue eyes. "Like you took care of your mom," she said proudly.

◆ ◆ ◆

Rodrick reached The Quarry first, and the tires of the Electra seemed to skate across the earth. Most of the dirt had been meticulously leveled by now from the war machines, and the slightest gradient sloped the entirety of the bowl to its center. Roddy parked near this epicenter, allowing headlights to illuminate the spot. He opened the trunk and reached past The Tourist to work gloves and shovels. By the time Tab arrived, Roddy had a foot's worth of coffin-shaped dirt removed. The Gypsy pulled the Chevy into position to add more light.

The ground was rich with dark earth and perfect for the task—chunky but loose enough for easy digging. It was done in minutes. Rodrick hoisted the lanky tarp from the trunk and into the hole, and the filling went even faster than the removal. Tab used the mass of the Chevy to roll over the grave again and again, tamping it to molecular density. They drove out the same way they came in, parking their vehicles at the entrance where the dirt stopped and the pavement began.

Gathering iron rakes from Roddy's trunk, the two walked back to the burial site. Using the rakes, they grazed the surface of the ground wherever they found foot or tire treads. This phase lasted three times as long as the burial. But here they were, tediously pawing at the soil as soldier ants slid to the center of a colossal basin, inching their way back to their vehicles.

A short gasp called the boy's attention to the door, and Rebel watched as Kip hurried toward him, balloons in hand. "You're awake!" she said. Steve was just behind, his arms loaded with flowers and candy.

"Shhh!" Laura said, smiling. "Charleen's still sleeping."

The Princess let go the balloons and hugged the boy, eliciting a painful grunt from the happy patient.

"Kip, you're going to break another rib," Laura scolded.

"Oh gosh, I'm sorry!" the girl pulled back.

"I'm aw'ight," Rebel smiled, reaching out for her to return.

"Babe, let's go get some coffee," Steve winked at his wife.

Laura gathered her purse as the man sat the gifts down. He surveyed the boy, squeezing his shoulder warmly. "Never looked better, champ. And hey, save me some candy," he said as he joined the woman.

The adults were gone. Rebel's mother was asleep beside him on the other side of the curtain, safe, and his hand was being held by the girl he loved. Aside from the piercing stitch in his side with each inhale, the boy felt invigorated.

"Thanks for com…"

Kip cut this pleasantry short with a kiss, making sure to avoid the gauze wrapping. Her lips were soft and warm just below his nose, and tears filled his eyes.

"Did I hurt you?" she asked.

"Naw," the boy tried smiling and then it did hurt. "I'm just glad to see ya."

"I shouldn't have yelled at you."

"It's okay."

"No, it's not," The Princess insisted. "I was upset about my granddad and took it out on you."

"I don't care that you did," the boy squeezed her hand.

"I do," she said, fighting back tears of her own. Kip tapped her bottom lip softly with her finger. "So, my mom said the doctor put seven stitches in your lip."

"Great," Rebel sighed. "I'll be lookin' like Frankenstein by the time it's all over with."

Kip glanced quickly to make sure Charleen was still asleep, then leaned down to steal another kiss. "It'll make you look tough," she grinned.

"That's something Lee would say," Rebel said, allowing his eyes to rest.

◆ ◆ ◆

The next morning, the film of thin sand and scattered dirt at the entrance of The Quarry was warm. It would get hotter as the day progressed, layered moist with humidity. Massive trucks soon rolled over any trace of where Rodrick and Tab had been the night before, ushering tons upon tons of concrete into the bowl. This was a special day for The Quarry—what was would never be again. The belly of the vast caldron teemed with men in work shirts and hardhats and orange vests. These men pointed and yelled and watched as others worked.

Diesel after diesel made the loop, dumping their thick liquid haul until empty, then rolled away to make room for the next. The grave of The Tourist was covered first, bearing the heaviest, most impenetrable dose of the stuff. Trucks poured their way out of the bowl, using the same technique as the grave diggers. Soon the majority of it was glazed deep in liquid stone, sectioned by wood framings and rebar throughout.

The Quarry was now a galactic-sized egg scooped clean, and only the smoothness of its shell remained. One month later water would rise to its rim, and the vision the boy had seen in his head would be nearly complete.

The pine row closest to Kip's house had been cleared, and construction was underway on houses twice the size of her own. These would have envious views overlooking the lake. From the ridge line The Princess' house was now easily visible, the saucer-shaped treehouse standing out like a white-powdered donut through the distant trees.

The jungle was plowed and the lone sturdy sapling long since cut, making way for what would become the first proper golf course Clanton ever had. Where the jungle had been, miles of land now stretched over low hills, before unseen. Each day it was becoming apparent where sand traps would go, and a massive tract was staked with flags for the club house. Snake-like patterns weaved through the pines, denoting the paths of golf carts.

New princesses would be raised around The Quarry. And they, visited by new boys from Old Manookie.

CHAPTER 24

The Undiscovered

The boy clawed at the high weed with Isaac's old garden hoe, pulling clumps from the ground back toward the tree line and away from the barn. Behind him was the long, curving trail of his labor, and he was almost done.

With her finger Kip hooked a strip of hair from her mouth, freeing it to fall in line with the rest, buoyed by the wind as she pedaled. The Princess caught a glint of sun bouncing from the water that filled The Quarry, and marveled at how quickly these newer, larger homes were going up.

◆ ◆ ◆

Charleen examined herself nervously in the bedroom mirror, pulling down on a skirt she feared was too short. A soft white blouse fit her elegantly, however, and she supposed the professionalism of the top would compensate for any uncertainty of the bottom. She sighed at her reflection, touching up lipstick and cupping hands at feathered hair one last time.

◆

The dog leapt into the back of the sky-blue Chevy, sliding until his thick shoulders bounced off the back of the cab. Tab was not far behind, adjusting the weight of a large duffle on her shoulder as she walked. Her hair was ponied and pulled tight through a trucker hat, and she looked half-rocker, half-construction worker in ripped jeans and a sleeveless Def Leopard tee. She flung the duffle into the bed of the truck and glanced at her apartment one last time.

◆

A stocky man tapped on the glass of the open door and Laura lowered the paint roller from the wall. She stepped over boxes of inventory on her way to meet him, apologizing for her appearance. In rolled up, paint-stained jeans she was still arresting. She signed the man's form. Outside, Steve directed movers on where to deliver a bulky new soda machine. Laura eased around the stocky man and stood beneath the refurbished *Grayson's* sign, instructing her husband on how the machine would fit more easily through the back of the store.

◆

Charleen shuffled towards the entrance of the bank, tugging at the skirt as she went, her purse bouncing against her hip. A woman with a kind face opened the door and waved. Charleen wondered if her blouse was nice enough after all as she shook the woman's hand. Inside, the woman talked while pointing to a row of bank tellers behind a long counter. One of the teller seats was empty, and the woman invited Charleen to sit.

Lines of white flashed by the tires of the Chevy, morphing into one elongated blur. Tab let her arm swim the wind through the open window and the pickup whooshed beneath an interstate sign that read: *Lafayette 70.* She pulled the cap from her head and tousled her mane, allowing waves of black to float throughout the cab. Roscoe propped himself upright, licking the sable bands as they danced about.

The beach comber slid through the dirt of the drive seamlessly, and Kip could see the barn far in the distance. She slowed to a stop when she got to the trailer and dismounted. The girl walked the bicycle alongside her, avoiding the deepest holes of the yard. She saw the rust that clung to the edges of the trailer's frame, and the cinder blocks upon which the entire home sat. She saw also the sun-bleached green of its walls and the faulty repair job of the front door. As she passed, she imagined the boy inside of it, playing hide and seek with Lee or watching television with Tab while his mother was at work. All her visions were pleasant ones. In them, her friend was smiling or laughing or doing something creative within the small space. Several strays approached her barking, and she was startled, but in the end their tails wagged and she moved on.

On the beaten trail leading to the barn, brush met her in

places where the bike took up too much room, and she felt the whip and snag of briar at her shins. This was the first time she'd ever been to Rebel's home, much less the barn, and her excitement was such that she didn't mind the discomfort. She only wanted to see him. To be with her best friend and perhaps kiss him again. Perhaps inside the barn. By now this place had become a living, mythical thing for The Princess. And finally, here it was, before her now: a graying red leviathan. Thinly veiled and hallowed by time.

She could hear the boy toiling on the far side of it. "Rebel!" Kip called out, and her friend appeared immediately; sweat-drenched and smiling. He was filthy from digging, but the girl was growing accustomed to seeing him this way. An unexpected flush of arousal came at the top of her legs and she looked away, forcing her mind to the nuance of the barn. "So this is it, huh?"

"This is it," the boy replied, pushing wet bangs from his eyes. "Whatcha thank?" he asked proudly.

The Princess moved to stand directly in front of the structure, admiring the place she'd heard the boy speak about so many times. Rebel noticed she was in the exact spot Lee had stood weeks before—erect and proud, wearing a limp coyote around his neck like a regal pimp.

Kip stared up at the bay window, squinting from the brightness of the sun, and opened her hand for it to be held. Rebel wiped what grime he could onto his jeans. The boy took the girl's hand, envisioning the largeness of the barn as a magnificent cathedral. One in which they would eventually marry. They might just walk toward it now, hand in hand, wet from heat and tanned of sun. And as they passed through the barn doors they would transform: cleansed and groomed and fitted with the finest clothes either of them had ever worn. She would look down at her dress and smile, and the boy would marvel at how well the caramel of her skin matched the brilliance of the white. She would look at the boy then, never so handsome, his hair combed and cheeks flushed. A suit that made him appear older than he was. Someday.

"Thanks for comin'," Rebel said, annoyed by the sudden emotion in his voice.

"Of course," Kip said, and squeezed the dirty hand holding hers.

"You sure about this?"

Rebel pulled the girl close, hugging her as tightly as he ever had. She squeezed him in return.

"Yeah," he said, relaxing his hold of her. He kissed the side of her face—her sweet spot, he'd decided. A subtle tenderness situated above her jaw and beside her ear, making itself known only when she tucked her hair behind her ears. There, he could smell the essence of her, between hair and skin. There, he could lose himself in the warm softness of it, taken away to another place.

"I'll be back," Rebel said, disappearing into the barn. Kip surveyed the grounds, noticing the trail of barren dirt Rebel had etched out. It lay roughly ten yards from the building and ran the circumference of the barn. She walked alongside it, following its pattern, and noticed that at any point this shallow ditch was at least a foot wide, cleared of the slightest twig, blade or root.

By the time she traced the entire trail she found herself back where she started. Rebel was waiting. At his feet were a half-dozen gas cans, old and new. Several had been used to hold diesel for Isaac's tractor. These were rusted and ancient. Others contained aged gasoline designated for two defunct lawnmowers that lay now in cobwebs.

The boy breathed deeply, looked into the girl's face, and they shared a knowing smile. Each grabbed hold of a container and ran to the barn, splashing its walls with fuel. The sun-faded red of the cathedral screamed to life as liquid saturated the old wood. That which was fossilized soon appeared to breathe in a rich, glowing crimson. As one can emptied, another was gathered, and the pair bathed the beast thoroughly, sloshing as high as their arms could reach.

They worked the margin of the building, laughing as they went, racing to see who might empty their cans first. Soon it was finished. Rebel and Kip met in front of the barn once more, and together, looked down at the last remaining can. This one was smaller than the rest, the newest and most manageable. The boy squatted down and took the small jug in his hand.

So close to the earth, not far from the high weed and cast beneath a yawning sapphire, a thousand thoughts seemed to come to the child at once. Conclusions he was afraid to admit, even now. Reasonings and logic that gnawed at his gut. He would make himself abide the unanswered questions he had for The Vampire and the insinuations of The Walrus. Some day he would cross. He would see Jesus there.

Then he would know everything.

Rebel placed his forehead against the can, as if he might cobble those conceits into one great whirring spiral, and then will that spiral into the fuel itself. All would burn and he would be glad.

The boy stood and looked at the girl. He took a generous crow-hop, then hurled the can up and through The Trellis, out of sight. From below they heard the container burst, and the slop of gasoline splashing onto the boards of the loft. They ran to the edge of the brush and sat down together cross-legged, each picking up an empty Coke bottle. Rebel stuffed each glass with a bottle rocket as he dug one of Tab's cigarette lighters from his hip. He extended it to Kip. "You first," he smiled.

The girl grinned and lit the firework just before it fell into the bottle, holding it out toward the barn. Squinting as it caught fire, she jerked, but the boy held her fast. The rocket shot from the glass, flying hard at the building, only to bounce off the wall and flail to the ground. The firecracker ignited suddenly in the grass, and they laughed.

Rebel lit his own, training his aim meticulously at the bay. The rocket screeched away, finding home through the corner of the large square. Kip gasped and clenched the boy's arm as they waited. A muffled pop from within the loft and nothing more. "Come on!" Rebel giggled, and stood to load another.

The boy positioned himself as a sharpshooter, holding the bottle with both hands. "Light it for me," he grinned. Kip reached out and snapped the lighter to life, then the wick. She watched it burn as the boy studied The Trellis. Rebel closed one eye for focus, and through the iris of the other, flashed the memory of a thousand adventures.

The rocket shot clean, leaving a cloud of coal smoke swirling inside the bottle. They watched it sail high, then arch, vanishing into the center of the window's shadow. A breathless silence as they held onto one another, A pop from the cracker, then a sweeping, sonorous rumble emanated from the second floor. Flames licked through the bay and the children stumbled back toward the brush behind them.

A dense grey smoke rose immediately through the opening, searching for freedom. From within, streaks of bright orange flared lawlessly. Soon the saturation of the exterior walls caught alight. In a matter of seconds, the whole of the barn was engulfed as flames raced and crossed one another, cascading heavenward.

The friends stood in wonder. Then came loud pops of weakening timber and the burgeoning stress of bearing upright. Rebel and Kip lowered themselves to the ground, arm in arm. They watched the great leviathan groan and writhe about for a long time; collapsing first at its edges.

The bay window remained and the boy stood, pulling The Princess up with him. They mounted their bikes, Kip on the comber, the boy on the dirt bike littered with pink stickers. The girl led out toward the trailer, navigating the trail that was no longer new. Just before the first bend in the path the boy slowed, anchoring himself to the ground with a foot. Rebel looked back as smoke caressed the sky in long, billowing waves. He knew someone would soon come, just as they had for Lee.

And yet, The Trellis remained. A derelict vanguard, as if all else might burn to ash but it would stay. Fixed and suspended within sky for all time.

Sunlight on the boy's shoulder began to curve, bleeding into something new. Pony Time edged gently onto the tops of the pines.

He stared at the blood frame and could swear that within he saw the rawboned form of his brother—a waxen Dalí hanging neck to truss. Lee glowed tenebrous within a gossamer chrysalis. Immutable seed sown deep inside the guts of a scarlet dragon.

A heartening breath slid from the boy's chest. He pedaled on. Soon Rebel caught sight of the girl he loved. He imagined them riding on together. Past high weed and the dirt road. Past tumult and penance and the jurisdiction of cares. Until they reached the undiscovered.

EPILOGUE

Lifting his nose from the dirt, he snorted free the stuck bits trapped in his nostrils. That earth smelled of old leather. He creased his eyes and discerned a blur of movement in the distance. At first there was darkness, and the light he could sense came only from a familiar moon. A strident ringing ebbed in his ears, transmuting slowly into the raucous clangor of tribes. Various tongues and dialects and guttural sounds. Some words he could make out, others came as grunting snuffs or howls intermittent. The soft glow of distant fire.

The long man pushed his body upright by the palms, and the space encircling him became clearer. Thick jungle lay behind, and he saw natives there. Muscled, naked bodies layered in war paint with bones tied upon. Hemp bindings holding the ears and scalps of enemies.

Above these warriors, enshrouded on a great mound of kudzu, was a Cherokee Witch-Queen. Her dark face was laced in a crackled white, marred by rituals centuries old. The queen was curvaceous and fleshy, the bulk of her torso covered by two enormous breasts that lay pierced and naked before the stars. In her hand was a staff made from the spine of a bear, and it wrapped in tendrils from the intestines of a boar.

Next to the Cherokee was a dense, teeming population of gorillas. Between conversation and the pummeling of their chests, a low roar hovered in constant above their lodgings. They were led by an oversized silverback named Bete Sage who over years proved surprisingly measured in his decisions, especially as they affected the greater welfare of The Quarry.

Farther along, nestled in the first long curve of the bowl, was the Angel's Round: an unadorned nook set aside for the outlying traffic of Heaven. These beings came and went as they pleased, absent more often than not from most Appraisals, as was the case now.

The Alzahrion encamped directly across from The Round in the opposing bend. They sat like monks among the sand hills, conscientiously measuring the temperature within the dunes, ensuring their giants reached term.

The Bärenwölfe were next. The man in the dirt recognized this was the area from which the howling had emanated. These were a lascivious bunch, viewed largely as a necessary evil since they served as The Quarry's perimeter guard. Towering, long-fanged beasts. The abominations of long-term inbreeding of wolf and bear.

Finally, along the high ridge of the pine row, opposite the Cherokee, was The Vampire. The dead boy, however, was new as the day of his death, neck scuffed fresh red from a wrenching violence. He sat on a pinewood throne, flanked on either side by hundreds of buried oaks, flanged and spike-carved at their tops like so many sharpened pencils.

Buttressing his throne and among the oak spikes were gatherings of dwarves, rapscallions all. They busied themselves with drink and women and gambling. This revelry was illuminated by torches that ran the circumference of the bowl, casting glows of orange and red onto its belly. And onto the man in the dirt.

Slowly, the breadth of the basin recognized the awakening of the long man, and soon the rumblings and clatter and boorish makings of every faction grew quiet. The man in the dirt struggled to stand. A soreness throughout his midsection and back from something he could not name.

"Order!" The Vampire shouted, pounding a gavel on the armrest of his throne. Grumbling from the apes. "I said order, gyatdammit!" Lee screamed as he stood. He moved to the edge of a wooden platform where he took his position behind a lectern. "Bete, will you git'cher shit under control ove'ere!"

The silverback bowed upright that he might peer over his army and let out a guttural bark. Every ape came to rest.

"Fuckin' hairy-ass savages. Rude as hell," Lee mumbled to himself. The dead boy looked down from the pine row at the man in the center of The Quarry. A glint shown in the eyes of The Vampire from the torches along the ridge line. The long man strained harder to see, and realized The Vampire was, indeed, leashed. The rope from the noose around his neck led over the dead boy's shoulder to the hand of an enormous dark winged War Angel. Imposing, even within shadow. This great being sat on a stool and drank Wild Turkey from the bottle, with no small amount running the length of a dense Nordic beard. He rested a scarred, meaty forearm on one knee, unconcerned with these proceedings.

"Aw'ight," Lee said loudly, "Appraisal's officially in session fer 'is sum'bitch."

The man in the dirt hobbled awkwardly, turning a slow circle as he tried to determine what each creature was and who might come for him and from which direction.

"Dennis Roy Cleckley, forty-four years of age, from Who-The-Hell-Fuckin'-Cares, stands accused of livin' a shit life and bein' a all-round asshole," The Vampire stated. "Appraisal's up... Bärenwölfe has the floor."

And so it went, each faction saying their piece. The Bärenwölfe proposed Rip-Share, wherein at the drop of Lee's hand, whoever reached the epicenter first ripped the accused asunder, retaining the selection of their choice. What remained would be shared among the other tribes based upon who arrived second, third, and so on.

The Alzahrion preferred abstention, as usual, deflecting communal responsibility unless it directly affected the incubation of their sand giants.

The Witch-Queen Nilahasi Tayyi was in rare form and screamed at The Vampire from her kudzu palace. She was incensed, insistent that the white man's Appraisal should happen elsewhere since the Alzahrion would not vote and the angels— aside from The Vampire's handler—were absent yet again. There were more pressing matters to discuss and Quarry decisions to be made, she protested.

The man in the basin observed all of this with growing alarm. "I... I know you," The Tourist said, pointing a shaky finger up at Lee.

"Shut the fuck up! You don't know shit, motherfucker," the dead boy fired back. "'You don't talk, aw'ight? You just sit there and wait fer what's comin', bitch."

"What is this place?" Dennis asked.

"Where chickens come to roost, you fuckin' cocksucker!" The Vampire hissed, igniting a fume of profane laughter from the dwarves.

Suddenly, a bottomless reverberation shook the ground. It swelled, this sound, causing pines to shimmy needles to the ground. Clumps of soil broke free from the walls of The Quarry and descended the bowl as the tribes became restless.

Far behind the sand dunes he appeared, the Great Giant,

eclipsing moon and star. The ancient man was careful not to crush all that had grown up in his absence, stopping short of entering The Quarry for fear of obliteration. He squatted, and wind from this movement cascaded through the basin like a breathy tsunami. The man in the dirt stared up at the giant, searching for the end of him.

The dead boy finally spoke. "Well, I be damn!" Lee laughed, clapping his hands. "Where in the hell have you been? You know what—I don't even give a shit. Yer here, so yer votin'." The Vampire shook his head in disbelief as he looked behind to the War Angel. "This motherfucker's gon show up after fifty gotdamn years like he ain't missed a beat. What hell kinda person does such as 'at?"

The dark winged Viking only turned up the bottle. Locks of hair the length of fields swung from the Great Giant's head as he nodded toward the lectern. Lee scanned his surroundings, mocking acknowledgment. "What? What t'hell you lookin' at me for? We all sittin' here lookin' at'cher big ass, waitin' on you."

The Great Man took in a deep breath which made every tree along the ridge lean his direction. For a moment, he studied the speck of flesh in the dirt. Then he lifted his heavy head and spoke in an ancient tongue. When he finished, the tribes conferred independently. One by one, each faction signaled agreement using the same gesture.

"Aw'ight then," Lee said, "'at's it."

The Tourist swung to face The Vampire. "What does that mean? What happened?" he asked, surveying the basin. The man searched for insight from the faces of other beings and found none. A vague whirring then. A hum indecipherable. Dennis' fear seemed to pivot, and in its place, a familiar rage he'd known since he was a child.

"Who the fuck do you think you are?" the man growled at

Lee, and spit toward the lectern. "You little shit. Why don't you come down here and say whatever you gotta say to my face? Huh? Come on!" The sound swelled—an urgent, rushing buzz high above the quarry. "Come down here so all your friends can watch me beat your scrawny ass!" the dirt man screamed. The more frenetic he became the more the tribes calmed.

Waiting. This unsettled The Tourist, and he began to pace, observing as the Witch-Queen stared blankly into the night sky. The man tried tracing her gaze, but all he could discern were stars fixed within a blanket of blue ink. He turned once more to the dead boy. "You think you're in control here?" Dennis sneered. He spun about, yelling to all the tribes, "Who the fuck put this little prick in charge? Huh?"

Lee slid his butterfly knife from his pocket and flipped it open. Back and forth and oscillating, The Vampire turned the blade and handles over in his hand. A sharp pain gripped Dennis' ribs and he grimaced, constricting at the waist. The noise came loudly from above, slicing through cloud and sky.

The Tourist glared up at the dead boy. "You know, I wish you'd been there."

With every flip of the blade in the hand of the dead boy, blood appeared on the torso of the man in the dirt. Dozens of wounds. At his sides and on his back, bleeding through, soiling his clothes. He grabbed at the cuts. Too many to hold. "Oh yeah. You should'a been there." the bleeding man said, "You could'a heard your bitch mother yelp like the cunt she is. And watch me beat the shit out of your little brother."

An ear-splitting crash blunted the man's voice to nothing as the load reached its destination. The sky-blue Chevy exploded as it landed, with parts of the pickup rocketing out in every direction. Shoots of blood and entrails spurt from beneath the wreckage, spreading most of the long man out and onto the virgin earth.

One of the Chevy's tires bounced wildly toward the gorilla nest, and Bete Sage used his large body as a shield as it flew overhead. The Bärenwölfe thrust themselves onto mounds of dirt and rock and howled into the night, tearing at their chests until they bled. A war cry erupted from The Cherokee, and a host of warriors raced to encircle the crash site, scooping globs of The Tourist into their hands. They slung the soupy mess toward the moon as they chanted aloud.

Piles of gravel stirred near the sand dunes, and slowly the Rekishi Lords appeared. They slid ghost-sail from the rocks, assuming form and ushering themselves toward the center of the bowl. All parted as they approached, allowing the wraiths room to perform their duties. The Rekishi gathered around the crumpled mass of metal and blood and made their marks on leather strips with gelatinous claws.

The earth of the basin groaned and rose at its center with the pain of contraction, lifting up the smashed truck like a wave. The epicenter suddenly dropped as quickly as it had swelled, concaving in violence until the soil stretched wide its yawning mouth and swallowed the wreckage whole. The Lords waited patiently for the coffers that would hold record of these events. Finally, they emerged: clay vessels primeval, offering their innards as a vault for eternity.

The wraiths placed their bindings inside the chests and hovered away, wisps of nothing fusing once again into the crags of the rocks.

The tribes thundered euphoric around the open mouth of this rotund depression, screaming and dancing and wailing in song as the chests began to close. At the sealing of the last there was a detonating clap, and at once the breadth of the basin was still and void. There was nothing in the whole of it; no trace of tribe or clan. The leashed Vampire and the Viking Angel vanished. Empty, save a single sapling that stood within the length of that hallowed earth. And under the sapling, a log. This log served as the throne of a princess, and carved crudely within the wood were initials that read: R+K.

ACKNOWLEDGMENTS

I'd like to thank my wife Delaine for championing me in everything I get excited about. The sheer amount of time it takes to write anything of length is a gift a spouse extends to a writer, and I love that you encouraged me to start and to finish. You are my best friend and my treasure.

To my kids: Ginsyn, Taegan, and Sylas. You all watched me toil away at that black desk behind the pool table on Shakespeare Lane more times than any of us can count. Thank you for being so supportive. Dillon Campbell and Noah Cardenas, you two are the best sons-in-law a man could ask for. Your interest in the book and desire to read it was more encouraging than you know.

To my father, Terry Crim. You and Sally have loved me so well. Your confidence in me gives me hope.

To my mother, Debbie Shirey. The artist in you cultivated a love for art and creativity in me and that is an invaluable part of my life.

To my publisher, Keith Glines. Who knew that conversation in the green room at 3Circle would lead us here? Thank you for this partnership. Thank you for this adventure. And thank you for the best steak I've ever eaten in my entire life. More cigars around the fire and more books are in our future.

To my editor, Stephanie Glines. You are a saint for the work you have poured into this project and I can never repay you. The way you opened your heart to this story fueled something in me.

To The Back Porch Publishing Team. I'm indebted to you all for the efforts toward this book. From layout to cover design, marketing and more—thank you.

Dairek and Emily Rose Morgan. You both are our ride-or-die and your encouragement over the years was so incredibly appreciated.

Ben and Camille-Claire Grayson, Emily Moss and Greg Wilson, Anton Seim, Reid Gormly, Jen Lee—the OG LA gang. This book is a culmination of our collective grind and hustle to pursue dreams.

To the *Beta Crew*: Brett Mims, Jake Buettner, Carley Chastain, Beth Shaver. You all took the time to read early drafts and give invaluable notes and insight. I'm indebted.

Wayne Porter. As my high school Lit teacher, you made more of an impression on me than you will ever know. For me, you helped make literature a love and writing an ambition.

Barney March and Ryan Smith. Discussions regarding this book seemed never-ending, but it's finally done! Thanks for your interest and much more, your friendship.

To Kim Nieme. You have been a promoter and advocate for my wife and myself since day one. Thank you for all the help with pitches and development deals over the years. You are a gem and we love you.

Lord Jesus
You are the way. You are the truth. You are the life.
The redeemer of all things lost.
gratias ago tibi pro salute

ABOUT THE AUTHOR

Travis Crim was born in Birmingham, Alabama, where he eventually graduated from the University of Alabama with a degree in Public Relations and English Literature. A former walk-on football player at UA, he spent twenty years in Los Angeles acting, producing, and writing screenplays. His literary inclinations rooted in Southern Gothic fiction were the impetus for his first novel.

Travis currently resides in Birmingham with his wife Delaine and their teenage son, Sylas. They have two older daughters, Ginsyn and Taegan, both married to outstanding young men.

Rebel Rising is his first book.